School's Out!

Ruskin Bond is known for his signature simplistic and witty writing style. He is the author of several bestselling short stories, novellas, collections, essays and children's books; and has contributed a number of poems and articles to various magazines and anthologies. At the age of 23, he won the prestigious John Llewellyn Rhys Prize for his first novel, *The Room on the Roof*. He was also the recipient of the Padma Shri in 1999, Lifetime Achievement Award by the Delhi Government in 2012 and the Padma Bhushan in 2014.

Born in 1934, Ruskin Bond grew up in Jamnagar, Shimla, New Delhi and Dehradun. Apart from three years in the UK, he has spent all his life in India and now lives in Landour, Mussoorie, with his adopted family.

RUSKIN BOND

School's Out!

RUPA

Published by
Rupa Publications India Pvt. Ltd 2025
7/16, Ansari Road, Daryaganj
New Delhi 110002

Sales centres:
Bengaluru Chennai
Hyderabad Jaipur Kathmandu
Kolkata Mumbai Prayagraj

P-ISBN: 978-93-7003-105-0
E-ISBN: 978-93-7003-560-7

First impression 2025

10 9 8 7 6 5 4 3 2 1

Printed in India

CONTENTS

INTRODUCTION

There are few joys as exhilarating and intense as the kind experienced on the last day of school before vacation. Fortunately, it has been decades since I have had to attend school, but even now, I cannot help but smile as I recall the trill of the bell announcing the end of the last period, the entire classroom immediately erupting into delighted chaos. This excitement would gradually settle into contentment as the vacation progressed, most of it spent in thinking up new ways to while away the time. And I was often the happiest when I was whiling it away in the banyan tree that grew behind my grandparents' house, hiding in its branches with a favourite book.

School's Out! brings together a collection of my stories that I hope will provide the same enjoyment to my readers during their vacations. I have included here stories like 'Romi and the Wildfire' and 'Angry River', which are about the resilience of young people, especially when working together with their friends to face challenges. 'All Creatures Great and Small', 'The Elephant and the Cassowary Bird' and 'The Last Tiger' are humorous and adventurous stories of domestic and wild animals. There are also stories like 'Coming Home to Dehra' and 'Growing Up with Trees', which recount some of my own vacation days. And lastly, I have included some of my favourite stories written for young readers, such as 'The Woman on Platform No. 8' and 'The Eyes Have It'.

The books I read during vacations, transporting me to a different world everyday even as I sat stationary, took me on some of the most memorable adventures I have ever had. I hope the stories here help you stave off the boredom too, at least until your own adventure begins!

Ruskin Bond

COMING HOME TO DEHRA

The faint queasiness I always feel towards the end of a journey probably has its origin in that first homecoming after my father's death.

It was the winter of 1944—yes, a long time ago—and the train was running through the thick sal forests near Dehra, bringing me at every click of the rails nearer to the mother I hadn't seen for four years and the stepfather I had seen just once or twice before my parents were divorced.

I was eleven and I was coming home to Dehra.

Three years earlier, after the separation, I had gone to live with my father. We were very happy together. He was serving in the RAF, at New Delhi, and we lived in a large tent somewhere near Humayun's Tomb. The area is now a very busy part of urban Delhi, but in those days it was still a wilderness of scrub jungle where black buck and nilgai roamed freely. We took long walks together, exploring the ruins of old tombs and forts, went to the pictures (George Formby comedies were special favourites of mine), collected stamps, bought books (my father had taught me to read and write before I started going to school), and made plans for going to England when the war was over.

Six months of bliss, even though it was summer and there weren't any fans, only a thick khus reed curtain that had to be splashed with water every hour by a *bhisti* who did the rounds of similar tents with his goat-skin water bag. I remember the tender refreshing fragrance of the khus, and also the smell of damp earth outside, where the water had spilt.

A happy time. But it had to end. My father's periodic bouts of malarial fever resulted in his having to enter hospital for a week. The bhisti's small son came to stay with me at night, and during the day I took my meals with an Anglo-Indian family across the road.

I would have been quite happy to continue with this arrangement whenever my father was absent, but someone at air headquarters must have advised him to put me in a boarding school.

Reluctantly he came to the decision that this would be the best thing—'until the war is over'—and in the June of 1943 he took me to Shimla, where I was incarcerated in a preparatory school for boys.

This is not the story of my life at boarding school. It might easily have been a public school in England; it did in fact pride itself on being the 'Eton of the East'. The traditions—such as ragging and flogging, compulsory games and chapel attendance, prefects larger than life, and honour boards for everything from school captaincy to choir membership—had all apparently been borrowed from *Tom Brown's Schooldays.*

My father wrote to me regularly, and his letters were the things I looked forward to more than anything else. I went to him for the winter holidays, and the following summer he came to Shimla during my mid-term break and took me out for the duration of the holidays. We stayed in a hotel called Craig-Dhu, on a spur north of Jacko Hill. It was an idyllic week; long walks, stories about phantom rickshaws, ice creams in the sun, browsings in bookshops, more plans: 'We will go to England next year.'

School seemed a stupid and heartless place after my father had gone away. He had been transferred to Calcutta and he wasn't keeping well there. Malaria again. And then jaundice. But his last letter sounded quite cheerful. He'd been selling part of his valuable stamp collection so as to have enough money for the fares to England.

One day my class teacher sent for me.

'I want to talk to you, Bond,' he said. 'Let's go for a walk.'

I knew immediately that something was wrong.

We took the path that went through the deodar forest, past Council Rock where scout meetings were held. As soon as my unfortunate teacher (no doubt cursing the headmaster for having given him this unpleasant task) started on the theme of 'God wanting your father in a higher and better place,' as though there could be any better place than Jacko Hill in mid-summer, I knew my father was dead, and burst into tears.

They let me stay in the school hospital for a few days until I felt better. The headmaster visited me there and took away the pile of my father's letters that I'd kept beside me.

'Your father's letters. You might lose them. Why not leave them with me? Then at the end of the year, before you go home, you can come and collect them.'

Unwillingly I gave him the letters. He told me he'd heard from my mother that I would be going home to her at the end of the year. He seemed surprised that I evinced no interest in this prospect.

At the end of the year, the day before school closed, I went to the headmaster's office and asked for my letters.

'What letters?' he said. His desk was piled with papers and correspondence, and he was irritated by my interruption.

'My father's letters,' I explained. 'I gave them to you to keep for me, sir—when he died...'

'Letters. Are you sure you gave them to me?'

He grew more irritated. 'You must be mistaken, Bond. Why should I want to keep your father's letters?'

'I don't know, sir. You said I could collect them before going home.'

'Look, I don't remember any letters and I'm very busy just now, so run along. I'm sure you're mistaken, but if I find your letters, I'll send them to you.'

I don't suppose he meant to be unkind, but he was the first man who aroused in me feelings of hate...

As the train drew into Dehra, I looked out of the window to see if there was anyone on the platform waiting to receive me. The station was crowded enough, as most railway stations are in India, with overloaded travellers, shouting coolies, stray dogs, stray stationmasters... Pandemonium broke loose as the train came to a halt and people debouched from the carriages. I was thrust on the platform with my tin trunk and small attaché case. I sat on the trunk and waited for someone to find me.

Slowly the crowd melted away. I was left with one elderly coolie who was too feeble to carry heavy luggage and had decided that my trunk was just the right size and weight for his head and shoulders. I waited another ten minutes, but no representative of my mother or stepfather appeared. I permitted the coolie to lead me out of the station to the tonga stand.

Those were the days when everyone, including high-ranking officials, went about in tongas. Dehra had just one taxi. I was quite happy sitting beside a rather smelly, paan-spitting tonga driver, while his weary, underfed pony clip-clopped along the quiet tree-lined roads.

Dehra was always a good place for trees. The valley soil is very fertile, the rainfall fairly heavy; almost everything grows there, if given the chance. The roads were lined with neem and mango trees, eucalyptus, Persian lilac, jacaranda, amaltas (laburnum) and many others. In the gardens of the bungalows were mangoes, litchis and guavas; sometimes jackfruit and papaya. I did not notice all these trees at once; I came to know them as time passed.

The tonga first took me to my grandmother's house. I was under the impression that my mother still lived there.

A lovely, comfortable bungalow that spread itself about the grounds in an easy-going, old-fashioned way. There was even smoke coming from the chimneys, reminding me of the smoke from my grandfather's pipe. When I was eight, I had spent several months there with my grandparents. In retrospect it had been an idyllic interlude. But Grandfather was dead. Grandmother lived alone.

White-haired, but still broad in the face and even broader behind, she was astonished to see me getting down from the tonga.

'Didn't anyone meet you at the station?' she asked.

I shook my head. Grandmother said: 'Your mother doesn't livc here any more. You can come in and wait, but she may be worried about you, so I'd better take you to her placc. Come on, help me up into the tonga... I might have known it would be a white horse. It always makes me nervous sitting in a tonga behind a white horse.'

'Why, Granny?'

'I don't know, I suppose white horses are nervous, too. Anyway, they are always trying to topple me out. Not so fast, driver!' she called out, as the tonga man cracked his whip and the pony changed from a slow shuffle to a brisk trot.

It took us about twenty-five minutes to reach my stepfather's house which was in the Dalanwala area, not far from the dry bed of the seasonal Rispana river. My grandmother, seeing that I was in need of moral support, got down with me, while the tonga driver carried my bedding roll and tin trunk on to the verandah.

The front door was bolted from inside. We had to knock on it repeatedly and call out before it was opened by a servant who did not look pleased at being disturbed. When he saw my grandmother he gave her a deferential salaam, then gazed at me with open curiosity.

'Where's the memsahib?' asked Grandmother.

'Out,' said the servant.

'I can see that but where have they gone?'

'They went yesterday to Motichur, for shikar. They will be back this evening.'

Grandmother looked upset, but motioned to the servant to bring in my things. 'Weren't they expecting the boy?' she asked. 'Yes,' he said looking at me again. 'But they said he would be arriving tomorrow.'

'They'd forgotten the date,' said Grandmother in a huff. 'Anyway, you can unpack and have a wash and change your clothes.'

Turning to the servant, she asked, 'Is there any lunch?'

'I will make lunch,' he said. He was staring at me again, and I felt uneasy with his eyes on me. He was tall and swarthy, with oily, jet-back hair and a thick moustache. A heavy scar ran down his left cheek, giving him a rather sinister appearance. He wore a torn shirt and dirty pyjamas. His broad, heavy feet were wet. They left marks on the uncarpeted floor.

A baby was crying in the next room, and presently a woman

(who turned out to be the cook's wife) appeared in the doorway, jogging the child in her arms.

'They've left the baby behind, too,' said Grandmother, becoming more and more irate. 'He is your young brother. Only six months old.' I hadn't been told anything about a younger brother. The discovery that I had one came as something of a shock. I wasn't prepared for a baby brother, least of all a baby half-brother. I examined the child without much enthusiasm. He looked healthy enough and he cried with gusto.

'He's a beautiful baby,' said Grandmother. 'Well, I've got work to do. The servants will look after you. You can come and see me in a day or two. You've grown since I last saw you. And you're getting pimples.'

This reference to my appearance did not displease me as Grandmother never indulged in praise. For her to have observed my pimples indicated that she was fond of me.

The tonga driver was waiting for her. 'I suppose I'll have to use the same tonga,' she said. 'Whenever I need a tonga, they disappear, except for the ones with white ponies. When your mother gets back, tell her I want to see her. Shikar, indeed. An infant to look after, and they've gone shooting.'

Grandmother settled herself in the tonga, nodded in response to the cook's salaam, and took a tight grip of the armrests of her seat. The driver flourished his whip and the pony set off at the same listless, unhurried trot, while my grandmother, feeling quite certain that she was going to be hurtled to her doom by a wild white pony, set her teeth and clung tenaciously to the tonga seat. I was sorry to see her go.

My mother and stepfather returned in the evening from their hunting trip with a pheasant which was duly handed over to the cook, whose name was Mangal Singh. My mother gave me a perfunctory kiss. I think she was pleased to see me, but I was accustomed to a more intimate caress from my father, and the strange reception I had received made me realize the extent of my loss. Boarding school life had been routine. Going home was something that I had always looked forward to. But going home had meant my father, and now he had vanished and I was left quite desolate.

I suppose if one is present when a loved one dies, or sees him dead and laid out and later buried, one is convinced of the finality of the thing and finds it easier to adapt to the changed circumstances. But when you hear of a death, a father's death, and have only the faintest idea of the manner of his dying, it is rather a lot for the imagination to cope with—especially when the imagination is a small boy's. There being no tangible evidence of my father's death, it was, for me, not a death but a vanishing. And although this enabled me to remember him as a living, smiling, breathing person, it meant that I was not wholly reconciled to his death, and subconsciously expected him to turn up (as he often did, when I most needed him) and deliver me from any unpleasant situation.

My stepfather barely noticed me. The first thing he did on coming into the house was to pour himself a whisky and soda. My mother, after inspecting the baby, did likewise. I was left to unpack and settle in my room.

I was fortunate in having my own room. I was as desirous of my own privacy as much as my mother and stepfather were desirous of theirs. My stepfather, a local businessman, was ready to put up with me provided I did not get in the way. And, in a different way, I was ready to put up with him, provided he left me alone. I was even willing that my mother should leave me alone. There was a big window to my room, and I opened it to the evening breeze, and gazed out on to the garden, a rather unkempt place where marigolds and a sort of wild blue everlasting grew rampant among the litchi trees.

THE PHOTOGRAPH

I was ten years old. My grandmother sat on the string bed under the mango tree. It was late summer and there were sunflowers in the garden and a warm wind in the trees. My grandmother was knitting a woollen scarf for the winter months. She was very old, dressed in a plain white sari. Her eyes were not very strong now but her fingers moved quickly with the needles and the needles kept clicking all afternoon. Grandmother had white hair but there were very few wrinkles on her skin.

I had come home after playing cricket in the maidan. I had taken my meal and now I was rummaging through a box of old books and family heirlooms that had just that day been brought out of the attic by my mother. Nothing in the box interested me very much except for a book with colourful pictures of birds and butterflies. I was going through the book, looking at the pictures, when I found a small photograph between the pages. It was a faded picture, a little yellow and foggy. It was the picture of a girl standing against a wall and behind the wall there was nothing but sky. But from the other side a pair of hands reached up, as though someone was going to climb the wall. There were flowers growing near the girl but I couldn't tell what they were. There was a creeper too but it was just a creeper.

I ran out into the garden. 'Granny!' I shouted. 'Look at this picture! I found it in the box of old things. Whose picture is it?'

I jumped on the bed beside my grandmother and she walloped me on the bottom and said, 'Now I've lost count of my stitches and the next time you do that I'll make you finish the scarf yourself.'

Granny was always threatening to teach me how to knit, which I thought was a disgraceful thing for a boy to do. It was a good deterrent for keeping me out of mischief. Once, I had torn the drawing-room curtains and Granny had put a needle and thread in my hand and made me stitch the curtain together, even though I made long, two-inch stitches, which had to be taken out by my mother and done again.

She took the photograph from my hand and we both stared at it for quite a long time. The girl had long, loose hair and she wore a long dress that nearly covered her ankles, and sleeves that reached her wrists, and there were a lot of bangles on her hands. But despite all this drapery, the girl appeared to be full of freedom and movement. She stood with her legs apart and her hands on her hips and had a wide, almost devilish smile on her face.

'Whose picture is it?' I asked.

'A little girl's, of course,' said Grandmother. 'Can't you tell?'

'Yes, but did you know the girl?'

'Yes, I knew her,' said Granny, 'but she was a very wicked girl and I shouldn't tell you about her. But I'll tell you about the photograph. It was taken in your grandfather's house about sixty years ago. And that's the garden wall and over the wall there was a road going to town.'

'Whose hands are they,' I asked, 'coming up from the other side?'

Grandmother squinted and looked closely at the picture, and shook her head. 'It's the first time I've noticed,' she said.

'They must have been the sweeper boy's. Or maybe they were your grandfather's.'

'They don't look like Grandfather's hands,' I said. 'His hands are all bony.'

'Yes, but this was sixty years ago.'

'Didn't he climb up the wall after the photo?'

'No, nobody climbed up. At least, I don't remember.'

'And you remember well, Granny.'

'Yes, I remember...I remember what is not in the photograph. It was a spring day and there was a cool breeze blowing, nothing like this. Those flowers at the girl's feet, they were marigolds, and the bougainvillea creeper, it was a mass of purple. You cannot see these colours in the photo and even if you could, as nowadays, you wouldn't be able to smell the flowers or feel the breeze.'

'And what about the girl?' I said. 'Tell me about the girl.'

'Well, she was a wicked girl,' said Granny. 'You don't know the trouble they had getting her into those fine clothes she's wearing.'

'I think they are terrible clothes,' I said.

'So did she. Most of the time, she hardly wore a thing. She used to go swimming in a muddy pool with a lot of ruffianly boys, and ride on the backs of buffaloes. No boy ever teased her, though, because she could kick and scratch and pull his hair out!'

'She looks like it too,' I said. 'You can tell by the way she's smiling. At any moment something's going to happen.'

'Something did happen,' said Granny. 'Her mother wouldn't let her take off the clothes afterwards, so she went swimming in them and lay for half an hour in the mud.'

I laughed heartily and Grandmother laughed too.

'Who was the girl?' I said. 'You must tell me who she was.'

'No, that wouldn't do,' said Grandmother, but I pretended I didn't know. I knew, because Grandmother still smiled in the same way, even though she didn't have as many teeth.

'Come on, Granny,' I said, 'tell me, tell me.'

But Grandmother shook her head and carried on with the knitting. And I held the photograph in my hand looking from it to my grandmother and back again, trying to find points in common between the old lady and the little pigtailed girl. A lemon-coloured butterfly settled on the end of Grandmother's knitting needle and stayed there while the needles clicked away. I made a grab at the butterfly and it flew off in a dipping flight and settled on a sunflower.

'I wonder whose hands they were,' whispered Grandmother to herself, with her head bowed, and her needles clicking away in the soft, warm silence of that summer afternoon.

THE LAST TONGA RIDE

It was a warm spring day in Dehra, and the walls of the bungalow were aflame with flowering bougainvillaea. The papayas were ripening. The scent of sweetpeas drifted across the garden. Grandmother sat in an easy chair in a shady corner of the verandah, her knitting needles clicking away, her head nodding now and then. She was knitting a pullover for my father. 'Delhi has cold winters,' she had said, and although the winter was still eight months away, she had set to work on getting our woollens ready.

In the Kathiawar states, touched by the warm waters of the Arabian Sea, it had never been cold but Dehra lies at the foot of the first range of the Himalayas.

Grandmother's hair was white, her eyes were not very strong but her fingers moved quickly with the needles and the needles kept clicking all morning.

When Grandmother wasn't looking, I picked geranium leaves, crushed them between my fingers and pressed them to my nose.

I had been in Dehra with my grandmother for almost a month and I had not seen my father during this time. We had never before been separated for so long. He wrote to me every week, and sent me books and picture postcards; and I would walk to the end of the road to meet the postman as early as possible, to see if there was any mail for us.

We heard the jingle of tonga-bells at the gate, and a familiar horse-buggy came rattling up the drive.

'I'll see who's come,' I said, and ran down the verandah steps and across the garden.

It was Bansi Lal in his tonga. There were many tongas and tonga-drivers in Dehra but Bansi was my favourite driver. He was young and handsome and he always wore a clean white shirt and pyjamas. His pony, too, was bigger and faster than the other tonga ponies. Bansi didn't have a passenger, so I asked him, 'What have you come for, Bansi?'

'Your grandmother sent for me, dost.' He did not call me 'chota sahib' or 'baba' but 'dost', and this made me feel much more important. Not every small boy could boast of a tonga-driver for his friend!

'Where are you going, Granny?' I asked, after I had run back to the verandah.

'I'm going to the bank.'

'Can I come too?'

'Whatever for? What will you do in the bank?'

'Oh, I won't come inside, I'll sit in the tonga with Bansi.'

'Come along, then.'

We helped Grandmother into the back seat of the tonga, and then I joined Bansi in the driver's seat. He said something to his pony, and the pony set off at a brisk trot, out of the gate and down the road.

'Now, not too fast, Bansi,' said Grandmother, who didn't like anything that went too fast—tonga, motor car, train or bullock cart.

'Fast?' said Bansi. 'Have no fear, Memsahib. This pony has never gone fast in its life. Even if a bomb went off behind us, we could go no faster. I have another pony, which I use for racing when customers are in a hurry. This pony is reserved for you, Memsahib.'

There was no other pony, but Grandmother did not know this, and was mollified by the assurance that she was riding in the slowest tonga in Dehra.

A ten-minute ride brought us to the bazaar. Grandmother's bank, the Allahabad Bank, stood near the clock tower. She was gone for about half an hour and during this period Bansi and I sauntered about in front of the shops. The pony had been left with some green stuff to munch.

'Do you have any money on you?' asked Bansi.

'Four annas,' I said.

'Just enough for two cups of tea,' said Bansi, putting his arm round my shoulders and guiding me towards a tea stall. The money passed from my palm to his.

'You can have tea, if you like,' I said. 'I'll have a lemonade.'

'So be it, friend. A tea and a lemonade, and be quick about it,' said Bansi to the boy in the stall and presently the drinks were set before us, and Bansi was making a sound rather like his pony when he drank, while I burped my way through some green, gaseous stuff that tasted more like soap than lemonade.

When Grandmother came out of the bank, she looked pensive, and did not talk much during the ride back to the house except to tell me to behave myself when I leaned over to pat the pony on its rump. After paying off Bansi, she marched straight indoors.

'When will you come again?' I asked Bansi.

'When my services are required, dost. I have to make a living, you know. But I tell you what, since we are friends, the next time I am passing this way after leaving a fare, I will jingle my bells at the gate and if you are free and would like a ride—a fast ride—you can join me. It won't cost you anything. Just bring some money for a cup of tea.'

'All right—since we are friends,' I said.

'Since we are friends.'

And touching the pony very lightly with the handle of his whip, he sent the tonga rattling up the drive and out of the gate. I could hear Bansi singing as the pony cantered down the road.

Ayah was waiting for me in the bedroom, her hands resting on her broad hips—sure sign of an approaching storm.

'So you went off to the bazaar without telling me,' she said. (It wasn't enough that I had Grandmother's permission!) 'And all this time I've been waiting to give you your bath.'

'It's too late now, isn't it?' I asked hopefully.

'No, it isn't. There's still an hour left for lunch. Off with your clothes!'

While I undressed, Ayah berated me for keeping the company of tonga-drivers like Bansi. I think she was a little jealous.

'He is a rogue, that man. He drinks, gambles and smokes opium. He has TB and other terrible diseases. So don't you be too friendly with him, understand, baba?'

I nodded my head sagely but said nothing. I thought Ayah was exaggerating, as she always did about people, and besides, I had no intention of giving up free tonga rides.

As my father had told me, Dehra was a good place for trees, and Grandmother's house was surrounded by several kinds—peepul, neem, mango, jackfruit, papaya and an ancient banyan tree. Some of the trees had been planted by my father and grandfather.

'How old is the jackfruit tree?' I asked Grandmother.

'Now let me see,' said Grandmother, looking very thoughtful. 'I should remember the jackfruit tree. Oh yes, your grandfather put it down in 1927. It was during the rainy season. I remember, because it was your father's birthday and we celebrated it by planting a tree. 14 July 1927. Long before you were born!'

The banyan tree grew behind the house. Its spreading branches, which hung to the ground and took root again, formed a number of twisting passageways in which I liked to wander. The tree was older than the house, older than my grandparents, as old as Dehra. I could hide myself in its branches behind thick, green leaves and spy on the world below.

It was an enormous tree, about sixty feet high, and the first time I saw it I trembled with excitement because I had never seen such a marvellous tree before. I approached it slowly, even cautiously, as I wasn't sure the tree wanted my friendship. It looked as though it had many secrets. There were sounds and movement in the branches but I couldn't see who or what made the sounds.

The tree made the first move, the first overture of friendship. It allowed a leaf to fall.

The leaf brushed against my face as it floated down, but before it could reach the ground I caught and held it. I studied the leaf, running my fingers over its smooth, glossy texture. Then I put out my hand and touched the rough bark of the tree and this felt good to me. So I removed my shoes and socks as people do when they enter a holy place; and finding first a foothold and then a handhold on that broad trunk, I pulled myself up with the help of the tree's aerial roots.

As I climbed, it seemed as though someone was helping me; invisible hands, the hands of the spirit in the tree, touched me and helped me climb.

But although the tree wanted me, there were others who were disturbed and alarmed by my arrival. A pair of parrots suddenly shot out of a hole in the trunk and, with shrill cries, flew across the garden—flashes of green and red and gold. A squirrel looked out from behind a branch, saw me, and went scurrying away to inform his friends and relatives.

I climbed higher, looked up, and saw a red beak poised above my head. I shrank away, but the hornbill made no attempt to attack me. He was relaxing in his home, which was a great hole in the tree trunk. Only the bird's head and great beak were showing. He looked at me in a rather bored way, drowsily opening and shutting his eyes.

'So many creatures live here,' I said to myself. 'I hope none of them are dangerous!'

At that moment, the hornbill lunged at a passing cricket. Bill and tree trunk met with a loud and resonant 'Tonk!'

I was so startled that I nearly fell out of the tree. But it was a difficult tree to fall out of! It was full of places where one could sit or even lie down. So I moved away from the hornbill, crawled along a branch that had sent out supports, and so moved quite a distance from the main body of the tree. I left its cold, dark depths for an area penetrated by shafts of sunlight.

No one could see me. I lay flat on the broad branch hidden by a screen of leaves. People passed by on the road below. A sahib in a sun-helmet. His memsahib twirling a coloured silk sun-umbrella. Obviously she did not want to get too brown and be mistaken for a country-born person. Behind them, a pram wheeled along by a nanny.

Then there were a number of Indians; some in white dhotis, some in western clothes, some in loincloths. Some with baskets on their heads. Others with coolies to carry their baskets for them.

A cloud of dust, the blare of a horn, and down the road, like an out-of-condition dragon, came the latest Morris touring car. Then cyclists. Then a man with a basket of papayas balanced on his head. Following him, a man with a performing monkey. This man rattled a little hand drum, and children followed the man and the monkey along the road. They stopped in the shade of a mango tree on the other side of the road. The little red monkey wore a frilled dress and a baby's bonnet. It danced for the children, while the man sang and played his drum.

The clip-clop of a tonga pony, and Bansi's tonga came rattling down the road. I called down to him and he reined in with a shout of surprise, and looked up into the branches of the banyan tree.

'What are you doing up there?' he cried.

'Hiding from Grandmother,' I said.

'And when are you coming for that ride?'

'On Tuesday afternoon,' I said.

'Why not today?'

'Ayah won't let me. But she has Tuesdays off.'

Bansi spat red paan juice across the road. 'Your ayah is jealous,' he said.

'I know,' I said. 'Women are always jealous, aren't they? I suppose it's because she doesn't have a tonga.'

'It's because she doesn't have a tonga-driver,' said Bansi, grinning up at me. 'Never mind. I'll come on Tuesday—that's the day after tomorrow, isn't it?'

I nodded down to him, and then started backing along my branch, because I could hear Ayah calling in the distance. Bansi leant forward and smacked his pony across the rump, and the tonga shot forward.

'What were you doing up there?' asked Ayah a little later.

'I was watching a snake cross the road,' I said. I knew she couldn't resist talking about snakes. There weren't as many in Dehra as there had been in Kathiawar and she was thrilled that I had seen one.

'Was it moving towards you or away from you?' she asked.

'It was going away.'

Ayah's face clouded over. 'That means poverty for the beholder,' she said gloomily.

Later, while scrubbing me down in the bathroom, she began to air all her prejudices, which included drunkards ('they die quickly anyway'), misers ('they get murdered sooner or later') and tonga-drivers ('they have all the vices').

'You are a very lucky boy,' she said suddenly, peering closely at my tummy.

'Why?' I asked. 'You just said I would be poor because I saw a snake going the wrong way.'

'Well, you won't be poor for long. You have a mole on your tummy, and that's very lucky. And there is one under your armpit, which means you will be famous. Do you have one on the neck? No, thank God! A mole on the neck is the sign of a murderer!'

'Do you have any moles?' I asked.

Ayah nodded seriously, and pulling her sleeve up to her shoulder, showed me a large mole high on her arm.

'What does that mean?' I asked.

'It means a life of great sadness,' said Ayah gloomily.

'Can I touch it?' I asked.

'Yes, touch it,' she said, and taking my hand, she placed it against the mole.

'It's a nice mole,' I said, wanting to make Ayah happy. 'Can I kiss it?'

'You can kiss it,' said Ayah.

I kissed her on the mole.

'That's nice,' she said.

Tuesday afternoon came at last, and as soon as Grandmother was asleep and Ayah had gone to the bazaar, I was at the gate, looking up and down the road for Bansi and his tonga. He was not long in coming. Before the tonga turned into the road, I could hear his voice, singing to the accompaniment of the carriage bells. He reached down, took my hand, and hoisted me onto the seat beside him. Then we went off down the road at a steady jogtrot. It was only when we reached the outskirts of the town that Bansi encouraged his pony to greater efforts. He rose in his seat, leaned forward and slapped the pony across the haunches. From a brisk trot we changed to a carefree canter. The tonga swayed from side to side. I clung to Bansi's free arm, while he grinned at me, his mouth red with paan juice.

'Where shall we go, dost?' he asked.

'Nowhere,' I said. 'Anywhere.'

'We'll go to the river,' said Bansi.

The 'river' was really a swift mountain stream that ran through the forests outside Dehra, joining the Ganga about fifteen miles away. It was almost dry during the winter and early summer; in flood during the monsoon.

The road out of Dehra was a gentle decline and soon we were rushing headlong through the tea gardens and eucalyptus forests, the pony's hoofs striking sparks off the metalled road, the carriage wheels groaning and creaking so loudly that I feared one of them would come off and that we would all be thrown into a ditch or into the small canal that ran beside the road. We swept through mango groves, through guava and litchi orchards, past broad-leaved sal and shisham trees. Once in the sal forest, Bansi turned the tonga on to a rough cart track, and we continued along it for about a furlong, until the road dipped down to the stream bed.

'Let us go straight into the water,' said Bansi. 'You and I and the pony!' And he drove the tonga straight into the middle of the stream, where the water came up to the pony's knees.

'I am not a great one for baths,' said Bansi, 'but the pony needs one, and why should a horse smell sweeter than its owner?' Saying which, he flung off his clothes and jumped into the water.

'Better than bathing under a tap!' he cried, slapping himself on the chest and thighs. 'Come down, dost, and join me!'

After some hesitation I joined him, but had some difficulty in keeping on my feet in the fast current. I grabbed at the pony's tail, and hung on to it, while Bansi began sloshing water over the patient animal's back.

After this, Bansi led both me and the pony out of the stream and together we gave the carriage a good washing down. I'd had a free ride and Bansi got the services of a free helper for the long overdue spring cleaning of his tonga. After we had finished the job, he presented me with a packet of aam papar—a sticky toffee made from mango pulp—and for some time I tore at it as a dog tears at a hit of old leather. Then I felt drowsy and lay down on the brown, sun-warmed grass. Crickets and grasshoppers were telephoning each other from tree and bush and a pair of bluejays rolled, dived and swooped acrobatically overhead.

Bansi had no watch. He looked at the sun and said, 'It is past three. When will that ayah of yours be home? She is more frightening than your grandmother!'

'She comes at four.'

'Then we must hurry back. And don't tell her where we've

been, or I'll never be able to come to your house again. Your grandmother's one of my best customers.'

'That means you'd be sorry if she died.'

'I would indeed, my friend.'

Bansi raced the tonga back to town. There was very little motor traffic in those days, and tongas and bullock carts were far more numerous than they are today.

We were back five minutes before Ayah returned. Before Bansi left, he promised to take me for another ride the following week.

◆

The house in Dehra had to be sold. My father had not left any money; he had never realized that his health would deteriorate so rapidly from the malarial fevers, which had grown in frequency. He was still planning for the future when he died. Now that my father had gone, Grandmother saw no point in staying on in India; there was nothing left in the bank and she needed money for our passages to England, so the house had to go. Dr Ghose, who had a thriving medical practice in Dehra, made her a reasonable offer, which she accepted.

Then things happened very quickly. Grandmother sold most of our belongings, because as she said, we wouldn't be able to cope with a lot of luggage. The *kabaris* came in droves, buying our crockery, furniture, carpets and clocks at throwaway prices. Grandmother hated parting with some of her possessions, such as the carved giltwood mirror, her walnut-wood armchair and her rosewood writing desk, but it was impossible to take them with us. They were carried away in a bullock cart.

Ayah was very unhappy at first but cheered up when Grandmother got her a job with a tea-planter's family in

Assam. It was arranged that she could stay with us until we left Dehra.

We left at the end of September, just as the monsoon clouds broke up, scattered, and were driven away by soft breezes from the Himalayas. There was no time to revisit the island where my father and I had planted our trees. And in the urgency and excitement of the preparations for our departure, I forgot to recover my small treasures from the hole in the banyan tree. It was only when we were in Bansi's tonga, on the way to the station, that I remembered my top, catapult and Iron Cross. Too late! To go back for them would mean missing the train.

'Hurry!' urged Grandmother nervously. 'We mustn't be late for the train, Bansi.'

Bansi flicked the reins and shouted to his pony, and for once in her life Grandmother submitted to being carried along the road at a brisk trot.

'It's five to nine,' she said, 'and the train leaves at nine.'

'Do not worry, Memsahib. I have been taking you to the station for fifteen years, and you have never missed a train!'

'No,' said Grandmother. 'And I don't suppose you'll ever take me to the station again, Bansi.'

'Times are changing, Memsahib. Do you know that there is now a taxi—a *motor car*—competing with the tongas of Dehra? You are lucky to be leaving. If you stay, you will see me starve to death!'

'We will all starve to death if we don't catch that train,' said Grandmother.

'Do not worry about the train, it never leaves on time, and no one expects it to. If it left at nine o' clock, everyone would miss it.'

Bansi was right. We arrived at the station at five minutes

past nine, and rushed on to the platform, only to find that the train had not yet arrived.

The platform was crowded with people waiting to catch the same train or to meet people arriving on it. Ayah was there already, standing guard over a pile of miscellaneous luggage. We sat down on our boxes and became part of the platform life at an Indian railway station.

Moving among piles of bedding and luggage were sweating, cursing coolies; vendors of magazines, sweetmeats, tea and betel-leaf preparations; also stray dogs, stray people and sometimes a stray stationmaster. The cries of the vendors mixed with the general clamour of the station and the shunting of a steam engine in the yards. 'Tea, hot tea!' Sweets, papads, hot stuff, cold drinks, toothpowder, pictures of film stars, bananas, balloons, wooden toys, clay images of the gods. The platform had become a bazaar.

Ayah was giving me all sorts of warnings.

'Remember, baba, don't lean out of the window when the train is moving. There was that American boy who lost his head last year! And don't eat rubbish at every station between here and Bombay. And see that no strangers enter the compartment. Mr Wilkins was murdered *and* robbed last year!'

The station bell clanged, and in the distance there appeared a big, puffing steam engine, painted green and gold and black. A stray dog, with a lifetime's experience of trains, darted away across the railway lines. As the train came alongside the platform, doors opened, window shutters fell, faces appeared in the openings, and even before the train had come to a stop, people were trying to get in or out.

For a few moments there was chaos. The crowd surged backward and forward. No one could get out. No one could get in. A hundred people were leaving the train, two hundred were getting into it. No one wanted to give way.

The problem was solved by a man climbing out of a window. Others followed his example and the pressure at the doors eased and people started squeezing into their compartments.

Grandmother had taken the precaution of reserving berths in a first-class compartment, and assisted by Bansi and half a dozen coolies, we were soon inside with all our luggage. A whistle blasted and we were off! Bansi had to jump from the running train.

As the engine gathered speed, I ignored Ayah's advice and put my head out of the window to look back at the receding platform. Ayah and Bansi were standing on the platform, waving to me and I kept waving to them until the train rushed into the darkness and the bright lights of Dehra were swallowed up in the night. New lights, dim and flickering came into existence as we passed small villages. The stars too were visible and I saw a shooting star streaking through the heavens.

I remembered something that Ayah had once told me, that stars are the spirits of good men, and I wondered if that shooting star was a sign from my father that he was aware of our departure and would be with us on our journey. And I remembered something else that Ayah had said—that if one wished on a shooting star, one's wish would be granted, provided of course that one thrust all five fingers into the mouth at the same time!

'What on earth are you doing?' asked Grandmother staring at me as I thrust my hand into my mouth.

'Making a wish,' I said.

'Oh,' said Grandmother.

She was preoccupied, and didn't ask me what I was wishing for; nor did I tell her.

THE FOUR FEATHERS

Our school dormitory.was a very long room with about thirty beds, fifteen on either side of the room. This was good for pillow fights. Class V would take on Class VI (the two senior classes in our Prep school) and there would be plenty of space for leaping, struggling small boys, pillows flying, feathers flying, until there was a cry of 'Here comes Fishy!' or 'Here comes Olly!' and either Mr Fisher, the Headmaster, or Mr Oliver, the Senior Master, would come striding in, cane in hand, to put an end to the general mayhem. Pillow fights were allowed, up to a point; nobody got hurt. But parents sometimes complained if, at the end of the term, a boy came home with a pillow devoid of cotton-wool or feathers.

In that last year at Prep school in Shimla, there were four of us who were close friends—Bimal, whose home was in Bombay; Riaz, who came from Lahore; Bran, who hailed from Vellore; and your narrator, who lived wherever his father (then in the Air Force) was posted.

We called ourselves the 'Four Feathers', the feathers signifying that we were companions in adventure, comrades-in-arms, and knights of the round table. Bimal adopted a peacock's feather as his emblem—he was always a bit showy. Riaz chose a falcon's feather—although we couldn't find one. Bran and I were at first offered crows or *murghi* feathers, but we protested vigorously and threatened a walkout. Finally, I settled for a parrot's feather (taken from Mrs Fisher's pet parrot), and Bran found a woodpecker's, which suited him, as he was always knocking things about.

Bimal was all thin legs and arms, so light and frisky that at times he seemed to be walking on air. We called him 'Bambi', after the delicate little deer in the Disney film. Riaz, on the other hand, was a sturdy boy, good at games though not very studious; but always good-natured, always smiling.

Bran was a dark, good-looking boy from the South; he was just a little spoilt—hated being given out in a cricket match and would refuse to leave the crease!—but he was affectionate and a loyal friend. I was the 'scribe'—good at inventing stories in order to get out of scrapes—but hopeless at sums, my highest marks being twenty-two out of one hundred.

On Sunday afternoons, when there were no classes or organized games, we were allowed to roam about on the hillside below the school. The Four Feathers would laze about on the short summer grass, sharing the occasional food parcel from home, reading comics (sometimes a book), and making plans for the long winter holidays. My father, who collected everything from stamps to seashells to butterflies, had given me a butterfly net and urged me to try and catch a rare species which, he said, was found only near Chotta Shimla. He described it as a large purple butterfly with yellow and black borders on its wings. A Purple Emperor, I think it was called. As I wasn't very good at identifying butterflies, I would chase anything that happened to flit across the school grounds, usually ending up with Common Red Admirals, Clouded Yellows, or Cabbage Whites. But that Purple Emperor—that rare specimen being sought by collectors the world over—proved elusive. I would have to seek my fortune in some other line of endeavour.

One day, scrambling about among the rocks and thorny bushes below the school, I almost fell over a small bundle lying in the shade of a young spruce tree. On taking a closer look, I discovered that the bundle was really a baby, wrapped up in a tattered old blanket.

'Feathers, feathers!' I called, 'come here and look. A baby's been left here!'

The feathers joined me and we all stared down at the infant, who was fast asleep.

'Who would leave a baby on the hillside?' asked Bimal of no one in particular.

'Someone who doesn't want it,' said Bran.

'And hoped some good people would come along and keep it,' said Riaz.

'A panther might have come along instead,' I said. 'Can't leave it here.'

'Well, we'll just have to adopt it,' said Bimal.

'We can't adopt a baby,' said Bran.

'Why not?'

'We have to be married.'

'We don't.'

'Not us, you dope. The grown-ups who adopt babies.'

'Well, we can't just leave it here for grows-ups to come along,' I said.

'We don't even know if it's a boy or a girl,' said Riaz.

'Makes no difference. A baby's a baby. Let's take it back to school.'

'And keep it in the dormitory?'

'Of course not. Who's going to feed it? Babies need milk. We'll hand it over to Mrs Fisher. She doesn't have a baby.'

'Maybe she doesn't want one. Look, it's beginning to cry. Let's hurry!'

Riaz picked up the wide-awake and crying baby and gave it to Bimal who gave it to Bran who gave it to me. The Four Feathers marched up the hill to school with a very noisy baby.

'Now it's done potty in the blanket,' I complained. 'And some of it's on my shirt.'

'Never mind,' said Bimal. 'It's in a good cause. You're a Boy Scout, remember? You're supposed to help people in distress.'

The headmaster and his wife were in their drawing room, enjoying their afternoon tea and cakes. We trudged in, and Bimal announced, 'We've got something for Mrs Fisher.'

Mrs Fisher took one look at the bundle in my arms and let out a shriek. 'What have you brought here, Bond?'

'A baby, ma'am. I think it's a girl. Do you want to adopt it?'

Mrs Fisher threw up her arms in consternation, and turned to her husband. 'What are we to do, Frank? These boys are impossible. They've picked up someone's child!'

'We'll have to inform the police,' said Mr Fisher, reaching for the telephone. 'We can't have lost babies in the school.'

Just then there was a commotion outside, and a wild-eyed woman, her clothes dishevelled, entered at the front door accompanied by several menfolk from one of the villages. She ran towards us, crying out, 'My baby, my baby! Mera bachcha! You've stolen my baby!'

'We found it on the hillside,' I stammered.

'That's right,' said Bran. 'Finder's keepers!'

'Quiet, Adams,' said Mr Fisher, holding up his hand for order and addressing the villagers in a friendly manner. 'These boys found the baby alone on the hillside and brought it here before...before...'

'Before the hyenas got it,' I put in.

'Quite right, Bond. And why did you leave your child alone?' he asked the woman.

'I put her down for five minutes so that I could climb the plum tree and collect the plums. When I came down, the baby had gone! But I could hear it crying up on the hill. I called the menfolk and we come looking for it.'

'Well, here's your baby,' I said, thrusting it into her arms. By then I was glad to be rid of it! 'Look after it properly in future.'

'Kidnapper!' she screamed at me.

Mr Fisher succeeded in mollifying the villagers. 'These boys are good Scouts,' he told them. 'It's their business to help people.'

'Scout Law Number Three, sir,' I added. 'To be useful and helpful.'

And then the Headmaster turned the tables on the villagers. 'By the way, those plum trees belong to the school. So do the peaches and apricots. Now I know why they've been disappearing so fast!'

The villagers, a little chastened, went their way.

Mr Fisher reached for his cane. From the way he fondled it I knew he was itching to use it on our bottoms.

'No, Frank,' said Mrs Fisher, intervening on our behalf. 'It was really very sweet of them to look after that baby. And look at Bond—he's got baby-goo all over his clothes.'

'So he has. Go and take a bath, all of you. And what are you grinning about, Bond?'

'Scout Law Number Eight, sir. A Scout smiles and whistles under all difficulties.'

And so ended the first adventure of the Four Feathers.

THE WOMAN ON PLATFORM NO. 8

It was my second year at boarding school, and I was sitting on platform no. 8 at Ambala station, waiting for the northern-bound train. I think I was about twelve at the time. My parents considered me old enough to travel alone, and I had arrived by bus at Ambala early in the evening; now there was a wait till midnight before my train arrived. Most of the time I had been pacing up and down the platform, browsing through the bookstall, or feeding broken biscuits to stray dogs; trains came and went, the platform would be quiet for a while and then, when a train arrived, it would be an inferno of heaving, shouting, agitated human bodies. As the carriage doors opened, a tide of people would sweep down upon the nervous little ticket collector at the gate; and every time this happened I would be caught in the rush and swept outside the station. Now tired of this game and of ambling about the platform, I sat down on my suitcase and gazed dismally across the railway tracks.

Trolleys rolled past me, and I was conscious of the cries of the various vendors—the men who sold curds and lemon, the sweetmeat seller, the newspaper boy—but I had lost interest in all that was going on along the busy platform, and continued to stare across the railway tracks, feeling bored and a little lonely.

'Are you all alone, my son?' asked a soft voice close behind me.

I looked up and saw a woman standing near me. She was leaning over, and I saw a pale face and dark, kind eyes. She wore no jewels, and was dressed very simply in a white sari.

'Yes, I am going to school,' I said, and stood up respectfully. She seemed poor, but there was a dignity about her that commanded respect.

'I have been watching you for some time,' she said. 'Didn't your parents come to see you off?'

'I don't live here,' I said. 'I had to change trains. Anyway, I can travel alone.'

'I am sure you can,' she said, and I liked her for saying that, and I also liked her for the simplicity of her dress, and for her deep, soft voice and the serenity of her face.

'Tell me, what is your name?' she asked.

'Arun,' I said.

'And how long do you have to wait for your train?'

'About an hour, I think. It comes at twelve o'clock.'

'Then come with me and have something to eat.'

I was going to refuse, out of shyness and suspicion, but she took me by the hand, and then I felt it would be silly to pull my hand away. She told a coolie to look after my suitcase, and then she led me away down the platform. Her hand was gentle, and she held mine neither too firmly nor too lightly. I looked up at her again. She was not young. And she was not old. She must have been over thirty, but had she been fifty, I think she would have looked much the same.

She took me into the station dining room, ordered tea and samosas and jalebis, and at once I began to thaw and take a new interest in this kind woman. The strange encounter had little effect on my appetite. I was a hungry schoolboy, and I ate as much as I could in as polite a manner as possible. She took obvious pleasure in watching me eat, and I think it was the food that strengthened the bond between us and cemented our friendship, for under the influence of the tea and sweets I began to talk quite freely, and told her about my school, my friends, my likes and dislikes. She questioned me quietly from time to time, but preferred listening; she drew me out very well, and I had soon forgotten that we were strangers. But she did not ask me about my family or where I lived, and I did not ask her where she lived. I accepted her for what she had been to me—a quiet, kind and gentle woman who gave sweets to a lonely boy on a railway platform…

After about half an hour we left the dining room and began walking back along the platform. An engine was shunting up and down beside platform no. 8, and as it approached, a boy leapt off the platform and ran across the rails, taking a shortcut to the next platform. He was at a safe distance from the engine, but as he leapt across the rails, the woman clutched my arm. Her fingers dug into my flesh, and I winced with pain. I caught her fingers and looked up at her, and I saw a spasm of pain and fear and sadness pass across her face. She watched the boy as he climbed the platform, and it was not until he had disappeared in the crowd that she relaxed her hold on my arm. She smiled at me reassuringly and took my hand again, but her fingers trembled against mine.

'He was all right,' I said, feeling that it was she who needed reassurance.

She smiled gratefully at me and pressed my hand. We walked together in silence until we reached the place where I had left my suitcase. One of my school fellows, Satish, a boy of about my age, had turned up with his mother.

'Hello, Arun!' he called. 'The train's coming in late, as usual.

Did you know we have a new headmaster this year?'

We shook hands, and then he turned to his mother and said: 'This is Arun, Mother. He is one of my friends, and the best bowler in the class.'

'I am glad to know that,' said his mother, a large imposing woman who wore spectacles. She looked at the woman who held my hand and said: 'And I suppose you're Arun's mother?'

I opened my mouth to make some explanation, but before I could say anything the woman replied: 'Yes, I am Arun's mother.'

I was unable to speak a word. I looked quickly up at the woman, but she did not appear to be at all embarrassed, and was smiling at Satish's mother.

Satish's mother said, 'It's such a nuisance having to wait for the train right in the middle of the night. But one can't let the child wait here alone. Anything can happen to a boy at a big station like this—there are so many suspicious characters hanging about. These days one has to be very careful of strangers.'

'Arun can travel alone, though,' said the woman beside me, and somehow I felt grateful to her for saying that. I had already forgiven her for lying; and besides, I had taken an instinctive dislike to Satish's mother.

'Well, be very careful, Arun,' said Satish's mother, looking sternly at me through her spectacles. 'Be very careful when your mother is not with you. And never talk to strangers!'

I looked from Satish's mother to the woman who had given me tea and sweets, and back at Satish's mother.

'I like strangers,' I said.

Satish's mother definitely staggered a little, as obviously she was not used to being contradicted by small boys. 'There you are, you see! If you don't watch over them all the time, they'll walk straight into trouble. Always listen to what your mother tells you,' she said, wagging a fat little finger at me. 'And never, never talk to strangers.'

I glared resentfully at her, and moved closer to the woman who had befriended me. Satish was standing behind his mother, grinning at me, and delighting in my clash with his mother. Apparently he was on my side.

The station bell clanged, and the people who had till now been squatting resignedly on the platform began bustling about.

'Here it comes!' shouted Satish, as the engine whistle shrieked and the front lights played over the rails.

The train moved slowly into the station, the engine hissing and sending out waves of steam. As it came to a stop, Satish jumped on the footboard of a lighted compartment and shouted, 'Come on, Arun, this one's empty!' and I picked up my suitcase and made a dash for the open door.

We placed ourselves at the open windows, and the two women stood outside on the platform, talking up to us. Satish's mother did most of the talking.

'Now don't jump on and off moving trains as you did just now,' she said. 'And don't stick your heads out of the windows, and don't eat any rubbish on the way.' She allowed me to share the benefit of her advice, as she probably didn't think my 'mother' a very capable person. She handed Satish a bag of fruit, a cricket bat and a big box of chocolates, and told him to share the food with me. Then she stood back from the window to watch how my 'mother' behaved.

I was smarting under the patronizing tone of Satish's mother, who obviously thought mine a very poor family; and I did not intend giving the other woman away. I let her take my hand in hers, but I could think of nothing to say. I was conscious of Satish's mother staring at us with hard, beady eyes, and I found myself hating her with a firm, unreasoning hate. The guard walked up the platform, blowing his whistle for the train to leave. I looked straight into the eyes of the woman who held my hand, and she smiled in a gentle, understanding way. I leaned out of the window then, and put my lips to her cheek and kissed her.

The carriage jolted forward, and she drew her hand away.

'Goodbye, Mother!' said Satish, as the train began to move slowly out of the station. Satish and his mother waved to each other.

'Goodbye,' I said to the other woman, 'goodbye—Mother…' I didn't wave or shout, but sat still in front of the window, gazing at the woman on the platform. Satish's mother was talking to her, but she didn't appear to be listening; she was looking at me as the train took me away. She stood there on the busy platform, a pale sweet woman in white, and I watched her until she was lost in the milling crowd.

THE FIGHT

Ranji had been less than a month in Rajpur when he discovered the pool in the forest. It was the height of summer and his school had not yet opened and, having as yet made no friends in this semi-hill station, he wandered about a good deal by himself into the hills and forests that stretched away interminably on all sides of the town. It was hot, very hot, at that time of year, and Ranji walked about in his vest and shorts, his brown feet white with the chalky dust that flew up from the ground. The earth was parched, the grass brown, the trees listless, hardly stirring, waiting for a cool wind or a refreshing shower of rain.

It was on such a day—a hot, tired day—that Ranji found the pool in the forest. The water had a gentle translucency and you could see the smooth round pebbles at the bottom of the pool. A small stream emerged from a cluster of rocks to feed the pool. During the monsoon, this stream would be a gushing torrent, cascading down from the hills, but during the summer it was barely a trickle. The rocks, however, held the water in the pool, and it did not dry up like the pools in the plains.

When Ranji saw the pool, he did not hesitate to get into it. He had often gone swimming, alone or with friends, when he had lived with his parents in a thirsty town in the middle of the Rajputana desert. There, he had known only sticky, muddy pools, where buffaloes wallowed and women washed clothes. He had never seen a pool like this—so clean and cold and inviting. He threw off all his clothes, as he had done when he went swimming in the plains, and leapt into the water. His limbs were supple, free of any fat, and his dark body glistened in patches of sunlit water.

The next day he came again to quench his body in the cool waters of the forest pool. He was there for almost an hour, sliding in and out of the limpid green water, or lying stretched out on the smooth yellow rocks in the shade of broad-leaved sal trees. It was while he lay thus, naked on a rock, that he noticed another boy standing a little distance away, staring at him in a rather hostile manner. The other boy was a little older than Ranji, taller, thick-set, with a broad nose and thick, red lips. He had only just noticed Ranji, and he stood at the edge of the pool, wearing a pair of bathing shorts, waiting for Ranji to explain himself.

When Ranji did not say anything, the other called out, 'What are you doing here, mister?'

Ranji, who was prepared to be friendly, was taken aback at the hostility of the other's tone.

'I am swimming,' he replied. 'Why don't you join me?'

'I always swim alone,' said the other. 'This is my pool, I did not invite you here. And why are you not wearing any clothes?'

'It is not your business if I do not wear clothes. I have nothing to be ashamed of.'

'You skinny fellow, put on your clothes.'

'Fat fool, take yours off.'

This was too much for the stranger to tolerate. He strode up to Ranji, who still sat on the rock and, planting his broad feet firmly on the sand, said (as though this would settle the matter once and for all), 'Don't you know I am a Punjabi? I do not take replies from villagers like you!'

'So you like to fight with villagers?' said Ranji. 'Well, I am not a villager. I am a Rajput!'

'I am a Punjabi!'

'I am a Rajput!'

They had reached an impasse. One had said he was a Punjabi, the other had proclaimed himself a Rajput. There was little else that could be said.

'You understand that I am a Punjabi?' said the stranger, feeling that perhaps this information had not penetrated Ranji's head.

'I have heard you say it three times,' replied Ranji.

'Then why are you not running away?'

'I am waiting for *you* to run away!'

'I will have to beat you,' said the stranger, assuming a violent attitude, showing Ranji the palm of his hand.

'I am waiting to see you do it,' said Ranji.

'You will see me do it,' said the other boy.

Ranji waited. The other boy made a strange, hissing sound. They stared each other in the eye for almost a minute. Then the Punjabi boy slapped Ranji across the face with all the force he could muster. Ranji staggered, feeling quite dizzy. There were thick, red finger marks on his cheek.

'There you are!' exclaimed his assailant. 'Will you be off now?'

For answer, Ranji swung his arm up and pushed a hard, bony fist into the other's face.

And then they were at each other's throats, swaying on the rock, tumbling on to the sand, rolling over and over, their legs and arms locked in a desperate, violent struggle. Gasping and cursing, clawing and slapping, they rolled right into the shallows of the pool.

Even in the water the fight continued as, spluttering and covered with mud, they groped for each other's head and throat. But after five minutes of frenzied, unscientific struggle, neither boy had emerged victorious. Their bodies heaving with exhaustion, they stood back from each other, making tremendous efforts to speak.

'Now…now do you realize…I am a Punjabi?' gasped the stranger.

'Do you know I am a Rajput?' said Ranji with difficulty.

They gave a moment's consideration to each other's answers, and in that moment of silence there was only their heavy breathing and the rapid beating of their hearts.

'Then you will not leave the pool?' said the Punjabi boy.

'I will not leave it,' said Ranji.

'Then we shall have to continue the fight,' said the other.

'All right,' said Ranji.

But neither boy moved, neither took the initiative.

The Punjabi boy had an inspiration.

'We will continue the fight tomorrow,' he said. 'If you dare to come here again tomorrow, we will continue this fight and I will not show you mercy as I have done today.'

'I will come tomorrow,' said Ranji. 'I will be ready for you.'

They turned from each other then and, going to their respective rocks, put on their clothes and left the forest by different routes.

When Ranji got home, he found it difficult to explain the cuts and bruises that showed on his face, legs and arms. It was difficult to conceal the fact that he had been in an unusually violent fight, and his mother insisted on his staying at home for the rest of the day. That evening, though, he slipped out of the house and went to the bazaar, where he found comfort and solace in a bottle of vividly coloured lemonade and a banana leaf full of hot, sweet jalebis. He had just finished the lemonade when he saw his adversary coming down the road. His first impulse was to turn away and look elsewhere, his second to throw the lemonade bottle at his enemy. But he did neither of these things. Instead, he stood his ground and scowled at his passing adversary. And the Punjabi boy said nothing either, but scowled back with equal ferocity.

The next day was as hot as the previous one. Ranji felt weak and lazy and not at all eager for a fight. His body was stiff and sore after the previous day's encounter. But he could not refuse the challenge. Not to turn up at the pool would be an acknowledgement of defeat. From the way he felt just then, he knew he would be beaten in another fight. But he could not acquiesce in his own defeat. He must defy his enemy to the last, or outwit him, for only then could he gain his respect. If he surrendered now, he would be beaten for all time; but to fight and be beaten today left him free to fight and be beaten again. As long as he fought, he had a right to the pool in the forest.

He was half hoping that the Punjabi boy would have forgotten the challenge, but these hopes were dashed when he saw his opponent sitting, stripped to the waist, on a rock on the other side of the pool. The Punjabi boy was rubbing oil on his body, massaging it into his broad thighs. He saw Ranji beneath the sal trees, and called a challenge across the waters of the pool.

'Come over on this side and fight!' he shouted.

But Ranji was not going to submit to any conditions laid down by his opponent.

'Come *this* side and fight!' he shouted back with equal vigour.

'Swim across and fight me here!' called the other. 'Or perhaps you cannot swim the length of this pool?'

But Ranji could have swum the length of the pool a dozen times without tiring, and here he would show the Punjabi boy his superiority. So, slipping out of his vest and shorts, he dived straight into the water, cutting through it like a knife, and surfaced with hardly a splash. The Punjabi boy's mouth hung open in amazement.

'You can dive!' he exclaimed.

'It is easy,' said Ranji, treading water, waiting for a further challenge. 'Can't you dive?'

'No,' said the other. 'I jump straight in. But if you will tell me how, I will make a dive.'

'It is easy,' said Ranji. 'Stand on the rock, stretch your arms out and allow your head to displace your feet.'

The Punjabi boy stood up, stiff and straight, stretched out his arms, and threw himself into the water. He landed flat on his belly, with a crash that sent the birds screaming out of the trees.

Ranji dissolved into laughter.

'Are you trying to empty the pool?' he asked, as the Punjabi boy came to the surface, spouting water like a small whale.

'Wasn't it good?' asked the boy, evidently proud of his feat.

'Not very good,' said Ranji. 'You should have more practice. See, I will do it again.'

And pulling himself up on a rock, he executed another perfect dive. The other boy waited for him to come up, but, swimming underwater, Ranji circled him and came upon him from behind.

'How did you do that?' asked the astonished youth.

'Can't you swim underwater?' asked Ranji.

'No, but I will try it.'

The Punjabi boy made a tremendous effort to plunge to the bottom of the pool and indeed he thought he had gone right down, though his bottom, like a duck's, remained above the surface.

Ranji, however, did not discourage him.

'It was not bad,' he said. 'But you need a lot of practice.'

'Will you teach me?' asked his enemy.

'If you like, I will teach you.'

'You must teach me. If you do not teach me, I will beat you. Will you come here every day and teach me?'

'If you like,' said Ranji. They had pulled themselves out of the water, and were sitting side by side on a smooth grey rock.

'My name is Suraj,' said the Punjabi boy. 'What is yours?'

'It is Ranji.'

'I am strong, am I not?' asked Suraj, bending his arm so that a ball of muscle stood up stretching the white of his flesh.

'You are strong,' said Ranji. 'You are a real *pahelwan.*'

'One day I will be the world's champion wrestler,' said Suraj, slapping his thighs, which shook with the impact of his hand. He looked critically at Ranji's hard, thin body.

'You are quite strong yourself,' he conceded. 'But you are too bony. I know you people do not eat enough. You must come and have your food with me.

'I drink one *seer* of milk every day. We have got our own cow! Be my friend, and I will make you a pahelwan like me! I know—if you teach me to dive and swim underwater, I will make you a pahelwan! That is fair, isn't it?'

'That is fair!' said Ranji, though he doubted if he was getting the better of the exchange.

Suraj put his arm around the younger boy and said, 'We are friends now, yes?'

They looked at each other with honest, unflinching eyes, and in that moment love and understanding were born.

'We are friends,' said Ranji.

The birds had settled again on their branches, and the pool was quiet and limpid in the shade of the sal trees.

'It is our pool,' said Suraj. 'Nobody else can come here without our permission. Who would dare?'

'Who would dare?' said Ranji, smiling with the knowledge that he had won the day.

THE NIGHT THE ROOF BLEW OFF

We are used to sudden storms, up here on the first range of the Himalayas. The old building in which we live has, for more than a hundred years, received the full force of the wind as it sweeps across the hills from the east.

We'd lived in the building for more than ten years without a disaster. It had even taken the shock of a severe earthquake. As my granddaughter Dolly said, 'It's difficult to tell the new cracks from the old!'

It's a two-storey building, and I live on the upper floor with my family: my three grandchildren and their parents. The roof is made of corrugated tin sheets, the ceiling of wooden boards. That's the traditional Mussoorie roof.

Looking back at the experience, it was the sort of thing that should have happened in a James Thurber story, like the dam that burst or the ghost who got in. But I wasn't thinking of Thurber at the time, although a few of his books were among the many I was trying to save from the icy rain pouring into my bedroom.

Our roof had held fast in many a storm, but the wind that night was really fierce. It came rushing at us with a high-pitched, eerie wail. The old roof groaned and protested. It took a battering for several hours while the rain lashed against the windows and the lights kept coming and going.

There was no question of sleeping, but we remained in bed for warmth and comfort. The fire had long since gone out, as the chimney had collapsed, bringing down a shower of sooty rainwater.

After about four hours of buffeting, the roof could take it no longer. My bedroom faces east, so my portion of the roof was the first to go.

The wind got under it and kept pushing until, with a ripping, groaning sound, the metal sheets shifted and slid off the rafters, some of them dropping with claps like thunder on to the road below.

So that's it, I thought. Nothing worse can happen. As long as the ceiling stays on, I'm not getting out of bed. We'll collect our roof in the morning.

Icy water splashing down on my face made me change my mind in a hurry. Leaping from the bed, I found that much of the ceiling had gone, too. Water was pouring on my open typewriter as well as on the bedside radio and bed cover.

Picking up my precious typewriter (my companion for forty years), I stumbled into the front sitting room (and library), only to find a similar situation there. Water was pouring through the slats of the wooden ceiling, raining down on the open bookshelves.

By now I had been joined by the children, who had come to my rescue. Their section of the roof hadn't gone as yet. Their parents were struggling to close a window against the driving rain.

'Save the books!' shouted Dolly, the youngest, and that became our rallying cry for the next hour or two.

Dolly and her brother Mukesh picked up armfuls of books and carried them into their room. But the floor was awash, so the books had to be piled on their beds. Dolly was helping me gather some of my papers when a large field rat jumped on to the desk in front of her. Dolly squealed and ran for the door.

'It's all right,' said Mukesh, whose love of animals extends even to field rats. 'It's only sheltering from the storm.'

Big brother Rakesh whistled for our dog, Tony, but Tony wasn't interested in rats just then. He had taken shelter in the kitchen, the only dry spot in the house.

Two rooms were now practically roofless, and we could see the sky lit up by flashes of lightning.

There were fireworks indoors, too, as water spluttered and crackled along a damaged wire. Then the lights went out altogether.

Rakesh, at his best in an emergency, had already lit two kerosene lamps. And by their light, we continued to transfer books, papers and clothes to the children's room.

We noticed that the water on the floor was beginning to subside a little.

'Where is it going?' asked Dolly.

'Through the floor,' said Mukesh. 'Down to the flat below!'

Cries of concern from our downstairs neighbours told us that they were having their share of the flood.

Our feet were freezing because there hadn't been time to put on proper footwear. And besides, shoes and slippers were awash by now. All chairs and tables were piled high with books. I hadn't realized the extent of my library until that night!

The available beds were pushed into the driest corner of the children's room, and there, huddled in blankets and quilts, we spent the remaining hours of the night while the storm continued.

Towards morning the wind fell, and it began to snow. Through the door to the sitting room, I could see snowflakes drifting through the gaps in the ceiling, settling on picture-frames. Ordinary things like a glue bottle and a small clock took on a certain beauty when covered with soft snow.

Most of us dozed off.

When dawn came, we found the windowpanes encrusted with snow and icicles. The rising sun struck through the gaps in the ceiling and turned everything golden. Snow crystals glistened on the empty bookshelves. But the books had been saved.

Rakesh went out to find a carpenter and tinsmith, while the rest of us started putting things in the sun to dry. By evening we'd put much of the roof back on.

It's a much-improved roof now, and we look forward to the next storm with confidence!

THE FUNERAL

'I don't think he should go,' said Aunt M.

'He's too young,' concurred Aunt B. 'He'll get upset and probably throw a tantrum. And you know Padre Lal doesn't like having children at funerals.'

The boy said nothing. He sat in the darkest corner of the darkened room, his face revealing nothing of what he thought and felt. His father's coffin lay in the next room, the lid fastened forever over the tired, wistful countenance of the man who had meant so much to the boy. Nobody else had mattered—neither uncles nor aunts nor fond grandparents. Least of all the mother who was hundreds of miles away with another husband. He hadn't seen her since he was four—that was just over five years ago—and he did not remember her very well.

The house was full of people—friends, relatives, neighbours. Some had tried to fuss over him but had been discouraged by his silence, the absence of tears. The more understanding of them had kept their distance.

Scattered words of condolence passed back and forth like dragonflies in the wind. 'Such a tragedy!'

'Only forty.'

'No one realized how serious it was.'

'Devoted to the child.'

It seemed to the boy that everyone who mattered in the

hill station was present. And for the first time they had the run of the house for his father had not been a sociable man. Books, music, flowers and his stamp collection had been his main preoccupations, apart from the boy.

A small hearse, drawn by a hill pony, was led in at the gate and several able-bodied men lifted the coffin and manoeuvred it into the carriage. The crowd drifted away. The cemetery was about a mile down the road and those who did not have cars would have to walk the distance.

The boy stared through a window at the small procession passing through the gate. He'd been forgotten for the moment—left in care of the servants, who were the only ones to stay behind. Outside it was misty. The mist had crept up the valley and settled like a damp towel on the face of the mountain. Everyone was wet although it hadn't rained.

The boy waited until everyone had gone and then he left the room and went out onto the verandah. The gardener, who had been sitting in a bed of nasturtiums, looked up and asked the boy if he needed anything. But the boy shook his head and retreated indoors. The gardener, looking aggrieved because of the damage done to the flower beds by the mourners, shambled off to his quarters. The sahib's death meant that he would be out of a job very soon. The house would pass into other hands. The boy would go to an orphanage. There weren't many people who kept gardeners these days. In the kitchen, the cook was busy preparing the only big meal ever served in the house. All those relatives, and the padre too, would come back famished, ready for a sombre but nevertheless substantial meal. He, too, would be out of a job soon; but cooks were always in demand.

The boy slipped out of the house by a back door and made his way into the lane through a gap in a thicket of dog roses.

When he reached the main road, he could see the mourners wending their way around the hill to the cemetery. He followed at a distance.

It was the same road he had often taken with his father during their evening walks. The boy knew the name of almost every plant and wildflower that grew on the hillside. These, and various birds and insects, had been described and pointed out to him by his father.

Looking northwards, he could see the higher ranges of the Himalayas and the eternal snows. The graves in the cemetery were so laid out that if their incumbents did happen to rise one day, the first thing they would see would be the glint of the sun on those snow-covered peaks. Possibly the site had been chosen for the view. But to the boy it did not seem as if anyone would be able to thrust aside those massive tombstones and rise from their graves to enjoy the view. Their rest seemed as eternal as the snows. It would take an earthquake to burst those stones asunder and thrust the coffins up from the earth. The boy wondered why people hadn't made it easier for the dead to rise. They were so securely entombed that it appeared as though no one really wanted them to get out.

'God has need of your father…' With those words a well-meaning missionary had tried to console him.

And had God, in the same way, laid claim to the thousands of men, women and children who had been put to rest here in these neat and serried rows? What could he have wanted them for? Of what use are we to God when we are dead, wondered the boy.

The cemetery gate stood open but the boy leant against the old stone wall and stared down at the mourners as they shuffled about with the unease of a batsman about to face a very fast bowler. Only this bowler was invisible and would come up stealthily and from behind.

Padre Lal's voice droned on through the funeral service and then the coffin was lowered—down, deep down. The boy was surprised at how far down it seemed to go! Was that other, better world down in the depths of the earth? How could anyone, even a Samson, push his way back to the surface again? Superman did it in comics but his father was a gentle soul who wouldn't fight too hard against the earth and the grass and the roots of tiny trees. Or perhaps he'd grow into a tree and escape that way! 'If ever I'm put away like this,' thought the boy, 'I'll get into the root of a plant and then I'll become a flower and then maybe a bird will come and carry my seed away... I'll get out somehow!'

A few more words from the padre and then some of those present threw handfuls of earth over the coffin before moving away.

Slowly, in twos and threes, the mourners departed. The mist swallowed them up. They did not see the boy behind the wall. They were getting hungry.

He stood there until they had all gone. Then he noticed that the gardeners or caretakers were filling in the grave. He did not know whether to go forward or not. He was a little afraid. And it was too late now. The grave was almost covered.

He turned and walked away from the cemetery. The road stretched ahead of him, empty, swathed in mist. He was alone. What had his father said to him once? 'The strongest man in the world is he who stands alone.'

Well, he was alone, but at the moment he did not feel very strong.

For a moment he thought his father was beside him, that they were together on one of their long walks. Instinctively he put out his hand, expecting his father's warm, comforting touch. But there was nothing there, nothing, no one...

He clenched his fists and pushed them deep down into his pockets. He lowered his head so that no one would see his tears. There were people in the mist but he did not want to go near them for they had put his father away.

'He'll find a way out,' the boy said fiercely to himself. 'He'll get out somehow!'

A LONG WALK FOR BINA

I

A leopard, lithe and sinewy, drank at the mountain stream, and then lay down on the grass to bask in the late February sunshine. Its tail twitched occasionally and the animal appeared to be sleeping. At the sound of distant voices, it raised its head to listen, then stood up and leapt lightly over the boulders in the stream, disappearing among the trees on the opposite bank.

A minute or two later, three children came walking down the forest path. They were a girl and two boys, and they were singing in their local dialect an old song they had learnt from their grandparents.

Five more miles to go!
We climb through rain and snow.
A river to cross...
A mountain to pass...
Now we've four more miles to go!

Their school satchels looked new, their clothes had been washed and pressed. Their loud and cheerful singing startled a spotted forktail. The bird left its favourite rock in the stream and flew down the dark ravine.

'Well, we have only three more miles to go,' said the bigger boy, Prakash, who had been this way hundreds of times. 'But first we have to cross the stream.'

He was a sturdy twelve-year-old with eyes like black currants and a mop of bushy hair that refused to settle down on his head. The girl and her small brother were taking this path for the first time.

'I'm feeling tired, Bina,' said the little boy.

Bina smiled at him, and Prakash said, 'Don't worry, Sonu, you'll get used to the walk. There's plenty of time.' He glanced at the old watch he'd been given by his grandfather. It needed constant winding. 'We can rest here for five or six minutes.'

They sat down on a smooth boulder and watched the clear water of the shallow stream tumbling downhill. Bina examined the old watch on Prakash's wrist. The glass was badly scratched and she could barely make out the figures on the dial. 'Are you sure it still gives the right time?' she asked.

'Well, it loses five minutes every day, so I put it ten minutes ahead at night. That means by morning it's quite accurate! Even our teacher, Mr Mani, asks me for the time. If he doesn't ask, I tell him! The clock in our classroom keeps stopping.'

They removed their shoes and let the cold mountain water run over their feet. Bina was the same age as Prakash. She had pink cheeks, soft brown eyes and hair that was just beginning to lose its natural curls. Hers was a gentle face, but a determined little chin showed that she could be a strong person. Sonu, her younger brother, was ten. He was a thin boy who had been sickly as a child but was now beginning to fill out. Although he did not look very athletic, he could run like the wind.

II

Bina had been going to school in her own village of Koli, on the other side of the mountain. But it had been a primary school, finishing at Class 5. Now, in order to study in Class 6, she would have to walk several miles every day to Nauti, where there was a high school going up to Class 8. It had been decided that Sonu would also shift to the new school, to give Bina company. Prakash, their neighbour in Koli, was already a pupil at the Nauti school. His mischievous nature, which sometimes got him into trouble, had resulted in his having to repeat a year.

But this didn't seem to bother him. 'What's the hurry?' he had told his indignant parents. 'You're not sending me to a foreign land when I finish school. And our cows aren't running away, are they?'

'You would prefer to look after the cows, wouldn't you?' asked Bina, as they got up to continue their walk.

'Oh, school's all right. Wait till you see old Mr Mani. He always gets our names mixed up, as well as the subjects he's supposed to be teaching. At our last lesson, instead of maths, he gave us a geography lesson!'

'More fun than maths,' said Bina.

'Yes, but there's a new teacher this year. She's very young they say, just out of college. I wonder what she'll be like.'

Bina walked faster, and Sonu had some trouble keeping up with them. She was excited about the new school and the prospect of different surroundings. She had seldom been outside her own village, with its small school and single ration shop. The day's routine never varied—helping her mother in the fields or with household tasks like fetching water from the spring or cutting grass and fodder for the cattle. Her father, who was a soldier, was away for nine months in the year, and Sonu was still too small for the heavier tasks.

As they neared Nauti Village, they were joined by other children coming from different directions. Even where there were no major roads, the mountains were full of little lanes and shortcuts. Like a game of snakes and ladders, these narrow paths zigzagged around the hills and villages, cutting through fields and crossing narrow ravines until they came together to form a fairly busy road along which mules, cattle and goats joined the throng.

Nauti was a fairly large village, and from here a broader but dustier road started for Tehri. There was a small bus, several trucks and (for part of the way) a road roller. The road hadn't been completed because the heavy diesel roller couldn't take the steep climb to Nauti. It stood on the roadside halfway up the road from Tehri.

Prakash knew almost everyone in the area, and exchanged greetings and gossip with other children as well as with muleteers, bus drivers, milkmen and labourers working on the road. He loved telling everyone the time, even if they weren't interested.

'It's nine o'clock,' he would announce, glancing at his wrist. 'Isn't your bus leaving today?'

'Off with you!' the bus driver would respond, 'I'll leave when I'm ready.'

As the children approached Nauti, the small flat school buildings came into view on the outskirts of the village, fringed by a line of long-leaved pines. A small crowd had assembled on the one playing field. Something unusual seemed to have happened. Prakash ran forward to see what it was all about. Bina and Sonu stood aside, waiting in a patch of sunlight near the boundary wall.

Prakash soon came running back to them. He was bubbling over with excitement.

'It's Mr Mani!' he gasped. 'He's disappeared! People are saying a leopard must have carried him off!'

III

Mr Mani wasn't really old. He was about fifty-five and was expected to retire soon. But for the children, most adults over forty seemed ancient! And Mr Mani had always been a bit absent-minded, even as a young man.

He had gone out for his early morning walk, saying he'd be back by eight o'clock, in time to have his breakfast and be ready for class. He wasn't married, but his sister and her husband stayed with him. When it was past nine o'clock his sister presumed he'd stopped at a neighbour's house for breakfast (he loved tucking into other people's breakfast) and that he had gone on to school from there. But when the school bell rang at ten o'clock, and everyone but Mr Mani was present, questions were asked and guesses were made.

No one had seen him return from his walk, and enquiries made in the village showed that he had not stopped at anyone's house. For Mr Mani to disappear was puzzling; for him to disappear without his breakfast was extraordinary.

Then a milkman returning from the next village said he had seen a leopard sitting on a rock on the outskirts of the pine forest. There had been talk of a cattle-killer in the valley, of leopards and other animals being displaced by the construction of a dam. But as yet no one had heard of a leopard attacking a man. Could Mr Mani have been its first victim? Someone found a strip of red cloth entangled in a blackberry bush and went running through the village showing it to everyone. Mr Mani had been known to wear red pyjamas. Surely he had been seized and eaten! But where were his remains? And why had he been in his pyjamas?

Meanwhile, Bina and Sonu and the rest of the children had followed their teachers into the school playground. Feeling a little lost, Bina looked around for Prakash. She found herself facing a dark, slender young woman wearing spectacles, who must have been in her early twenties—just a little too old to be another student. She had a kind, expressive face and she seemed a little concerned by all that had been happening.

Bina noticed that she had lovely hands; it was obvious that the new teacher hadn't milked cows or worked in the fields!

'You must be new here,' said the teacher, smiling at Bina. 'And is this your little brother?'

'Yes, we've come from Koli Village. We were at school there.'

'It's a long walk from Koli. You didn't see any leopards, did you? Well, I'm new too. Are you in the Class 6?'

'Sonu is in the third. I'm in the sixth.'

'Then I'm your new teacher. My name is Tania Ramola. Come along, let's see if we can settle down in our classroom.'

◆

Mr Mani turned up at twelve o'clock, wondering what all the fuss was about. No, he snapped, he had not been attacked by a leopard; and yes, he had lost his pyjamas, and would someone kindly return them to him?

'How did you lose your pyjamas, sir?' asked Prakash.

'They were blown off the washing line!' snapped Mr Mani.

After much questioning, Mr Mani admitted that he had gone further than he had intended, and that he had lost his way coming back. He had been a bit upset because the new teacher, a slip of a girl, had been given charge of the sixth, while he was still with the fifth, along with that troublesome boy Prakash, who kept on reminding him of the time! The headmaster had explained that as Mr Mani was due to retire at the end of the year, the school did not wish to burden him with a senior class. But Mr Mani looked upon the whole thing as a plot to get rid of him. He glowered at Miss Ramola whenever he passed her. And when she smiled back at him, he looked the other way!

Mr Mani had been getting even more absent-minded of late—putting on his shoes without his socks, wearing his homespun waistcoat inside out, mixing up people's names and of course, eating other people's lunches and dinners. His sister had made a mutton broth for the postmaster, who was down with 'flu', and had asked Mr Mani to take it over in a thermos. When the postmaster opened the thermos, he found only a few drops of broth at the bottom—Mr Mani had drunk the rest somewhere along the way.

When sometimes Mr Mani spoke of his coming retirement, it was to describe his plans for the small field he owned just behind the house. Right now, it was full of potatoes, which did not require much looking after; but he had plans for growing dahlias, roses, French beans, and other fruits and flowers.

The next time he visited Tehri, he promised himself, he would buy some dahlia bulbs and rose cuttings. The monsoon season would be a good time to put them down. And meanwhile, his potatoes were still flourishing.

IV

Bina enjoyed her first day at the new school. She felt at ease with Miss Ramola, as did most of the boys and girls in her class. Tania Ramola had been to distant towns such as Delhi and Lucknow—places they had only heard about—and it was said that she had a brother who was a pilot and flew planes all over the world. Perhaps he'd fly over Nauti some day!

Most of the children had of course seen planes flying overhead, but none of them had seen a ship, and only a few had been on a train. Tehri mountain was far from the railway and hundreds of miles from the sea. But they all knew about the big dam that was being built at Tehri, just forty miles away.

Bina, Sonu and Prakash had company for part of the way home, but gradually the other children went off in different directions. Once they had crossed the stream, they were on their own again.

It was a steep climb all the way back to their village. Prakash had a supply of peanuts that he shared with Bina and Sonu, and at a small spring they quenched their thirst.

When they were less than a mile from home, they met a postman who had finished his round of the villages in the area and was now returning to Nauti.

'Don't waste time along the way,' he told them. 'Try to get home before dark.'

'What's the hurry?' asked Prakash, glancing at his watch. 'It's only five o'clock.'

'There's a leopard around. I saw it this morning, not far from the stream. No one is sure how it got here. So don't take any chances. Get home early.'

'So, there really is a leopard,' said Sonu.

They took his advice and walked faster, and Sonu forgot to complain about his aching feet.

They were home well before sunset.

There was a smell of cooking in the air and they were hungry.

'Cabbage and roti,' said Prakash gloomily. 'But I could eat

anything today.' He stopped outside his small slate-roofed house, and Bina and Sonu waved goodbye and carried on across a couple of ploughed fields until they reached their small stone house.

'Stuffed tomatoes,' said Sonu, sniffing just outside the front door.

'And lemon pickle,' said Bina, who had helped cut, sun and salt the lemons a month previously.

Their mother was lighting the kitchen stove. They greeted her with great hugs and demands for an immediate dinner. She was a good cook who could make even the simplest of dishes taste delicious. Her favourite saying was 'Home-made bread is better than roast meat abroad,' and Bina and Sonu had to agree.

Electricity had yet to reach their village, and they took their meal by the light of a kerosene lamp. After the meal, Sonu settled down to do a little homework, while Bina stepped outside to look at the stars.

Across the fields, someone was playing a flute. 'It must be Prakash,' thought Bina. 'He always breaks off on the high notes.' But the flute music was simple and appealing, and she began singing softly to herself in the dark.

V

Mr Mani was having trouble with the porcupines. They had been getting into his garden at night and digging up and eating his potatoes. From his bedroom window—left open now that the mild April weather had arrived—he could listen to them enjoying the vegetables he had worked hard to grow. Scrunch, scrunch! *Katar, katar*, as their sharp teeth sliced through the largest and juiciest of potatoes. For Mr Mani it was as though they were biting through his own flesh. And the sound of them digging industriously as they rooted up those healthy, leafy plants made him tremble with rage and indignation. The unfairness of it all!

Yes, Mr Mani hated porcupines. He prayed for their destruction, their removal from the face of the earth. But, as his friends were quick to point out, 'The creator made porcupines too,' and in any case you could never see the creatures or catch them, they were completely nocturnal.

Mr Mani got out of bed every night, torch in one hand, a stout stick in the other but, as soon as he stepped into the garden, the crunching and digging stopped and he was greeted by the most infuriating of silences. He would grope around in the dark, swinging wildly with the stick, but not a single porcupine was to be seen or heard. As soon as he was back in bed, the sounds would start all over again—scrunch, scrunch, katar, katar...

Mr Mani came to his class tired and dishevelled, with rings under his eyes and a permanent frown on his face. It took some time for his pupils to discover the reason for his misery, but when they did, they felt sorry for their teacher and took to discussing ways and means of saving his potatoes from the porcupines.

It was Prakash who came up with the idea of a moat or water ditch. 'Porcupines don't like water,' he said knowledgeably.

'How do you know?' asked one of his friends.

'Throw water on one and see how it runs! They don't like getting their quills wet.'

There was no one who could disprove Prakash's theory, and the class fell in with the idea of building a moat, especially as it meant getting most of the day off.

'Anything to make Mr Mani happy,' said the headmaster, and the rest of the school watched with envy as the pupils of

Class 5, armed with spades and shovels collected from all parts of the village, took up their positions around Mr Mani's potato field and began digging a ditch.

By evening, the moat was ready, but it was still dry and the porcupines got in again that night and had a great feast.

'At this rate,' said Mr Mani gloomily, 'there won't be any potatoes left to save.'

But the next day, Prakash and the other boys and girls managed to divert the water from a stream that flowed past the village. They had the satisfaction of watching it flow gently into the ditch. Everyone went home in a good mood. By nightfall, the ditch had overflowed, the potato field was flooded, and Mr Mani found himself trapped inside his house. But Prakash and his friends had won the day. The porcupines stayed away that night!

◆

A month had passed, and wild violets, daisies and buttercups now sprinkled the hill slopes and, on her way to school, Bina gathered enough to make a little posy. The bunch of flowers fitted easily into an old ink well. Miss Ramola was delighted to find this little display in the middle of her desk.

'Who put these here?' she asked in surprise.

Bina kept quiet, and the rest of the class smiled secretively. After that, they took turns bringing flowers for the classroom.

On her long walks to school and home again, Bina became aware that April was the month of new leaves. The oak leaves were bright green above and silver beneath, and when they rippled in the breeze they were clouds of silvery green. The path was strewn with old leaves, dry and crackly. Sonu loved kicking them around.

Clouds of white butterflies floated across the stream. Sonu was chasing a butterfly when he stumbled over something dark and repulsive. He went sprawling on the grass. When he got to his feet, he looked down at the remains of a small animal.

'Bina! Prakash! Come quickly!' he shouted.

It was part of a sheep, killed some days earlier by a much larger animal.

'Only a leopard could have done this,' said Prakash.

'Let's get away, then,' said Sonu. 'It might still be around!'

'No, there's nothing left to eat. The leopard will be hunting elsewhere by now. Perhaps it's moved on to the next valley.'

'Still, I'm frightened,' said Sonu. 'There may be more leopards!'

Bina took him by the hand. 'Leopards don't attack humans!' she said.

'They will, if they get a taste for people!' insisted Prakash.

'Well, this one hasn't attacked any people as yet,' said Bina, although she couldn't be sure. Hadn't there been rumours of a leopard attacking some workers near the dam? But she did not want Sonu to feel afraid, so she did not mention the story. All she said was, 'It has probably come here because of all the activity near the dam.'

All the same, they hurried home. And for a few days, whenever they reached the stream, they crossed over very quickly, unwilling to linger too long at that lovely spot.

VI

A few days later, a school party was on its way to Tehri to see the new dam that was being built.

Miss Ramola had arranged to take her class, and Mr Mani, not wishing to be left out, insisted on taking his class as well.

That meant there were about fifty boys and girls taking part in the outing. The little bus could only take thirty. A friendly truck driver agreed to take some children if they were prepared to sit on sacks of potatoes. And Prakash persuaded the owner of the diesel roller to turn it around and head it back to Tehri—with him and a couple of friends up on the driving seat.

Prakash's small group set off at sunrise, as they had to walk some distance in order to reach the stranded road roller. The bus left at 9.00 a.m. with Miss Ramola and her class, and Mr Mani and some of his pupils. The truck was to follow later.

It was Bina's first visit to a large town, and her first bus ride.

The sharp curves along the winding, downhill road made several children feel sick. The bus driver seemed to be in a tearing hurry. He took them along at a rolling, rollicking speed, which made Bina feel quite giddy. She rested her head on her arms and refused to look out of the window. Hairpin bends and cliff edges, pine forests and snow-capped peaks, all swept past her, but she felt too ill to want to look at anything. It was just as well—those sudden drops, hundreds of feet to the valley below, were quite frightening. Bina began to wish that she hadn't come—or that she had joined Prakash on the road roller instead!

Miss Ramola and Mr Mani didn't seem to notice the lurching and groaning of the old bus. They had made this journey many times. They were busy arguing about the advantages and disadvantages of large dams—an argument that was to continue on and off for much of the day.

Meanwhile, Prakash and his friends had reached the roller. The driver hadn't turned up, but they managed to reverse it and get it going in the direction of Tehri. They were soon overtaken by both bus and truck but kept moving along at a steady chug. Prakash spotted Bina at the window of the bus and waved cheerfully. She responded feebly.

Bina felt better when the road levelled out near Tehri. As they crossed an old bridge over the wide river, they were startled by a loud bang that made the bus shudder. A cloud of dust rose above the town.

'They're blasting the mountain,' said Miss Ramola.

'End of a mountain,' said Mr Mani, mournfully.

While they were drinking cups of tea at the bus stop, waiting for the potato truck and the road roller, Miss Ramola and Mr Mani continued their argument about the dam. Miss Ramola maintained that it would bring electric power and water for irrigation to large areas of the country, including the surrounding area. Mr Mani declared that it was a menace, as it was situated in an earthquake zone. There would be a terrible disaster if the dam burst! Bina found it all very confusing. And what about the animals in the area, she wondered, what would happen to them?

The argument was becoming quite heated when the potato truck arrived. There was no sign of the road roller, so it was decided that Mr Mani should wait for Prakash and his friends while Miss Ramola's group went ahead.

◆

Some eight or nine miles before Tehri, the road roller had broken down, and Prakash and his friends were forced to walk. They had not gone far, however, when a mule train came along—five or six mules that had been delivering sacks of grain in Nauti. A boy rode on the first mule, but the others had no load.

'Can you give us a ride to Tehri?' called Prakash.

'Make yourselves comfortable,' said the boy.

There were no saddles, only gunny sacks strapped on to

the mules with rope. They had a rough but jolly ride down to the Tehri bus stop. None of them had ever ridden mules; but they had saved at least an hour on the road.

Looking around the bus stop for the rest of the party, they could find no one from their school. And Mr Mani, who should have been waiting for them, had vanished.

VII

Tania Ramola and her group had taken the steep road to the hill above Tehri. Half an hour's climbing brought them to a little plateau which overlooked the town, the river and the dam site.

The earthworks for the dam were only just coming up, but a wide tunnel had been bored through the mountain to divert the river into another channel. Down below, the old town was still spread out across the valley, and from a distance, it looked quite charming and picturesque.

'Will the whole town be swallowed up by the waters of the dam?' asked Bina.

'Yes, all of it,' said Miss Ramola. 'The clock tower and the old palace. The long bazaar, and the temples, the schools and the jail and hundreds of houses, for many miles up the valley. All those people will have to go—thousands of them! Of course, they'll be resettled elsewhere.'

'But the town's been here for hundreds of years,' said Bina. 'They were quite happy without the dam, weren't they?'

'I suppose they were. But the dam isn't just for them—it's for the millions who live further downstream, across the plains.'

'And it doesn't matter what happens to this place?'

'The local people will be given new homes somewhere else.' Miss Ramola found herself on the defensive and decided to change the subject. 'Everyone must be hungry. It's time we had our lunch.'

Bina kept quiet. She didn't think the local people would want to go away. And it was a good thing, she mused, that there was only a small stream and not a big river running past her village. To be uprooted like this—a town and hundreds of villages—and put down somewhere on the hot, dusty plains—seemed to her unbearable.

'Well, I'm glad I don't live in Tehri,' she said.

She did not know it, but all the animals and most of the birds had already left the area. The leopard had been among them.

◆

They walked through the colourful, crowded bazaar, where fruit sellers did business beside silversmiths, and pavement vendors sold everything from umbrellas to glass bangles. Sparrows attacked sacks of grain, monkeys made off with bananas, and stray cows and dogs rummaged in refuse bins, but nobody took any notice. Music blared from radios. Buses blew their horns. Sonu bought a whistle to add to the general din, but Miss Ramola told him to put it away. Bina had kept five rupees aside, and now she used it to buy a cotton headscarf for her mother.

As they were about to enter a small restaurant for a meal, they were joined by Prakash and his companions; but of Mr Mani there was still no sign.

'He must have met one of his relatives,' said Prakash. 'He has relatives everywhere.'

After a simple meal of rice and lentils, they walked the length of the bazaar without finding Mr Mani. At last, when they were about to give up the search, they saw him emerge from a by-lane, a large sack slung over his shoulder.

'Sir, where have you been?' asked Prakash. 'We have been looking for you everywhere.'

On Mr Mani's face was a look of triumph.

'Help me with this bag,' he said breathlessly.

'You've bought more potatoes, sir,' said Prakash.

'Not potatoes, boy. Dahlia bulbs!'

VIII

It was dark by the time they were all back in Nauti. Mr Mani had refused to be separated from his sack of dahlia bulbs, and had been forced to sit in the back of the truck with Prakash and most of the boys.

Bina did not feel so ill on the return journey. Going uphill was definitely better than going downhill! But by the time the bus reached Nauti it was too late for most of the children to walk back to the more distant villages. The boys were put up in different homes, while the girls were given beds in the school verandah.

The night was warm and still. Large moths fluttered around the single bulb that lit the verandah. Counting moths, Sonu soon fell asleep. But Bina stayed awake for some time, listening to the sounds of the night. A nightjar went tonk-tonk in the bushes, and somewhere in the forest an owl hooted softly. The sharp call of a barking deer travelled up the valley from the direction of the stream. Jackals kept howling. It seemed that there were more of them than ever before.

Bina was not the only one to hear the barking deer. The leopard, stretched full length on a rocky ledge, heard it too. The leopard raised its head and then got up slowly. The deer was its natural prey. But there weren't many left, and that was why the leopard, robbed of its forest by the dam, had taken to attacking dogs and cattle near the villages.

As the cry of the barking deer sounded nearer, the leopard left its lookout point and moved swiftly through the shadows towards the stream.

IX

In early June, the hills were dry and dusty, and forest fires broke out, destroying shrubs and trees, killing birds and small animals. The resin in the pines made these trees burn more fiercely, and the wind would take sparks from the trees and carry them into the dry grass and leaves, so that new fires would spring up before the old ones had died out. Fortunately, Bina's village was not in the pine belt; the fires did not reach it. But Nauti was surrounded by a fire that raged for three days, and the children had to stay away from school.

And then, towards the end of June, the monsoon rains arrived and there was an end to forest fires. The monsoon lasts three months and the lower Himalayas would be drenched in rain, mist and cloud for the next three months.

The first rain arrived while Bina, Prakash and Sonu were returning home from school. Those first few drops on the dusty path made them cry out with excitement. Then the rain grew heavier and a wonderful aroma rose from the earth.

'The best smell in the world!' exclaimed Bina.

Everything suddenly came to life. The grass, the crops, the trees, the birds. Even the leaves of the trees glistened and looked new.

That first wet weekend, Bina and Sonu helped their mother plant beans, maize and cucumbers. Sometimes, when the rain was very heavy, they had to run indoors. Otherwise they worked in the rain, the soft mud clinging to their bare legs.

Prakash now owned a dog, a black dog with one ear up and one ear down. The dog ran around getting in everyone's way, barking at cows, goats, hens and humans, without frightening any of them. Prakash said it was a very clever dog, but no one else seemed to think so. Prakash also said it would protect the village from the leopard, but others said the dog would be the first to be taken—he'd run straight into the jaws of Mr Spots!

In Nauti, Tania Ramola was trying to find a dry spot in the quarters she'd been given. It was an old building and the roof was leaking in several places. Mugs and buckets were scattered about the floor in order to catch the drips.

Mr Mani had dug up all his potatoes and presented them to the friends and neighbours who had given him lunches and dinners. He was having the time of his life, planting dahlia bulbs all over his garden.

'I'll have a field of many-coloured dahlias!' he announced. 'Just wait till the end of August!'

'Watch out for those porcupines,' warned his sister. 'They eat dahlia bulbs too!'

Mr Mani made an inspection tour of his moat, no longer in flood, and found everything in good order. Prakash had done his job well.

◆

Now, when the children crossed the stream, they found that the water level had risen by about a foot. Small cascades had turned into waterfalls. Ferns had sprung up on the banks. Frogs chanted.

Prakash and his dog dashed across the stream. Bina and Sonu followed more cautiously. The current was much stronger now and the water was almost up to their knees. Once they had crossed the stream, they hurried along the path, anxious not to be caught in a sudden downpour.

By the time they reached school, each of them had two or three leeches clinging to their legs. They had to use salt to remove them. The leeches were the most troublesome part of the rainy season. Even the leopard did not like them. It could not lie in the long grass without getting leeches on its paws and face.

One day, when Bina, Prakash and Sonu were about to cross the stream they heard a low rumble, which grew louder every second. Looking up at the opposite hill, they saw several trees shudder, tilt outwards and begin to fall. Earth and rocks bulged out from the mountain, then came crashing down into the ravine.

'Landslide!' shouted Sonu.

'It's carried away the path,' said Bina. 'Don't go any further.'

There was a tremendous roar as more rocks, trees and bushes fell away and crashed down the hillside.

Prakash's dog, who had gone ahead, came running back, tail between his legs.

They remained rooted to the spot until the rocks had stopped falling and the dust had settled. Birds circled the area, calling wildly. A frightened barking deer ran past them.

'We can't go to school now,' said Prakash. 'There's no way around.'

They turned and trudged home through the gathering mist.

In Koli, Prakash's parents had heard the roar of the landslide. They were setting out in search of the children when they saw them emerge from the mist, waving cheerfully.

X

They had to miss school for another three days, and Bina was afraid they might not be able to take their final exams. Although Prakash was not really troubled at the thought of missing exams, he did not like feeling helpless just because their path had been swept away. So he explored the hillside until he found a goat-track going around the mountain. It joined up with another path near Nauti. This made their walk longer by a mile, but Bina did not mind. It was much cooler now that the rains were in full swing.

The only trouble with the new route was that it passed close to the leopard's lair. The animal had made this area its own since being forced to leave the dam area.

One day, Prakash's dog ran ahead of them barking furiously. Then he ran back whimpering.

'He's always running away from something,' observed Sonu. But a minute later he understood the reason for the dog's fear.

They rounded a bend and Sonu saw the leopard standing in their way. They were struck dumb—too terrified to run. It was a strong, sinewy creature. A low growl rose from its throat. It seemed ready to spring.

They stood perfectly still, afraid to move or say a word. And the leopard must have been equally surprised. It stared at them for a few seconds, then bounded across the path and into the oak forest.

Sonu was shaking. Bina could hear her heart hammering. Prakash could only stammer: 'Did you see the way he sprang? Wasn't he beautiful?'

He forgot to look at his watch for the rest of the day.

A few days later, Sonu stopped and pointed to a large outcrop of rock on the next hill.

The leopard stood far above them, outlined against the sky. It looked strong, majestic. Standing beside it were two young cubs.

'Look at those little ones!' exclaimed Sonu.

'So it's a female, not a male,' said Prakash.

'That's why she was killing so often,' said Bina. 'She had to feed her cubs too.'

They remained still for several minutes, gazing up at the leopard and her cubs. The leopard family took no notice of them.

'She knows we are here,' said Prakash, 'but she doesn't care. She knows we won't harm them.'

'We are cubs too!' said Sonu.

'Yes,' said Bina. 'And there's still plenty of space for all of us. Even when the dam is ready there will still be room for leopards and humans.'

XI

The school exams were over. The rains were nearly over too. The landslide had been cleared, and Bina, Prakash and Sonu were once again crossing the stream.

There was a chill in the air, for it was the end of September.

Prakash had learnt to play the flute quite well, and he played on the way to school and then again on the way home. As a result, he did not look at his watch so often. One morning they found a small crowd in front of Mr Mani's house.

'What could have happened?' wondered Bina. 'I hope he hasn't got lost again.'

'Maybe he's sick,' said Sonu.

'Maybe it's the porcupines,' said Prakash.

But it was none of these things.

Mr Mani's first dahlia was in bloom, and half the village had turned up to look at it! It was a huge red double dahlia, so heavy that it had to be supported with sticks. No one had ever seen such a magnificent flower!

Mr Mani was a happy man. And his mood only improved over the coming week, as more and more dahlias flowered—

crimson, yellow, purple, mauve, white—button dahlias, pom-pom dahlias, spotted dahlias, striped dahlias... Mr Mani had them all! A dahlia even turned up on Tania Ramola's desk—he got along quite well with her now—and another brightened up the headmaster's study.

A week later, on their way home—it was almost the last day of the school term—Bina, Prakash and Sonu talked about what they might do when they grew up.

'I think I'll become a teacher,' said Bina. 'I'll teach children about animals and birds, and trees and flowers.'

'Better than maths!' said Prakash.

'I'll be a pilot,' said Sonu. 'I want to fly a plane like Miss Ramola's brother.'

'And what about you, Prakash?' asked Bina.

Prakash just smiled and said, 'Maybe I'll be a flute player,' and he put the flute to his lips and played a sweet melody.

'Well, the world needs flute players too,' said Bina, as they fell into step beside him.

The leopard had been stalking a barking deer. She paused when she heard the flute and the voices of the children. Her own young ones were growing quickly, but the girl and the two boys did not look much older.

They had started singing their favourite song again.

Five more miles to go!
We climb through rain and snow,
A river to cross...
A mountain to pass...
Now we've four more miles to go!

The leopard waited until they had passed, before returning to the trail of the barking deer.

THE TUNNEL

It was almost noon, and the jungle was very still, very silent. Heat waves shimmered along the railway embankment where it cut a path through the tall evergreen trees. The railway lines were two straight black serpents disappearing into the tunnel in the hillside.

Suraj stood near the cutting, waiting for the mid-day train. It wasn't a station, and he wasn't catching a train. He was waiting so that he could watch the steam-engine come roaring out of the tunnel.

He had cycled out of the town and taken the jungle path until he had come to a small village. He had left the cycle there, and walked over a low, scrub-covered hill and down to the tunnel exit.

Now he looked up. He had heard, in the distance, the shrill whistle of the engine. He couldn't see anything because the train was approaching from the other side of the hill; but presently a sound, like distant thunder, issued from the tunnel, and he knew the train was coming through.

A second or two later, the steam-engine shot out of the tunnel, snorting and puffing like some green, black and gold dragon, some beautiful monster out of Suraj's dreams. Showering sparks left and right, it roared a challenge to the jungle.

Instinctively, Suraj stepped back a few paces. And then the

train had gone, leaving only a plume of smoke to drift lazily over tall shisham trees.

The jungle was still again. No one moved. Suraj turned from his contemplation of the drifting smoke and began walking along the embankment, towards the tunnel.

The tunnel grew darker as he walked further into it. When he had gone about twenty yards, it became pitch black. Suraj had to turn and look back at the opening to reassure himself that there was still daylight outside. Ahead of him, the tunnel's other opening was just a small round circle of light.

The tunnel was still full of smoke from the train, but it would be several hours before another train came through. Till then, it belonged to the jungle again.

Suraj didn't stop, because there was nothing to do in the tunnel and nothing to see. He had simply wanted to walk through, so that he would know what the inside of a tunnel was really like. The walls were damp and sticky. A bat flew past. A lizard scuttled between the lines.

Coming straight from the darkness into the light, Suraj was dazzled by the sudden glare. He put a hand up to shade his eyes and looked up at the tree-covered hillside. He thought he saw something moving between the trees.

It was just a flash of orange and gold, and a long swishing tail. It was there between the trees for a second or two, and then it was gone.

About fifty feet from the entrance to the tunnel stood the watchman's hut. Marigolds grew in front of the hut, and at the back there was a small vegetable patch. It was the watchman's duty to inspect the tunnel and keep it clear of obstacles. Every day, before the train came through, he would walk the length of the tunnel. If all was well, he would return to his hut and take a nap. If something was wrong, he would walk back up the line and wave a red flag and the engine-driver would slow down. At night, the watchman lit an oil lamp and made a similar inspection of the tunnel. Of course, he could not stop the train if there was a porcupine on the line. But if there was any danger to the train, he'd go back up the line and wave his lamp to the approaching engine. If all was well, he'd hang his lamp at the door of the hut and go to sleep.

He was just settling down on his cot for an afternoon nap when he saw the boy emerge from the tunnel. He waited until Suraj was only a few feet away and then said: 'Welcome, welcome, I don't often have visitors. Sit down for a while, and tell me why you were inspecting my tunnel.'

'Is it your tunnel?' asked Suraj.

'It is,' said the watchman. 'It is truly my tunnel, since no one else will have anything to do with it. I have only lent it to the government.'

Suraj sat down on the edge of the cot.

'I wanted to see the train come through,' he said. 'And then, when it had gone, I thought I'd walk through the tunnel.'

'And what did you find in it?'

'Nothing. It was very dark. But when I came out, I thought I saw an animal—up on the hill—but I'm not sure, it moved away very quickly.'

'It was a leopard you saw,' said the watchman. 'My leopard.'

'Do you own a leopard too?'

'I do.'

'And do you lend it to the government?'

'I do not.'

'Is it dangerous?'

'No, it's a leopard that minds its own business. It comes

to this range for a few days every month.'

'Have you been here a long time?' asked Suraj.

'Many years. My name is Sunder Singh.'

'My name's Suraj.'

'There's one train during the day. And another during the night. Have you seen the night mail come through the tunnel?'

'No. At what time does it come?'

'About nine o'clock, if it isn't late. You could come and sit here with me, if you like. And after it has gone, I'll take you home.'

'I shall ask my parents,' said Suraj. 'Will it be safe?'

'Of course. It's safer in the jungle than in the town. Nothing happens to me out here, but last month when I went into the town, I was almost run over by a bus.'

Sunder Singh yawned and stretched himself out on the cot. 'And now I'm going to take a nap, my friend. It is too hot to be up and about in the afternoon.'

'Everyone goes to sleep in the afternoon,' complained Suraj. 'My father lies down as soon as he's had his lunch.'

'Well, the animals also rest in the heat of the day. It is only the tribe of boys who cannot, or will not, rest.'

Sunder Singh placed a large banana leaf over his face to keep away the flies, and was soon snoring gently. Suraj stood up, looking up and down the railway tracks. Then he began walking back to the village.

The following evening, towards dusk, as the flying foxes swooped silently out of the trees, Suraj made his way to the watchman's hut.

It had been a long hot day, but now the earth was cooling, and a light breeze was moving through the trees. It carried with it a scent of mango blossoms, the promise of rain.

Sunder Singh was waiting for Suraj. He had watered his small garden, and the flowers looked cool and fresh. A kettle was boiling on a small oil-stove.

'I'm making tea,' he said. 'There's nothing like a glass of hot tea while waiting for a train.'

They drank their tea, listening to the sharp notes of the tailorbird and the noisy chatter of the seven-sisters. As the brief twilight faded, most of the birds fell silent. Sunder Singh lit his oil-lamp and said it was time for him to inspect the tunnel. He moved off towards the tunnel, while Suraj sat on the cot, sipping his tea. In the dark, the trees seemed to move closer to him. And the night life of the forest was conveyed on the breeze—the sharp call of a barking-deer, the cry of a fox, the quaint tonk-tonk of a nightjar. There were some sounds that Suraj couldn't recognize—sounds that came from the trees, creakings and whisperings, as though the trees were coming alive, stretching their limbs in the dark, shifting a little, reflexing their fingers.

Sunder Singh stood inside the tunnel, trimming his lamp. The night sounds were familiar to him and he did not give them much thought; but something else—a padded footfall, a rustle of dry leaves—made him stand alert for a few seconds, peering into the darkness. Then, humming softly to himself, he returned to where Suraj was waiting. Another ten minutes remained for the night mail to arrive.

As Sunder Singh sat down on the cot beside Suraj, a new sound reached both of them quite distinctly—a rhythmic sawing sound, as if someone was cutting through the branch of a tree.

'What's that?' whispered Suraj.

'It's the leopard,' said Sunder Singh.

'I think it's in the tunnel.'

'The train will soon be here,' reminded Suraj.

'Yes, my friend. And if we don't drive the leopard out of the tunnel, it will be run over and killed. I can't let that happen.'

'But won't it attack us if we try to drive it out?' asked Suraj, beginning to share the watchman's concern.

'Not this leopard. It knows me well. We have seen each other many times. It has a weakness for goats and stray dogs, but it won't harm us. Even so, I'll take my axe with me. You stay here, Suraj.'

'No, I'm going with you. It'll be better than sitting here alone in the dark!'

'All right, but stay close behind me. And remember, there's nothing to fear.'

Raising his lamp high, Sunder Singh advanced into the tunnel, shouting at the top of his voice to try and scare away the animal. Suraj followed close behind, but he found he was unable to do any shouting. His throat was quite dry.

They had gone just about twenty paces into the tunnel when the light from the lamp fell upon the leopard. It was crouching between the tracks, only fifteen feet away from them. It was not a very big leopard, but it looked lithe and sinewy. Baring its teeth and snarling, it went down on its belly, tail twitching.

Suraj and Sunder Singh both shouted together. Their voices rang through the tunnel. And the leopard, uncertain as to how many terrifying humans were there in the tunnel with him, turned swiftly and disappeared into the darkness.

To make sure that it had gone, Sunder Singh and Suraj walked the length of the tunnel. When they returned to the entrance, the rails were beginning to hum. They knew the train was coming.

Suraj put his hand to the rails and felt its tremor. He heard the distant rumble of the train. And then the engine came round the bend, hissing at them, scattering sparks into the darkness, defying the jungle as it roared through the steep sides of the cutting. It charged straight at the tunnel, and into it, thundering past Suraj like the beautiful dragon of his dreams.

And when it had gone, the silence returned and the forest seemed to breathe, to live again. Only the rails still trembled with the passing of the train.

And they trembled to the passing of the same train, almost a week later, when Suraj and his father were both travelling in it.

Suraj's father was scribbling in a notebook, doing his accounts. Suraj sat at an open window staring out at the darkness. His father was going to Delhi on a business trip and had decided to take the boy along. 'I don't know where he gets to, most of the time,' he'd complained. 'I think it's time he learnt something about my business.'

The night mail rushed through the forest with its hundreds of passengers. Tiny flickering lights came and went, as they passed small villages on the fringe of the jungle.

Suraj heard the rumble as the train passed over a small bridge. It was too dark to see the hut near the cutting, but he knew they must be approaching the tunnel. He strained his eyes looking out into the night; and then, just as the engine let out a shrill whistle, Suraj saw the lamp.

He couldn't see Sunder Singh, but he saw the lamp, and he knew that his friend was out there.

The train went into the tunnel and out again. It left the jungle behind and thundered across the endless plains; and Suraj stared out at the darkness, thinking of the lonely cutting in the forest, and the watchman with the lamp who would always remain a firefly for those travelling thousands, as he lit up the darkness for steam-engines and leopards.

OUR GREAT ESCAPE

It had been a lonely winter for a fourteen-year-old. I had spent the first few weeks of the vacation with my mother and stepfather in Dehra. Then they left for Delhi, and I was pretty much on my own. Of course, the servants were there to take care of my needs, but there was no one to keep me company. I would wander off in the mornings, taking some path up the hills, come back home for lunch, read a bit, and then stroll off again till it was time for dinner. Sometimes I walked up to my grandparents' house, but it seemed so different now, with people I didn't know occupying the house.

The three-month winter break over, I was almost eager to return to my boarding school in Shimla.

It wasn't as though I had many friends at school. I needed a friend but it was not easy to find one among a horde of rowdy, pea-shooting eighth formers, who carved their names on desks and stuck chewing gum on the class teacher's chair. Had I grown up with other children, I might have developed a taste for schoolboy anarchy; but in sharing my father's loneliness after his separation from my mother, and in being bereft of any close family ties, I had turned into a premature adult.

After a month in the eighth form, I began to notice a new boy, Omar, and then only because he was a quiet, almost taciturn person who took no part in the form's feverish attempt to imitate the Marx Brothers at the circus. He showed no resentment at the prevailing anarchy, nor did he make a move to participate in it. Once he caught me looking at him, and he smiled ruefully, tolerantly. Did I sense another adult in the class? Someone who was a little older than his years?

Even before we began talking to each other, Omar and I developed an understanding of sorts, and we'd nod almost respectfully to each other when we met in the classroom corridors or the environs of the dining hall or the dormitory. We were not in the same house. The house system practised its own form of apartheid, whereby a member of one house was not expected to fraternize with someone belonging to another. Those public schools certainly knew how to clamp you into compartments. However, these barriers vanished when Omar and I found ourselves selected for the School Colts' hockey team, Omar as a full-back, I as the goalkeeper.

The taciturn Omar now spoke to me occasionally, and we combined well on the field of play. A good understanding is needed between a goalkeeper and a full-back. We were on the same wavelength. I anticipated his moves; he was familiar with mine. Years later, when I read Conrad's *The Secret Sharer*, I thought of Omar.

It wasn't until we were away from the confines of school, classroom and dining hall that our friendship flourished. The hockey team travelled to Sanawar on the next mountain range, where we were to play a couple of matches against our old rivals, the Lawrence Memorial Royal Military School. This had been my father's old school, so I was keen to explore its grounds and peep into its classrooms.

Omar and I were thrown together a good deal during the visit to Sanawar, and in our more leisurely moments, strolling undisturbed around a school where we were guests and not pupils, we exchanged life histories and other confidences. Omar, too, had lost his father—had I sensed that before?—shot in some tribal encounter on the Frontier, for he hailed from the lawless lands beyond Peshawar. A wealthy uncle was seeing to Omar's education.

We wandered into the school chapel, and there I found my father's name—A. A. Bond—on the school's roll of honour board: old boys who had lost their lives while serving during the two World Wars.

'What did his initials stand for?' asked Omar.

'Aubrey Alexander.'

'Unusual names, like yours. Why did your parents call you Rusty?'

'I am not sure.' I told him about the book I was writing. It was my first one and was called *Nine Months* (the length of the school term, not a pregnancy), and it described some of the happenings at school and lampooned a few of our teachers. I had filled three slim exercise books with this premature literary project, and I allowed Omar to go through them. He must have been my first reader and critic.

'They're very interesting,' he said, 'but you'll get into trouble if someone finds them, especially Mr Fisher.'

I have to admit it wasn't great literature. I was better at hockey and football. I made some spectacular saves, and we won our matches against Sanawar. When we returned to Shimla, we were school heroes for a couple of days and lost some of our reticence; we were even a little more forthcoming with other boys. And then Mr Fisher, my housemaster, discovered my literary opus, *Nine Months*, under my mattress, and took it away and read it (as he told me later) from cover to cover.

Corporal punishment then being in vogue, I was given six of the best with a springy Malacca cane, and my manuscript was torn up and deposited in Mr Fisher's wastepaper basket. All I had to show for my efforts were some purple welts on my bottom. These were proudly displayed to all who were interested, and I was a hero for another two days.

'Will you go away too when the British leave India?' Omar asked me one day.

'I don't think so,' I said. 'I don't have anyone to go back to in England, and my guardian, Mr Harrison, too seems to have no intention of going back.'

'Everyone is saying that our leaders and the British are going to divide the country. Shimla will be in India, Peshawar in Pakistan!'

'Oh, it won't happen,' I said glibly. 'How can they cut up such a big country?' But even as we chatted about the possibility, Nehru, Jinnah and Mountbatten, and all those who mattered, were preparing their instruments for major surgery.

Before their decision impinged on our lives and everyone else's, we found a little freedom of our own, in an underground tunnel that we discovered below the third flat.

It was really part of an old, disused drainage system, and when Omar and I began exploring it, we had no idea just how far it extended. After crawling along on our bellies for some twenty feet, we found ourselves in complete darkness. Omar had brought along a small pencil torch, and with its help we continued writhing forward (moving backwards would have been quite impossible) until we saw a glimmer of light at the end of the tunnel. Dusty, musty, very scruffy, we emerged at last onto a grassy knoll, a little way outside the school boundary.

It's always a great thrill to escape beyond the boundaries

that adults have devised. Here we were in unknown territory. To travel without passports—that would be the ultimate in freedom!

But more passports were on their way—and more boundaries.

Lord Mountbatten, viceroy and governor-general-to-be, came for our Founder's Day and gave away the prizes. I had won a prize for something or the other, and mounted the rostrum to receive my book from this towering, handsome man in his pinstripe suit. Bishop Cotton's was then the premier school of India, often referred to as the 'Eton of the East'. Viceroys and governors had graced its functions. Many of its boys had gone on to eminence in the civil services and armed forces. There was one 'old boy' about whom they maintained a stolid silence—General Dyer, who had ordered the massacre at Amritsar and destroyed the trust that had been building up between Britain and India.

Now Mountbatten spoke of the momentous events that were happening all around us—the War had just come to an end, the United Nations held out the promise of a world living in peace and harmony, and India, an equal partner with Britain, would be among the great nations...

A few weeks later, Bengal and the Punjab provinces were bisected. Riots flared up across northern India, and there was a great exodus of people crossing the newly-drawn frontiers of Pakistan and India. Homes were destroyed, thousands lost their lives.

The common room radio and the occasional newspaper kept us abreast of events, but in our tunnel, Omar and I felt immune from all that was happening, worlds away from all the pillage, murder and revenge. And outside the tunnel, on the pine knoll below the school, there was fresh untrodden grass, sprinkled with clover and daisies; the only sounds we heard were the hammering of a woodpecker and the distant insistent call of the Himalayan Barbet. Who could touch us there?

'And when all the wars are done,' I said, 'a butterfly will still be beautiful.'

'Did you read that somewhere?'

'No, it just came into my head.'

'Already you're a writer.'

'No, I want to play hockey for India or football for Arsenal. Only winning teams!'

'You can't win forever. Better to be a writer.'

When the monsoon arrived, the tunnel was flooded, the drain choked with rubble. We were allowed out to the cinema to see Laurence Olivier's *Hamlet*, a film that did nothing to raise our spirits on a wet and gloomy afternoon; but it was our last picture that year, because communal riots suddenly broke out in Shimla's Lower Bazaar, an area that was still much as Kipling had described it—'a man who knows his way there can defy all the police of India's summer capital'—and we were confined to school indefinitely.

One morning after prayers in the chapel, the headmaster announced that the Muslim boys—those who had their homes in what was now Pakistan—would have to be evacuated, sent to their homes across the border with an armed convoy.

The tunnel no longer provided an escape for us. The bazaar was out of bounds. The flooded playing field was deserted. Omar and I sat on a damp wooden bench and talked about the future in vaguely hopeful terms, but we didn't solve any problems. Mountbatten and Nehru and Jinnah were doing all the solving.

It was soon time for Omar to leave—he left along with some fifty other boys from Lahore, Pindi and Peshawar. The rest of us—Hindus, Christians, Parsis—helped them load their luggage into the waiting trucks. A couple of boys broke down and wept. So did our departing school captain, a Pathan who had been known for his stoic and unemotional demeanour. Omar waved cheerfully to me and I waved back. We had vowed to meet again some day.

The convoy got through safely enough. There was only one casualty—the school cook, who had strayed into an off-limits area in the foothill town of Kalika and been set upon by a mob. He wasn't seen again.

Towards the end of the school year, just as we were all getting ready to leave for the school holidays, I received a letter from Omar. He told me something about his new school and how he missed my company and our games and our tunnel to freedom. I replied and gave him my home address, but I did not hear from him again.

Some seventeen or eighteen years later, I did get news of Omar, but in an entirely different context. India and Pakistan were at war, and in a bombing raid over Ambala, not far from Shimla, a Pakistani plane was shot down. Its crew died in the crash. One of them, I learnt later, was Omar.

Did he, I wonder, get a glimpse of the playing fields we knew so well as boys? Perhaps memories of his schooldays flooded back as he flew over the foothills. Perhaps he remembered the tunnel through which we were able to make our little escape to freedom.

But there are no tunnels in the sky.

GROWING UP WITH TREES

Dehradun was a place for trees, and Grandfather's house was surrounded by several kinds—peepul, neem, mango, jackfruit and papaya. There was also an ancient banyan tree. I grew up amongst these trees, and some of them, planted by Grandfather, grew with me.

There were two types of trees that were of special interest to a boy—trees that were good for climbing, and trees that provided fruit.

The jackfruit tree was both these things. The fruit itself—the largest in the world—grew only on the trunk and main branches. I did not care much for the fruit, although cooked as a vegetable, it made a good curry. But the tree was large and leafy and easy to climb. It was a very dark tree and if I hid in it, I could not easily be seen from below. In a hole in the tree trunk I kept various banned items—a catapult, some lurid comics, and a large stock of chewing-gum. Perhaps they are still there, because I forgot to collect them when we finally went away.

The banyan tree grew behind the house. Its spreading branches, which hung to the ground and took root again, formed a number of twisting passageways which gave me endless pleasure. The tree was older than the house, older than my grandparents, as old as Dehra. I could hide myself in its branches, behind thick green leaves, and spy on the world below. I could read in it, too, propped up against the bole of the tree, with *Treasure Island* or the *Jungle Books* or comics like *Wizard* or *Hotspur* which, unlike the forbidden *Superman* and others like him, were full of clean-cut schoolboy heroes.

The banyan tree was a world in itself, populated with small beasts and large insects. While the leaves were still pink and tender, they would be visited by the delicate Map Butterfly, who committed her eggs to their care. The 'honey' on the leaves—an edible smear—also attracted the little striped squirrels, who soon grew used to my presence and became quite bold. Red-headed parakeets swarmed about the tree early in the mornings.

But the banyan really came to life during the monsoon, when the branches were thick with scarlet figs. These berries were not fit for human consumption, but the many birds that gathered in the tree—gossipy Rosy Pastors, quarrelsome Mynas, cheerful Bulbuls and Coppersmiths, and sometimes a raucous bullying crow—feasted on them. And when night fell, and the birds were resting, the dark Flying Foxes flapped heavily about the tree, chewing and munching as they clambered over the branches.

Among nocturnal visitors to the jackfruit and banyan trees was the Brainfever bird, whose real name is the Hawk-Cuckoo. 'Brainfever, brainfever!' it seems to call, and this shrill, nagging cry will keep the soundest of sleepers awake on a hot summer's night.

The British called it the Brainfever bird, but there are other names for it. The Marathas called it 'Paos-ala,' which means 'Rain is coming!' Perhaps Grandfather's interpretation of its call was the best. According to him, when the bird was tuning up for its main concert, it seemed to say: 'Oh dear, oh dear! How very hot it's getting! We feel it… we feel it… WE FEEL IT!'

Yes, the banyan tree was a noisy place during the rains. If the Brainfever bird made music by night, the crickets and cicadas orchestrated during the day. As musicians, the cicadas were in a class by themselves. All through the hot weather their chorus rang through the garden, while a shower of rain, far from damping their spirits, only roused them to a greater vocal effort.

The tree-crickets were a band of willing artistes who commenced their performance at almost any time of the day but preferably in the evenings. Delicate pale green creatures with transparent green wings, they were hard to find amongst the lush monsoon foliage; but once located, a tap on the leaf or bush on which they sat would put an immediate end to the performance.

At the height of the monsoon, the banyan tree was like an orchestra-pit with the musicians constantly turning up. Birds, insects and squirrels expressed their joy at the end of the hot weather and the cool quenching relief of the rains.

A flute in my hands, I would try adding my shrill piping to theirs. But they thought poorly of my musical ability, for, whenever I played on the flute, the birds and insects would subside into a pained and puzzled silence.

ROMI AND THE WILDFIRE

1

As Romi was about to mount his bicycle, he saw smoke rising from behind the distant line of trees.

'It looks like a forest fire,' said Prem, his friend and classmate.

'It's well to the east,' said Romi. 'Nowhere near the road.'

'There's a strong wind,' said Prem, looking at the dry leaves swirling across the road.

It was the middle of May, and it hadn't rained in the Terai for several weeks. The grass was brown, the leaves of the trees covered with dust. Even though it was getting on to six o'clock in the evening, the boys' shirts were damp with sweat.

'It will be getting dark soon,' said Prem. 'You'd better spend the night at my house.'

'No, I said I'd be home tonight. My father isn't keeping well. The doctor has given me some tablets for him.'

'You'd better hurry, then. That fire seems to be spreading.'

'Oh, it's far off. It will take me only forty minutes to ride through the forest. Bye, Prem—see you tomorrow!'

Romi mounted his bicycle and pedalled off down the main road of the village, scattering stray hens, stray dogs and stray villagers.

'Hey, look where you're going!' shouted an angry villager,

leaping out of the way of the oncoming bicycle. 'Do you think you own the road?'

'Of course I own it,' called Romi cheerfully, and cycled on.

His own village lay about seven miles distant, on the other side of the forest; but there was only a primary school in his village, and Romi was now in high school. His father, who was a fairly wealthy sugarcane farmer, had only recently bought him the bicycle. Romi didn't care too much for school and felt there weren't enough holidays; but he enjoyed the long rides, and he got on well with his classmates.

He might have stayed the night with Prem had it not been for the tablets which the *Vaid*—the village doctor—had given him for his father.

Romi's father was having back trouble, and the medicine had been specially prepared from local herbs.

Having been given such a fine bicycle, Romi felt that the least he could do in return was to get those tablets to his father as early as possible.

He put his head down and rode swiftly out of the village. Ahead of him, the smoke rose from the burning forest and the sky glowed red.

2

He had soon left the village far behind. There was a slight climb, and Romi had to push harder on the pedals to get over the rise. Once over the top, the road went winding down to the edge of the sub-tropical forest.

This was the part Romi enjoyed most. He relaxed, stopped pedalling, and allowed the bicycle to glide gently down the slope. Soon the wind was rushing past him, blowing his hair about his face and making his shirt billow out behind. He burst into song.

A dog from the village ran beside him, barking furiously. Romi shouted at the dog, encouraging him in the race.

Then the road straightened out, and Romi began pedalling again. The dog, seeing the forest ahead, turned back to the village. It was afraid of the forest.

The smoke was thicker now, and Romi caught the smell of burning timber. But ahead of him, the road was clear. He rode on.

It was a rough, dusty road, cut straight through the forest. Tall trees grew on either side, cutting off the last of the daylight. But the spreading glow of the fire on the right lit up the road, and giant tree-shadows danced before the boy on the bicycle.

Usually the road was deserted. This evening it was alive with wild creatures fleeing from the forest fire.

The first animal that Romi saw was a hare, leaping across the road in front of him. It was followed by several more hares. Then a band of monkeys streamed across, chattering excitedly.

They'll be safe on the other side, thought Romi. *The fire won't cross the road.*

But it was coming closer. And realizing this, Romi pedalled harder. In half-an-hour he should be out of the forest.

Suddenly, from the side of the road, several pheasants rose in the air, and with a *whoosh*, flew low across the path, just in front of the oncoming bicycle. Taken by surprise, Romi fell off. When he picked himself up and began brushing his clothes, he saw that his knee was bleeding. It wasn't a deep cut, but he allowed it to bleed a little, took out his handkerchief and bandaged his knee. Then he mounted the bicycle again.

He rode a bit slower now, because birds and animals kept coming out of the bushes.

Not only pheasants but smaller birds, too, were streaming

across the road—parrots, jungle crows, owls, magpies—and the air was filled with their cries.

Everyone's on the move, thought Romi. *It must be a really big fire.*

He could see the flames now, reaching out from behind the trees on his right, and he could hear the crackling as the dry leaves caught fire. The air was hot on his face. Leaves, still alight or turning to cinders, floated past.

A herd of deer crossed the road, and Romi had to stop until they had passed. Then he mounted again and rode on; but now, for the first time, he was feeling afraid.

3

From ahead came a faint clanging sound. It wasn't an animal sound, Romi was sure of that. A fire-engine? There were no fire-engines within fifty miles.

The clanging came nearer, and Romi discovered that the noise came from a small boy who was running along the forest path, two milk-cans clattering at his side.

'Teju!' called Romi, recognizing the boy from a neighbouring village. 'What are you doing out here?'

'Trying to get home, of course,' said Teju, panting along beside the bicycle.

'Jump on,' said Romi, stopping for him.

Teju was only eight or nine—a couple of years younger than Romi. He had come to deliver milk to some road-workers, but the workers had left at the first signs of the fire, and Teju was hurrying home with his cans still full of milk.

He got up on the crossbar of the bicycle, and Romi moved on again. He was quite used to carrying friends on the crossbar.

'Keep beating your milk-cans,' said Romi. 'Like that, the

animals will know we are coming. My bell doesn't make enough noise. I'm going to get a horn for my cycle!'

'I never knew there were so many animals in the jungle,' said Teju. 'I saw a python in the middle of the road. It stretched right across!'

'What did you do?'

'Just kept running and jumped right over it!'

Teju continued to chatter but Romi's thoughts were on the fire, which was much closer now. Flames shot up from the dry grass and ran up the trunks of trees and along the branches. Smoke billowed out above the forest.

Romi's eyes were smarting and his hair and eyebrows felt scorched. He was feeling tired but he couldn't stop now, he had to get beyond the range of the fire. Another ten or fifteen minutes of steady riding would get them to the small wooden bridge that spanned the little river separating the forest from the sugarcane fields.

Once across the river, they would be safe. The fire could not touch them on the other side because the forest ended at the river's edge. But could they get to the river in time?

4

Clang, clang, clang, went Teju's milk-cans. But the sound of the fire grew louder too.

A tall silk-cotton tree, its branches leaning across the road, had caught fire. They were almost beneath it when there was a crash and a burning branch fell to the ground a few yards in front of them.

The boys had to get off the bicycle and leave the road, forcing their way through a tangle of thorny bushes on the left, dragging and pushing at the bicycle and only returning to the road some distance ahead of the burning tree.

'We won't get out in time,' said Teju, back on the crossbar but feeling disheartened.

'Yes, we will,' said Romi, pedalling with all his might. 'The fire hasn't crossed the road as yet.'

Even as he spoke, he saw a small flame leap up from the grass on the left. It wouldn't be long before more sparks and burning leaves were blown across the road to kindle the grass on the other side.

'Oh, look!' exclaimed Romi, bringing the bicycle to a sudden stop.

'What's wrong now?' asked Teju, rubbing his sore eyes. And then, through the smoke, he saw what was stopping them.

An elephant was standing in the middle of the road.

Teju slipped off the crossbar, his cans rolling on the ground, bursting open and spilling their contents.

The elephant was about forty feet away. It moved about restlessly, its big ears flapping as it turned its head from side to side, wondering which way to go.

From far to the left, where the forest was still untouched, a herd of elephants moved towards the river. The leader of the herd raised his trunk and trumpeted a call. Hearing it, the elephant on the road raised its own trunk and trumpeted a reply. Then it shambled off into the forest, in the direction of the herd, leaving the way clear.

'Come, Teju, jump on!' urged Romi. 'We can't stay here much longer!'

5

Teju forgot about his milk-cans and pulled himself up on the crossbar. Romi ran forward with the bicycle, to gain speed, and mounted swiftly. He kept as far as possible to the left of the road, trying to ignore the flames, the crackling, the smoke and the scorching heat.

It seemed that all the animals who could get away, had done so. The exodus across the road had stopped.

'We won't stop again,' said Romi, gritting his teeth. 'Not even for an elephant!'

'We're nearly there!' said Teju. He was perking up again.

A jackal, overcome by the heat and smoke, lay in the middle of the path, either dead or unconscious. Romi did not stop. He swerved round the animal. Then he put all his strength into one final effort.

He covered the last hundred yards at top speed, and then they were out of the forest, free-wheeling down the sloping road to the river.

'Look!' shouted Teju. 'The bridge is on fire!'

Burning embers had floated down on to the small wooden bridge, and the dry, ancient timber had quickly caught fire. It was now burning fiercely.

Romi did not hesitate. He left the road, riding the bicycle over sand and pebbles. Then with a rush they went down the river-bank and into the water.

The next thing they knew, they were splashing around, trying to find each other in the darkness.

'Help!' cried Teju. 'I'm drowning!'

6

'Don't be silly,' said Romi. 'The water isn't deep—it's only up to the knees. Come here and grab hold of me.'

Teju splashed across and grabbed Romi by the belt.

'The water's so cold,' he said, his teeth chattering.

'Do you want to go back and warm yourself?' asked Romi. 'Some people are never satisfied. Come on, help me get the bicycle up. It's down here, just where we are standing.'

Together they managed to heave the bicycle out of the water and stand it upright.

'Now sit on it,' said Romi. 'I'll push you across.'

'We'll be swept away,' said Teju.

'No, we won't. There's not much water in the river at this time of the year. But the current is quite strong in the middle, so sit still. All right?'

'All right,' said Teju nervously.

Romi began guiding the bicycle across the river, one hand on the seat and one hand on the handlebar. The river was shallow and sluggish in midsummer; even so, it was quite swift in the middle. But having got safely out of the burning forest, Romi was in no mood to let a little river defeat him.

He kicked off his shoes, knowing they would be lost; and then gripping the smooth stones of the river-bed with his toes, he concentrated on keeping his balance and getting the bicycle and Teju through the middle of the stream. The water here came up to his waist, and the current would have been too strong for Teju. But when they reached the shallows, Teju got down and helped Romi push the bicycle.

They reached the opposite bank, and sank down on the grass.

'We can rest now,' said Romi. 'But not all night—I've got some medicine to give to my father.' He felt in his pockets and found that the tablets, in their envelope, had turned into a soggy mess. 'Oh well, he had to take them with water anyway,' he said.

They watched the fire as it continued to spread through the forest. It had crossed the road down which they had come. The sky was a bright red, and the river reflected the colour of the sky.

Several elephants had found their way down to the river. They were cooling off by spraying water on each other with their trunks. Further downstream there were deer and other animals.

Romi and Teju looked at each other in the glow from the fire. They hadn't known each other very well before. But now they felt they had been friends for years.

'What are you thinking about?' asked Teju.

'I'm thinking,' said Romi, 'that even if the fire is out in a day or two, it will be a long time before the bridge is repaired. So it will be a nice long holiday from school!'

'But you can walk across the river,' said Teju. 'You just did it.'

'Impossible,' said Romi. 'It's much too swift.'

KOKI PLAYS THE GAME

'There's a cricket match on Saturday, isn't there?' asked Koki.

'That's right,' said Ranji. 'We're playing the Public School team.'

'I might come and watch,' said Koki.

'As you like. It won't be much of a game. We'll beat them easily.'

Ranji's own cricket team was quite different from his school team. It consisted of boys big and small, long and short, from various walks of life. Even Koki, a girl, was allowed honorary membership, and had sometimes been 'twelfth man'—an extra. She knew the game well, and often bowled to Ranji in the mornings when he wanted batting practice. Only a couple of the teammates could afford to go to private schools like Ranji's; most of them went to the local government school, and two or three had stopped going to school altogether.

There was Bhartu, who delivered newspapers in the mornings; the brothers Mukesh and Rakesh, whose father kept a sweet shop; and a tailor's son, Amir Ali. There was Billy Jones, an Anglo-Indian boy; 'Lumboo', the Tall One; Sitaram, the washerman's son, and several others. And there was also Bhim, who couldn't play at all, but who made a good umpire (when his glasses weren't steamed over) and who accompanied the team wherever it went.

This Saturday they were playing on their 'home' ground, a patch of wasteland behind a new cinema called the Apsara ('Heavenly Dancer').

The Public School boys had all arrived first, which was only natural since they lived together in the same boarding school. The members of Ranji's team came from different directions, so it was some time before they had all assembled. Even then, they were two short. But Ranji won the toss and decided to bat, hoping that the missing team members would arrive in time to take their turn at the wicket.

'If Mukesh and Rakesh aren't here in time, we won't have them in the team,' said Ranji sternly.

'Don't sack them,' said Lumboo. 'They always bring us sweets and snacks from their father's shop. We need them in the team even if they don't score any runs.'

'Well, if they turn up *without* refreshments, they'll be sacked,' said Ranji, always ready to be fair.

The two umpires had gone out to set up the stumps—Bhim, on behalf of Ranji's team, and a teacher from the Public School.

'I don't like the look of that teacher,' said Amir Ali.

'Well, we won't take any risks.'

Billy Jones and Lumboo always opened the batting. Lumboo's height helped him to deal with the fast-rising ball. He took the first ball.

The Public School's opening bowler was speedy but inaccurate. This was because he was trying to bowl too fast. His first ball went for a wide, which gave Ranji's team its first run. The second ball wasn't quite so wide, but it was still about a foot from the leg stump. Lumboo took a swipe at it and missed. The third ball pitched halfway down the wicket and kept low. It struck Lumboo on the pads.

'How's that!' shouted the bowler, wicketkeeper, and slip-fielders in unison.

The Public School's umpire did not hesitate. Up went his finger. Lumboo was given out leg-before-wicket. Lumboo stood aghast. He looked down at where his feet were placed, then back at his stumps.

'I'm not in front of the wicket,' he complained to no one in particular.

'The umpire's word is law,' said the wicketkeeper.

Lumboo slowly walked back to where his teammates reclined against a pile of bricks.

'I wasn't out!' he protested.

'Never mind,' said Ranji, whose turn it was to bat. 'You'll get your chance when you come on to bowl.'

He walked to the wicket with a confident air, his bat resting on his shoulder. He took guard carefully and, tapping his bat on the ground, faced the bowler. He received a straight ball, fast, and met it on the half-volley, driving it straight back past the bowler. It sped to the boundary, amidst delighted cries from Ranji's teammates. Four runs.

The next ball was short, just outside the off stump. Ranji stepped back and square-cut it past point. Another four. There were more cheers, and this time Ranji distinctly heard a girl's voice shouting: 'Good shot, Ranji!'

He looked back to where his teammates were gathered. There was no girl among them. He turned and looked toward the opposite boundary, and there, under the giant cinema hoarding, stood Koki. She waved to him.

Ranji did not wave back. He felt acutely self-conscious. Settling down to face the bowler again, he was aware of two things at once—of the bowler making faces and charging up to bowl, and of Koki standing on the boundary and waiting for him to hit another four.

This loss of concentration caused him to misjudge the next ball. Instead of playing forward, he played back.

The ball took the edge of his bat and flew straight into the wicketkeeper's gloves.

'How's that!' shouted all the fielders, appealing for a catch.

Ranji did not wait for the umpire—in this case, Bhim, to give him out. He knew he'd touched the ball. Scowling, he walked back to his team. It was all Koki's fault!

Now, there was a good partnership between Sitaram and Bhartu. Sitaram, who helped his father with the town's washing on Sundays, was in the habit of laying out clothes on a flat stone and pounding them with a stout stick—the method followed by most washermen.

He dealt with the cricket ball in much the same way—clouting it hard, and sending it to various points of the compass. He hit up 25 valuable runs before he was out, caught off a big hit. Bhartu pushed and prodded, merely keeping one end going, until he too was out to an LBW decision. Billy Jones had gone the same way, taking the ball on his pads. No one was happy with the LBW decisions.

'We must have neutral umpires,' said Amir Ali.

'But who wants to be an umpire?' said Ranji. 'We won't find anyone. We'll have to use our own team members—or let the other side provide *both* umpires!'

'Not after today,' said Lumboo.

Meanwhile, Mukesh and Rakesh had arrived, carrying paper bags full of samosas and jalebis. As a result, everyone cheered up. Wickets fell almost as rapidly as the snacks and sweets were consumed. Mukesh and Rakesh, who were the last men in, held out for several overs until Rakesh was given out—LBW! Ranji's team was all out for 87 runs—not really a match-winning score, except on a tricky wicket.

It was the Public School team's turn to bat. One of their opening batsmen was bowled by Lumboo for naught. The other batsman was twice rapped on the pads by balls from Ranji, but his loud appeals for LBW were turned down—by the Public School's umpire, naturally! Muttering to himself, Ranji hurled down a thunderbolt of a ball. It rose sharply and struck the batsman on the hand. Howling with pain, he dropped his bat and wrung his hand. Then he showed everyone a swollen finger and decided to 'retire hurt'.

'There's more than one way of getting them out,' muttered Ranji, as he passed the umpire.

The next two batsmen were good players, not as nervous as the openers. One of them got what might have been a faint tickle to an out-swinger from Lumboo, but he was given the benefit of the doubt by Bhim—who, as umpires went, was as impartial as a star. He showed no favours to his own team, no matter what the other umpire did. It just isn't fair, thought Ranji.

The number three and four batsmen put on 40 runs between them, and by mid-afternoon Ranji's players were feeling tired and hungry. Then three quick wickets fell to Sitaram's spinners. Three wickets remained, and 20 runs were needed by the Public School for victory.

This was when Bhartu, running to take a catch, collided with chubby Mukesh. Both of them went sprawling on the grass, and when they got up the ball was found lodged in the back of Mukesh's pants. How it got there no one could tell, but after much discussion the umpires had to agree that it qualified as a catch and the batsman was given out. But Bhartu had to leave the ground with a bleeding nose.

Ranji looked around for a replacement. There was no one in sight except Koki.

'Come and field,' said Ranji brusquely.

Koki needed no persuading. She slipped off her sandals and dashed barefoot on to the field, taking up Bhartu's position near the boundary.

The tail-end batsmen were now swinging at the ball in a desperate attempt to hit the remaining runs. A hard-hit drive sped past Koki and went for four runs. Ranji gave her a hard look. Then the two batsmen got into a muddle while trying to take a quick run, and one of them was run out.

The last man came in. The Public School was 8 runs behind. But a couple of boundaries would take care of that.

The batsmen ran two. And then one of them, over-confident and sure of victory, swung out at a slow, tempting ball from Sitaram, and the ball flew towards Koki in a long, curving arc.

Koki had to run a few yards to her left. Then she leapt like a gazelle and took the ball in both hands. Ranji's team had won, and Koki had made the winning catch.

It was her last appearance as 'twelfth man'. From that day onwards she was a regular member of the team.

THE FLUTE PLAYER

Down the main road passed big yellow buses, cars, pony-drawn tongas, motorcycles and bullock carts. This steady flow of traffic seemed, somehow, to form a barrier between the city on one side of the Trunk Road, and the distant sleepy villages on the other. It seemed to cut India in half—the India Kamla knew slightly, and the India she had never seen.

Kamla's grandmother lived on the outskirts of the city of Jaipur, and just across the road from the house there were fields and villages stretching away for hundreds of miles. But Kamla had never been across the main road. This separated the busy city from the flat green plains stretching endlessly towards the horizon.

Kamla was used to city life. In England, it was London and Manchester. In India, it was Delhi and Jaipur. Rainy Manchester was, of course, different in many ways from sun-drenched Jaipur, and Indian cities had stronger smells and more vibrant colours than their English counterparts. Nevertheless, they had much in common: busy people always on the move, money constantly changing hands, buses to catch, schools to attend, parties to go to, TV to watch. Kamla had seen very little of the English countryside, even less of India outside the cities.

Her parents lived in Manchester where her father was a doctor in a large hospital. She went to school in England. But this year, during the summer holidays, she had come to India to stay with her grandmother. Apart from a maidservant and a grizzled old nightwatchman, Grandmother lived quite alone in a small house on the outskirts of Jaipur. During the winter months, Jaipur's climate was cool and bracing but in the summer, a fierce sun poured down upon the city from a cloudless sky.

None of the other city children ventured across the main road into the fields of millet, wheat and cotton, but Kamla was determined to visit the fields before she returned to England. From the flat roof of the house, she could see them stretching away for miles, the ripening wheat swaying in the hot wind. Finally, when there were only two days left before she went to Delhi to board a plane for London, she made up her mind and crossed the main road.

She did this in the afternoon, when Grandmother was asleep and the servants were in the bazaar. She slipped out of the back door and her slippers kicked up the dust as she ran down the path to the main road. A bus roared past and more dust rose from the road and swirled about her. Kamla ran through the dust, past the jacaranda trees that lined the road, and into the fields.

Suddenly, the world became an enormous place, bigger and more varied than it had seemed from the air, also mysterious and exciting—and just a little frightening.

The sea of wheat stretched away till it merged with the hot blinding blue of the sky. Far to her left were a few trees and the low white huts of a village. To her right lay hollow pits of red dust and a blackened chimney where bricks used to be made. In front, some distance away, Kamla could see a camel moving round a well, drawing up water for the fields. She set out in the direction of the camel.

Her grandmother had told her not to wander off on her

own in the city; but this wasn't the city, and as far as she knew, camels did not attack people.

It took her a long time to get to the camel. It was about half a mile away, though it seemed much nearer. And when Kamla reached it, she was surprised to find that there was no one else in sight. The camel was turning the wheel by itself, moving round and round the well, while the water kept gushing up in little trays to run down the channels into the fields. The camel took no notice of Kamla, did not look at her even once, just carried on about its business.

There must be someone here, thought Kamla, walking towards a mango tree that grew a few yards away. Ripe mangoes dangled like globules of gold from its branches. Under the tree, fast asleep, was a boy.

All he wore was a pair of dirty white shorts. His body had been burnt dark by the sun; his hair was tousled, his feet chalky with dust. In the palm of his outstretched hand was a flute. He was a thin boy, with long bony legs, but Kamla felt that he was strong too, for his body was hard and wiry.

Kamla came nearer to the sleeping boy, peering at him with some curiosity, for she had not seen a village boy before. Her shadow fell across his face. The coming of the shadow woke the boy. He opened his eyes and stared at Kamla. When she did not say anything, he sat up, his head a little to one side, his hands clasping his knees, and stared at her.

'Who are you?' he asked a little gruffly. He was not used to waking up and finding strange girls staring at him.

'I'm Kamla. I've come from England, but I'm really from India. I mean I've come home to India, but I'm really from England.' This was getting to be rather confusing, so she countered with an abrupt, 'Who are you?'

'I'm the strongest boy in the village,' said the boy, deciding to assert himself without any more ado. 'My name is Romi. I can wrestle and swim and climb any tree.'

'And do you sleep a lot?' asked Kamla innocently.

Romi scratched his head and grinned.

'I must look after the camel,' he said. 'It is no use staying awake for the camel. It keeps going round the well until it is tired, and then it stops. When it has rested, it starts going round again. It can carry on like that all day. But it eats a lot.'

Mention of the camel's food reminded Romi that he was hungry. He was growing fast these days and was nearly always hungry. There were some mangoes lying beside him, and he offered one to Kamla. They were silent for a few minutes. You cannot suck mangoes and talk at the same time. After they had finished, they washed their hands in the water from one of the trays.

'There are parrots in the tree,' said Kamla, noticing three or four green parrots conducting a noisy meeting in the topmost branches. They reminded her a bit of a pop group she had seen and heard at home.

'They spoil most of the mangoes,' said Romi.

He flung a stone at them, missed, but they took off with squawks of protest, flashes of green and gold wheeling in the sunshine.

'Where do you swim?' asked Kamla. 'Down in the well?'

'Of course not. I'm not a frog. There is a canal not far from here. Come, I will show you!'

As they crossed the fields, a pair of blue jays flew out of a bush, rockets of bright blue that dipped and swerved, rising and falling as they chased each other.

Remembering a story that Grandmother had told her, Kamla said, 'They are sacred birds, aren't they? Because of their blue throats.' She told him the story of the God Shiva having a blue throat because he had swallowed a poison that would have destroyed the world; he had kept the poison in his throat and would not let it go further. 'And so his throat is blue, like the blue jay's.'

Romi liked this story. His respect for Kamla greatly increased. But he was not to be outdone, and when a small grey squirrel dashed across the path he told her that squirrels, too, were sacred. Krishna, the god who had been born into a farmer's family like Romi's, had been fond of squirrels and would take them in his arms and stroke them. 'That is why squirrels have four dark lines down their backs,' said Romi. 'Krishna was very dark, as dark as I am, and the stripes are the marks of his fingers.'

'Can you catch a squirrel?' asked Kamla.

'No, they are too quick. But I caught a snake once. I caught it by its tail and dropped it in the old well. That well is full of snakes. Whenever we catch one, instead of killing it, we drop it in the well! They can't get out.'

Kamla shuddered at the thought of all those snakes swimming and wriggling about at the bottom of the deep well. She wasn't sure that she wanted to return to the well with him. But she forgot about the snakes when they reached the canal.

It was a small canal, about ten metres wide, and only waist-deep in the middle, but it was very muddy at the bottom. She had never seen such a muddy stream in her life.

'Would you like to get in?' asked Romi.

'No,' said Kamla. 'You get in.'

Romi was only too ready to show off his tricks in the water. His toes took a firm hold on the grassy bank, the muscles of his calves tensed, and he dived into the water with a loud splash, landing rather awkwardly on his belly. It was a poor dive, but Kamla was impressed.

Romi swam across to the opposite bank and then back again. When he climbed out of the water, he was covered with mud. It made him look quite fierce. 'Come on in,' he invited. 'It's not deep.'

'It's dirty,' said Kamla, but felt tempted all the same.

'It's only mud,' said Romi. 'There's nothing wrong with mud. Camels like mud. Buffaloes love mud.'

'I'm not a camel—or a buffalo.'

'All right. You don't have to go right in, just walk along the sides of the channel.'

After a moment's hesitation, Kamla slipped her feet out of her slippers, and crept cautiously down the slope till her feet were in the water. She went no further, but even so, some of the muddy water splashed on to her clean white skirt. What would she tell Grandmother? Her feet sank into the soft mud and she gave a little squeal as the water reached her knees. It was with some difficulty that she got each foot out of the sticky mud.

Romi took her by the hand, and they went stumbling along the side of the channel while little fish swam in and out of their legs, and a heron, one foot raised, waited until they had passed before snapping a fish out of the water. The little fish glistened in the sun before it disappeared down the heron's throat.

Romi gave a sudden exclamation and came to a stop. Kamla held on to him for support.

'What is it?' she asked, a little nervously.

'It's a tortoise,' said Romi. 'Can you see it?'

He pointed to the bank of the canal, and there, lying quite still, was a small tortoise. Romi scrambled up the bank and, before Kamla could stop him, had picked up the tortoise. As soon as he touched it, the animal's head and legs disappeared into its shell. Romi turned it over, but from behind the breastplate only the head and a spiky tail were visible.

'Look!' exclaimed Kamla, pointing to the ground where the tortoise had been lying. 'What's in that hole?'

They peered into the hole. It was about half a metre deep, and at the bottom were five or six white eggs, a little smaller than a hen's eggs.

'Put it back,' said Kamla. 'It was sitting on its eggs.'

Romi shrugged and dropped the tortoise back on its hole. It peeped out from behind its shell, saw the children were still present, and retreated into its shell again.

'I must go,' said Kamla. 'It's getting late. Granny will wonder where I have gone.'

They walked back to the mango tree, and washed their hands and feet in the cool clear water from the well; but only after Romi had assured Kamla that there weren't any snakes in the well—he had been talking about an old disused well on the far side of the village. Kamla told Romi she would take him to her house one day, but it would have to be next year, or perhaps the year after, when she came to India again.

'Is it very far, where you are going?' asked Romi.

'Yes, England is across the seas. I have to go back to my parents. And my school is there, too. But I will take the plane from Delhi. Have you ever been to Delhi?'

'I have not been further than Jaipur,' said Romi. 'What is England like? Are there canals to swim in?'

'You can swim in the sea. Lots of people go swimming in the sea. But it's too cold most of the year. Where I live, there are shops and cinemas and places where you can eat anything you like. And people from all over the world come to live there. You can see red faces, brown faces, black faces, white faces!'

'I saw a red face once,' said Romi. 'He came to the village to take pictures. He took one of me sitting on the camel. He said he would send me the picture, but it never came.'

Kamla noticed the flute lying on the grass. 'Is it your flute?' she asked.

'Yes,' said Romi. 'It is an old flute. But the old ones are best. I found it lying in a field last year. Perhaps it was the God Krishna's! He was always playing the flute.'

'And who taught you to play it?'

'Nobody. I learnt by myself. Shall I play it for you?'

Kamla nodded, and they sat down on the grass, leaning against the trunk of the mango tree, and Romi put the flute to his lips and began to play.

It was a slow, sweet tune, a little sad, a little happy, and the notes were taken up by the breeze and carried across the fields. There was no one to hear the music except the birds and the camel, and Kamla. Whether the camel liked it or not, we shall never know; it just kept going round and round the well, drawing up water for the fields. And whether the birds liked it or not, we cannot say, although it is true that they were all suddenly silent when Romi began to play. But Kamla was charmed by the music, and she watched Romi while he played, and the boy smiled at her with his eyes and ran his fingers along the flute. When he stopped playing, everything was still, everything silent, except for the soft wind sighing in the wheat and the gurgle of water coming up from the well.

Kamla stood up to leave.

'When will you come again?' asked Romi.

'I will try to come next year,' said Kamla.

'That is a long time. By then you will be quite old. You may not want to come.'

'I will come,' said Kamla.

'Promise?'

'Promise.'

Romi put the flute in her hands and said, 'You keep it. I can get another one.'

'But I don't know how to play it,' said Kamla.

'It will play by itself,' said Romi.

She took the flute and put it to her lips and blew on it, producing a squeaky little note that startled a lone parrot out of the mango tree. Romi laughed, and while he was laughing, Kamla turned and ran down the path through the fields. And when she had gone some distance, she turned and waved to Romi with the flute. He stood near the well and waved back at her.

Cupping his hands to his mouth, he shouted across the fields, 'Don't forget to come next year!'

And Kamla called back, 'I won't forget.' But her voice was faint, and the breeze blew the words away and Romi did not hear them.

Was England home? wondered Kamla. Or was this Indian city home? Or was her true home in that other India, across the busy Trunk Road? Perhaps she would find out one day.

Romi watched her until she was just a speck in the distance, and then he turned and shouted at the camel, telling it to move faster. But the camel did not even glance at him; it just carried on as before, as India has carried on for thousands of years, round and round and round the well, while the water gurgled and splashed over the smooth stones.

THE THIEF'S STORY

I was still a thief when I met Romi. And though I was only fifteen years old, I was an experienced and fairly successful hand. Romi was watching a wrestling match when I approached him. He was about twenty-five and he looked easygoing, kind and simple enough for my purpose. I was sure I would be able to win the young man's confidence.

'You look a bit of a wrestler yourself,' I said. There's nothing like flattery to break the ice!

'So do you,' he replied, which put me off for a moment because at that time I was rather thin and bony.

'Well,' I said modestly, 'I do wrestle a bit.'

'What's your name?'

'Hari Singh,' I lied. I took a new name every month, which kept me ahead of the police and former employers.

After these formalities Romi confined himself to commenting on the wrestlers, who were grunting, gasping and heaving each other about. When he walked away, I followed him casually.

'Hello again,' he said.

I gave him my most appealing smile. 'I want to work for you,' I said.

'But I can't pay you anything—not for some time, anyway.'

I thought that over for a minute. Perhaps I had misjudged my man. 'Can you feed me?' I asked.

'Can you cook?'

'I can cook,' I lied again.

'If you can cook, then maybe I can feed you.'

He took me to his room over the Delhi Sweet Shop and told me I could sleep on the balcony. But the meal I cooked that night must have been terrible because Romi gave it to a stray dog and told me to be off.

But I just hung around, smiling in my most appealing way, and he couldn't help laughing.

Later he said, never mind, he'd teach me to cook. He also taught me to write my name and said he would soon teach me to write whole sentences and to add figures. I was grateful. I knew that once I could write like an educated person, there would be no limit to what I could achieve.

It was quite pleasant working for Romi. I made tea in the morning and then took my time buying the day's supplies, usually making a profit of two or three rupees. I think he knew I made a little money this way, but he didn't seem to mind.

Romi made money by fits and starts. He would borrow one week, lend the next. He kept worrying about his next cheque, but as soon as it arrived he would go out and celebrate. He wrote for the *Delhi* and *Bombay* magazines: a strange way to make a living.

One evening he came home with a small bundle of notes, saying he had just sold a book to a publisher. That night I saw him put the money in an envelope and tuck it under the mattress.

I had been working for Romi for almost a month and, apart from cheating on the shopping, had not done anything big in my real line of work. I had every opportunity for doing so. I could come and go as I pleased, and Romi was the most trusting person I had ever met.

That was why it was so difficult to rob him. It was easy for me to rob a greedy man. But robbing a nice man could be a problem. And if he doesn't notice he's being robbed, then all the spice goes out of the undertaking!

Well, it's time I got down to some real work, I told myself. If I don't take the money, he'll only waste it on his so-called friends. After all, he doesn't even give me a salary.

Romi was sleeping peacefully. A beam of moonlight reached over the balcony and fell on his bed. I sat on the floor, considering the situation. If I took the money, I could catch the 10.30 express to Lucknow. Slipping out of my blanket, I crept over to the bed.

My hand slid under the mattress, searching for the notes. When I found the packet, I drew it out without a sound. Romi sighed in his sleep and turned on his side. Startled, I moved quickly out of the room.

Once on the road, I began to run. I had the money stuffed into a vest pocket under my shirt. When I'd gotten some distance from Romi's place, I slowed to a walk and, taking the envelope from my pocket, counted the money. Seven hundred rupees in fifties. I could live like a prince for a week or two!

When I reached the station, I did not stop at the ticket office (I had never bought a ticket in my life) but dashed straight onto the platform. The Lucknow Express was just moving out. The train had still to pick up speed and I should have been able to jump into one of the compartments, but I hesitated—for some reason I can't explain—and I lost the chance to get away.

When the train had gone, I found myself standing alone on the deserted platform. I had no idea where to spend the night. I had no friends, believing that friends were more trouble than help. And I did not want to arouse curiosity by staying at one of the small hotels nearby. The only person I knew really well was the man I had robbed. Leaving the station, I walked slowly through the bazaar.

In my short career, I had made a study of people's faces after they had discovered the loss of their valuables. The greedy showed panic; the rich showed anger; the poor, resignation. But I knew that Romi's face when he discovered the theft would show only a touch of sadness—not for the loss of money, but for the loss of trust.

The night was chilly—November nights can be cold in northern India—and a shower of rain added to my discomfort. I sat down in the shelter of the clock tower. A few beggars and vagrants lay beside me, rolled up tight in their blankets. The clock showed midnight. I felt for the notes; they were soaked through.

Romi's money. In the morning, he would probably have given me five rupees to go to the movies, but now I had it all: no more cooking meals, running to the bazaar, or learning to write sentences.

Sentences! I had forgotten about them in the excitement of the theft. Writing complete sentences, I knew, could one day bring me more than a few hundred rupees. It was a simple matter to steal. But to be a really big man, a clever and respected man, was something else. I should go back to Romi, I told myself, if only to learn to read and write.

I hurried back to the room feeling very nervous, for it is much easier to steal something than to return it undetected.

I opened the door quietly, then stood in the doorway in clouded moonlight. Romi was still asleep. I crept to the head of the bed, and my hand came up with the packet of notes. I felt his breath on my hand. I remained still for a few moments.

Then my fingers found the edge of the mattress, and I slipped the money beneath it.

I awoke late the next morning to find that Romi had already made the tea. He stretched out a hand to me. There was a fifty-rupee note between his fingers. My heart sank.

'I made some money yesterday,' he said. 'Now I'll be able to pay you regularly.'

My spirits rose. But when I took the note, I noticed that it was still wet from the night's rain.

So he knew what I'd done. But neither his lips nor his eyes revealed anything.

'Today we'll start writing sentences,' he said.

I smiled at Romi in my most appealing way. And the smile came by itself, without any effort.

THE BOY WHO BROKE THE BANK

Nathu, the sweeper-boy, grumbled to himself as he swept the steps of a small local bank, owned for the most part by Seth Govind Ram, a man of wealth whose haphazard business dealings had often brought him to the verge of ruin. Nathu used the small broom hurriedly and carelessly; the dust, after rising in a cloud above his head, settled down again on the steps. As Nathu was banging his pan against a dustbin, Sitaram, the washerman's son, passed by.

Sitaram was on his delivery round. He had a bundle of pressed clothes balanced on his head.

'Don't raise such a dust!' he called out to Nathu. 'Are you annoyed because they are still refusing to pay you another five rupees a month?'

'I don't want to talk about it,' complained the sweeper-boy. 'I haven't even received my regular pay. And this is the end of the month. Soon two months' pay will be due. Who would think this was a bank, holding up a poor man's salary? As soon as I get my money, I'm off! Not another week will I work in the place.'

And Nathu banged his pan against the dustbin two or three times more, just to emphasize his point and give himself confidence.

'Well, I wish you luck,' said Sitaram. 'I'll be on the look-out for a new job for you.' And he plodded barefoot along the road, the big bundle of clothes hiding most of his head and shoulders.

At the fourth house he visited, delivering the washing, Sitaram overheard the woman of the house saying how difficult it was to get someone to sweep the courtyard. Tying up his bundle, Sitaram said: 'I know a sweeper-boy who's looking for work. He might be able to work for you from next month. He's with Seth Govind Ram's bank just now, but they are not giving him his pay, and he wants to leave.'

'Oh, is that so?' said Mrs Prakash. 'And why aren't they paying him?'

'They must be short of money,' said Sitaram with a shrug. Mrs Prakash laughed, 'Well, tell him to come and see me when he's free.'

Sitaram, glad that he had been of some service both to a friend and to a customer, hoisted his bag on his shoulders and went on his way.

Mrs Prakash had to do some shopping. She gave instructions to her maidservant with regard to the baby and told the cook what she wanted for lunch. Her husband worked for a large company, and they could keep servants and do things in style. Having given her orders, she set out for the bazaar to make her customary tour of the cloth shops.

A large, shady tamarind tree grew near the clock tower, and it was here that Mrs Prakash found her friend, Mrs Bhushan, sheltering from the heat. Mrs Bhushan was fanning herself with a large peacock's feather. She complained that the summer was the hottest in the history of the town. She then showed Mrs Prakash a sample of the cloth she was going to buy, and for five minutes they discussed its shade, texture and design.

When they had exhausted the subject, Mrs Prakash said:

'Do you know, my dear, Seth Govind Ram's bank can't even pay its employees. Only this morning I heard a complaint from their sweeper-boy, who hasn't received his pay for two months!'

'It's disgraceful!' exclaimed Mrs Bhushan. 'If they can't pay their sweeper, they must be in a bad way. None of the others can be getting paid either.'

She left Mrs Prakash at the tamarind tree and went in search of her husband, who was found sitting under the fan in Jugal Kishore's electrical goods shop, playing cards with the owner.

'So there you are!' cried Mrs Bhushan. 'I've been looking for you for nearly an hour. Where did you disappear to?'

'Nowhere,' replied Mr Bhushan. 'Had you remained stationary in one shop, you might have found me. But you go from one to another, like a bee in a flower-garden.'

'Now don't start grumbling. The heat is bad enough. I don't know what's happening to this town. Even the bank is going bankrupt.'

'What did you say?' said Mr Jugal Kishore, sitting up suddenly. 'Which bank?'

'Why, Seth Govind Ram's bank, of course. I hear they've stopped paying their employees—no salary for over three months! Don't tell me you have an account with them, Mr Kishore?'

'No, but my neighbour has!' he said, and he called out to the keeper of the barber shop next door: 'Faiz Hussain, have you heard the latest? Seth Govind Ram's bank is about to collapse! You'd better take your money out while there's still time.'

Faiz Hussain, who was cutting the hair of an elderly gentleman, was so startled that his hand shook and he nicked his customer's ear. The customer yelped with pain and distress: pain, because of the cut, and distress, because of the awful news he had just heard. With one side of his neck still unshorn, he leapt out of his chair and sped across the road to a general merchant's store, where there was a telephone. He dialled Seth Govind Ram's number. The Seth was not at home. Where was he, then? The Seth was holidaying in Kashmir. Oh, was that so? The elderly gentleman did not believe it. He hurried back to the barber shop and told Faiz Hussain: 'The bird has flown! Seth Govind Ram has left town. Definitely, it means a collapse. I'll have the rest of my haircut another time.' And he dashed out of the shop and made a bee-line for his office and cheque book.

◆

The news spread through the bazaar with the rapidity of a forest fire. From the general merchant's it travelled to the tea-shop, circulated amongst the customers, and then spread with them in various directions, to the paan-seller, the tailor, the fruit-vendor, the jeweller, the beggar sitting on the pavement.

Old Ganpat, the beggar, had a crooked leg and had been squatting on the pavement for years, calling for alms. In the evening someone would come with a barrow and take him away. He had never been known to walk. But now, on learning that the bank was about to collapse, Ganpat astonished everyone by leaping to his feet and actually running at a good speed in the direction of the bank. It soon became known that he had well over a thousand rupees in savings.

Men stood in groups at street corners, discussing the situation. There hadn't been so much excitement since India last won a Test Match. The small town in the foot-hills seldom had a crisis, never had floods or earthquakes or droughts. And so the imminent crash of the local bank set everyone talking and speculating and rushing about in a frenzy.

Some boasted of their farsightedness, congratulating themselves on having taken out their money, or on never putting any in. Others speculated on the reasons for the crash, putting it all down to Seth Govind Ram's pleasure-loving ways. The Seth had fled the state, said one. He had fled the country, said another. He had a South American passport, said a third. Others insisted that he was hiding somewhere in the town. And there was a rumour that he had hanged himself from the tamarind tree, where he had been found that morning by the sweeper-boy.

Someone who had a relative working as a clerk in the bank decided to phone him and get the facts.

'I don't know anything about it,' said the clerk, 'except that half the town is here, trying to take their money out. Everyone seems to have gone mad!'

'There's a rumour that none of you have been paid.'

'Well, all the clerks have had their salaries. We wouldn't be working otherwise. It may be that some of the part-time workers are getting paid late, but that isn't due to a shortage of money—only a few hundred rupees—it's just that the clerk who looks after their payments is on sick leave. You don't expect me to do his work, do you?' And he put the telephone down.

By afternoon the bank had gone through all its ready money, and the harassed manager was helpless. Emergency funds could only be obtained from one of the government banks, and now it was nearly closing time. He wasn't sure he could persuade the crowd outside to wait until the following morning. And Seth Govind Ram could be of no help from his luxury houseboat in Kashmir, five hundred miles away.

The clerks shut down their counters. But the people gathered outside on the steps of the bank, shouting: 'We want our money!' 'Give it to us today, break in!' 'Fetch Seth Govind Ram, we know he's hiding in the vaults!'

Mischief-makers, who did not have a paisa in the bank, joined the crowd. The manager stood at the door and tried to calm his angry customers. He declared that the bank had plenty of money, that they could withdraw all they wanted the following morning.

'We want it now!' chanted the people. 'Now, now, now!'

A few stones were thrown, and the manager retreated indoors, closing the iron-grilled gate.

A brick hurtled through the air and smashed into the plate-glass window that advertised the bank's assets.

Then the police arrived. They climbed the steps of the bank and, using their long sticks, pushed the crowd back until people began falling over each other. Gradually everyone dispersed, shouting that they would be back in the morning.

◆

Nathu arrived next morning to sweep the steps of the bank.

He saw the refuse and the broken glass and the stones cluttering up the steps. Raising his hands in horror, he cried: 'Goondas! Hooligans! May they suffer from a thousand ills! It was bad enough being paid irregularly—now I must suffer an increase of work!' He smote the steps with his broom, scattering the refuse.

'Good morning, Nathu,' said Sitaram, the washer-man's son, getting down from his bicycle. 'Are you ready to take up a new job from the first of next month? You'll have to, I suppose, now that the bank is closing.'

'What did you say?' said Nathu.

'Haven't you heard? The bank's gone bankrupt. You'd better hang around until the others arrive, and then start demanding your money too. You'll be lucky if you get it!' He waved cheerfully, and pedalled away on his bicycle.

Nathu went back to sweeping the steps, muttering to himself. When he had finished, he sat down on the bottom step to await the arrival of the manager. He was determined to get his pay.

'Who would have thought the bank would collapse,' he said to himself, and looked thoughtfully across the street. 'I wonder how it could have happened.'

ANGRY RIVER

In the middle of the big river, the river that began in the mountains and ended in the sea, was a small island. The river swept round the island, sometimes clawing at its banks, but never going right over it. It was over twenty years since the river had flooded the island, and at that time no one had lived there. But for the last ten years a small hut had stood there, a mud-walled hut with a sloping thatched roof. The hut had been built into a huge rock, so only three of the walls were mud, and the fourth was rock.

Goats grazed on the short grass that grew on the island, and on the prickly leaves of thorn bushes. A few hens followed them about. There was a melon patch and a vegetable patch. In the middle of the island stood a peepul tree. It was the only tree there. Even during the Great Flood, when the island had been under water, the tree had stood firm.

It was an old tree. A seed had been carried to the island by a strong wind some fifty years back, had found shelter between two rocks, had taken root there, and had sprung up to give shade and shelter to a small family; and Indians love peepul trees, especially during the hot summer months when the heart-shaped leaves catch the least breath of air and flutter eagerly, fanning those who sit beneath.

A sacred tree, the peepul: the abode of spirits, good and bad.

'Don't yawn when you are sitting beneath the tree,' Grandmother used to warn Sita.

'And if you must yawn, always snap your fingers in front of your mouth. If you forget to do that, a spirit might jump down your throat!'

'And then what will happen?' asked Sita.

'It will probably ruin your digestion,' said Grandfather, who wasn't much of a believer in spirits.

The peepul had a beautiful leaf, and Grandmother likened it to the body of the mighty god Krishna—broad at the shoulders, then tapering down to a very slim waist.

It was an old tree, and an old man sat beneath it. He was mending a fishing net. He had fished in the river for ten years, and he was a good fisherman. He knew where to find the slim silver chilwa fish and the big, beautiful mahseer and the long-moustached singhara; he knew where the river was deep and where it was shallow; he knew which baits to use—which fish liked worms and which liked gram. He had taught his son to fish, but his son had gone to work in a factory in a city, nearly a hundred miles away. He had no grandson; but he had a granddaughter, Sita, and she could do all the things a boy could do, and sometimes she could do them better. She had lost her mother when she was very small. Grandmother had taught her all the things a girl should know, and she could do these as well as most girls. But neither of her grandparents could read or write, and as a result Sita couldn't read or write either.

There was a school in one of the villages across the river, but Sita had never seen it. There was too much to do on the island.

While Grandfather mended his net, Sita was inside the hut, pressing her grandmother's forehead, which was hot with fever.

Grandmother had been ill for three days and could not eat. She had been ill before, but she had never been so bad. Grandfather had brought her some sweet oranges from the market in the nearest town, and she could suck the juice from the oranges, but she couldn't eat anything else.

She was younger than Grandfather, but because she was sick, she looked much older. She had never been very strong.

When Sita noticed that Grandmother had fallen asleep, she tiptoed out of the room on her bare feet and stood outside.

The sky was dark with monsoon clouds. It had rained all night, and in a few hours it would rain again. The monsoon rains had come early, at the end of June. Now it was the middle of July, and already the river was swollen. Its rushing sound seemed nearer and more menacing than usual.

Sita went to her grandfather and sat down beside him beneath the peepul tree.

'When you are hungry, tell me,' she said, 'and I will make the bread.'

'Is your grandmother asleep?'

'She sleeps. But she will wake soon, for she has a deep pain.'

The old man stared out across the river, at the dark green of the forest, at the grey sky, and said, 'Tomorrow, if she is not better, I will take her to the hospital at Shahganj. There they will know how to make her well. You may be on your own for a few days—but you have been on your own before…'

Sita nodded gravely; she had been alone before, even during the rainy season. Now she wanted Grandmother to get well, and she knew that only Grandfather had the skill to take the small dugout boat across the river when the current was so strong. Someone would have to stay behind to look after their few possessions.

Sita was not afraid of being alone, but she did not like the look of the river. That morning, when she had gone down to fetch water, she had noticed that the level had risen. Those rocks which were normally spattered with the droppings of snipe and curlew and other water birds had suddenly disappeared.

They disappeared every year—but not so soon, surely?

'Grandfather, if the river rises, what will I do?'

'You will keep to the high ground.'

'And if the water reaches the high ground?'

'Then take the hens into the hut, and stay there.'

'And if the water comes into the hut?'

'Then climb into the peepul tree. It is a strong tree. It will not fall. And the water cannot rise higher than the tree!'

'And the goats, Grandfather?'

'I will be taking them with me, Sita. I may have to sell them to pay for good food and medicines for your grandmother. As for the hens, if it becomes necessary, put them on the roof. But do not worry too much'—and he patted Sita's head—'the water will not rise as high. I will be back soon, remember that.'

'And won't Grandmother come back?'

'Yes, of course, but they may keep her in the hospital for some time.'

◆

Towards evening, it began to rain again—big pellets of rain, scarring the surface of the river. But it was warm rain, and Sita could move about in it. She was not afraid of getting wet; she rather liked it. In the previous month, when the first monsoon shower had arrived, washing the dusty leaves of the tree and bringing up the good smell of the earth, she had exulted in it, had run about shouting for joy. She was used to it now, and indeed a little tired of the rain, but she did not mind getting wet. It was steamy indoors, and her thin dress would soon dry in the heat from the kitchen fire.

She walked about barefooted, bare-legged. She was very sure on her feet; her toes had grown accustomed to gripping all kinds of rocks, slippery or sharp. And though thin, she was surprisingly strong.

Black hair streaming across her face. Black eyes. Slim brown arms. A scar on her thigh—when she was small, visiting her mother's village, a hyena had entered the house where she was sleeping, fastened on to her leg and tried to drag her away, but her screams had roused the villagers and the hyena had run off.

She moved about in the pouring rain, chasing the hens into a shelter behind the hut. A harmless brown snake, flooded out of its hole, was moving across the open ground. Sita picked up a stick, scooped the snake up, and dropped it between a cluster of rocks. She had no quarrel with snakes. They kept down the rats and the frogs. She wondered how the rats had first come to the island—probably in someone's boat, or in a sack of grain. Now it was a job to keep their numbers down.

When Sita finally went indoors, she was hungry. She ate some dried peas and warmed up some goat's milk. Grandmother woke once and asked for water, and Grandfather held the brass tumbler to her lips.

◆

It rained all night.

The roof was leaking, and a small puddle formed on the floor. They kept the kerosene lamp alight. They did not need the light, but somehow it made them feel safer.

The sound of the river had always been with them, although

they were seldom aware of it; but that night they noticed a change in its sound. There was something like a moan, like a wind in the tops of tall trees and a swift hiss as the water swept round the rocks and carried away pebbles. And sometimes there was a rumble, as loose earth fell into the water.

Sita could not sleep.

She had a rag doll, made with Grandmother's help out of bits of old clothing. She kept it by her side every night. The doll was someone to talk to, when the nights were long and sleep elusive. Her grandparents were often ready to talk—and Grandmother, when she was well, was a good storyteller—but sometimes Sita wanted to have secrets, and though there were no special secrets in her life, she made up a few, because it was fun to have them. And if you have secrets, you must have a friend to share them with, a companion of one's own age. Since there were no other children on the island, Sita shared her secrets with the rag doll whose name was Mumta.

Grandfather and Grandmother were asleep, though the sound of Grandmother's laboured breathing was almost as persistent as the sound of the river.

'Mumta,' whispered Sita in the dark, starting one of her private conversations.

'Do you think Grandmother will get well again?'

Mumta always answered Sita's questions, even though the answers could only be heard by Sita.

'She is very old,' said Mumta.

'Do you think the river will reach the hut?' asked Sita.

'If it keeps raining like this, and the river keeps rising, it will reach the hut.'

'I am a little afraid of the river, Mumta. Aren't you afraid?'

'Don't be afraid. The river has always been good to us.'

'What will we do if it comes into the hut?'

'We will climb on to the roof.'

'And if it reaches the roof?'

'We will climb the peepul tree. The river has never gone higher than the peepul tree.'

As soon as the first light showed through the little skylight, Sita got up and went outside. It wasn't raining hard, it was drizzling, but it was the sort of drizzle that could continue for days, and it probably meant that heavy rain was falling in the hills where the river originated.

Sita went down to the water's edge. She couldn't find her favourite rock, the one on which she often sat dangling her feet in the water, watching the little chilwa fish swim by. It was still there, no doubt, but the river had gone over it.

She stood on the sand, and she could feel the water oozing and bubbling beneath her feet.

The river was no longer green and blue and flecked with white, but a muddy colour.

She went back to the hut. Grandfather was up now. He was getting his boat ready.

Sita milked a goat. Perhaps it was the last time she would milk it.

◆

The sun was just coming up when Grandfather pushed off in the boat. Grandmother lay in the prow. She was staring hard at Sita, trying to speak, but the words would not come. She raised her hand in a blessing.

Sita bent and touched her grandmother's feet, and then Grandfather pushed off. The little boat—with its two old people and three goats—riding swiftly on the river, moved slowly, very slowly, towards the opposite bank. The current was so swift now that Sita realized the boat would be carried about half a mile downstream before Grandfather could get it to dry land.

It bobbed about on the water, getting smaller and smaller, until it was just a speck on the broad river.

And suddenly Sita was alone.

There was a wind, whipping the raindrops against her face; and there was the water, rushing past the island; and there was the distant shore, blurred by rain; and there was the small hut; and there was the tree.

Sita got busy. The hens had to be fed. They weren't bothered about anything except food. Sita threw them handfuls of coarse grain and potato peelings and peanut shells.

Then she took the broom and swept out the hut, lit the charcoal burner, warmed some milk, and thought, 'Tomorrow there will be no milk…' She began peeling onions. Soon her eyes started smarting and, pausing for a few moments and glancing around the quiet room, she became aware again that she was alone. Grandfather's hookah stood by itself in one corner. It was a beautiful old hookah, which had belonged to Sita's great-grandfather. The bowl was made out of a coconut encased in silver. The long winding stem was at least four feet in length. It was their most valuable possession. Grandmother's sturdy shisham wood walking stick stood in another corner.

Sita looked around for Mumta, found the doll beneath the cot, and placed her within sight and hearing.

Thunder rolled down from the hills. BOOM—BOOM—BOOM…

'The gods of the mountains are angry,' said Sita. 'Do you think they are angry with me?'

'Why should they be angry with you?' asked Mumta.

'They don't have to have a reason for being angry. They are angry with everything, and we are in the middle of everything. We are so small—do you think they know we are here?'

'Who knows what the gods think?'

'But I made you,' said Sita, 'and I know you are here.'

'And will you save me if the river rises?'

'Yes, of course. I won't go anywhere without you, Mumta.'

Sita couldn't stay indoors for long. She went out, taking Mumta with her, and stared out across the river, to the safe land on the other side. But was it safe there? The river looked much wider now. Yes, it had crept over its banks and spread far across the flat plain. Far away, people were driving their cattle through waterlogged, flooded fields, carrying their belongings in bundles on their heads or shoulders, leaving their homes, making for the high land. It wasn't safe anywhere.

She wondered what had happened to Grandfather and Grandmother. If they had reached the shore safely, Grandfather would have to engage a bullock cart, or a pony-drawn carriage, to get Grandmother to the district town, five or six miles away, where there was a market, a court, a jail, a cinema and a hospital.

She wondered if she would ever see Grandmother again. She had done her best to look after the old lady, remembering the times when Grandmother had looked after her, had gently touched her fevered brow, and had told her stories—stories about the gods: about the young Krishna, friend of birds and animals, so full of mischief, always causing confusion among the other gods; and Indra, who made the thunder and lightning; and Vishnu, the preserver of all good things, whose steed was a great white bird; and Ganesh, with the elephant's head; and Hanuman, the monkey god, who helped the young Prince Rama in his war with the King of Ceylon. Would Grandmother return to tell her more about them, or would she have to find out for herself?

The island looked much smaller now. In parts, the mud banks had dissolved quickly, sinking into the river. But in the middle of the island there was rocky ground, and the rocks would never crumble, they could only be submerged. In a space in the middle of the rocks grew the tree.

Sita climbed up the tree to get a better view. She had climbed the tree many times and it took her only a few seconds to reach the higher branches. She put her hand to her eyes to shield them from the rain, and gazed upstream.

There was water everywhere. The world had become one vast river. Even the trees on the forested side of the river looked as though they had grown from the water, like mangroves. The sky was banked with massive, moisture-laden clouds. Thunder rolled down from the hills and the river seemed to take it up with a hollow, booming sound.

Something was floating down with the current, something big and bloated. It was closer now, and Sita could make out the bulky object—a drowned buffalo, being carried rapidly downstream.

So the water had already inundated the villages further upstream. Or perhaps the buffalo had been grazing too close to the rising river.

Sita's worst fears were confirmed when, a little later, she saw planks of wood, small trees and bushes, and then a wooden bedstead, floating past the island.

How long would it take for the river to reach her own small hut?

As she climbed down from the tree, it began to rain more heavily. She ran indoors, shooing the hens before her. They flew into the hut and huddled under Grandmother's cot. Sita thought it would be best to keep them together now. And having them with her took away some of the loneliness.

There were three hens and a cock bird. The river did not bother them. They were interested only in food, and Sita kept them happy by throwing them a handful of onion skins.

She would have liked to close the door and shut out the swish of the rain and the boom of the river, but then she would have no way of knowing how fast the water rose.

She took Mumta in her arms, and began praying for the rain to stop and the river to fall. She prayed to the god Indra, and, just in case he was busy elsewhere, she prayed to other gods too. She prayed for the safety of her grandparents and for her own safety. She put herself last but only with great difficulty.

She would have to make herself a meal. So she chopped up some onions, fried them, then added turmeric and red chilli powder and stirred until she had everything sizzling; then she added a tumbler of water, some salt, and a cup of one of the cheaper lentils. She covered the pot and allowed the mixture to simmer. Doing this took Sita about ten minutes. It would take at least half an hour for the dish to be ready.

When she looked outside, she saw pools of water amongst the rocks and near the tree. She couldn't tell if it was rainwater or overflow from the river.

She had an idea.

A big tin trunk stood in a corner of the room. It had belonged to Sita's mother. There was nothing in it except a cotton-filled quilt, for use during the cold weather. She would stuff the trunk with everything useful or valuable, and weigh it down so that it wouldn't be carried away—just in case the river came over the island... Grandfather's hookah went into the trunk. Grandmother's walking stick went in too. So did a number of small tins containing the spices used in cooking—nutmeg, caraway seeds, cinnamon, coriander and pepper—a bigger tin of flour and a tin of raw sugar. Even if Sita had to spend several hours in the tree, there would be something to eat when she came down again.

A clean white cotton shirt of Grandfather's, and Grandmother's only spare sari also went into the trunk. Never mind if they got stained with yellow curry powder! Never mind if they got to smell of salted fish, some of that went in too.

Sita was so busy packing the trunk that she paid no attention to the lick of cold water at her heels. She locked the trunk, placed the key high on the rock wall, and turned to give her attention to the lentils. It was only then that she discovered that she was walking about on a watery floor.

She stood still, horrified by what she saw. The water was oozing over the threshold, pushing its way into the room.

Sita was filled with panic. She forgot about her meal and everything else. Darting out of the hut, she ran splashing through ankle-deep water towards the safety of the peepul tree. If the tree hadn't been there, such a well-known landmark, she might have floundered into deep water, into the river.

She climbed swiftly into the strong arms of the tree, made herself secure on a familiar branch and thrust the wet hair away from her eyes.

◆

She was glad she had hurried. The hut was now surrounded by water. Only the higher parts of the island could still be seen—a few rocks, the big rock on which the hut was built, a hillock on which some thorny bilberry bushes grew.

The hens hadn't bothered to leave the hut. They were probably perched on the cot now.

Would the river rise still higher? Sita had never seen it like this before. It swirled around her, stretching in all directions.

More drowned cattle came floating down. The most unusual things went by on the water—an aluminium kettle, a cane chair, a tin of tooth powder, an empty cigarette packet, a wooden slipper, a plastic doll…

A doll!

With a sinking feeling, Sita remembered Mumta.

Poor Mumta! She had been left behind in the hut. Sita, in her hurry, had forgotten her only companion.

Well, thought Sita, if I can be careless with someone I've made, how can I expect the gods to notice me, alone in the middle of the river?

The waters were higher now, the island fast disappearing.

Something came floating out of the hut.

It was an empty kerosene tin, with one of the hens perched on top. The tin came bobbing along on the water, not far from the tree, and was then caught by the current and swept into the river. The hen still managed to keep its perch.

A little later, the water must have reached the cot because the remaining hens flew up to the rock ledge and sat huddled there in the small recess.

The water was rising rapidly now, and all that remained of the island was the big rock that supported the hut, the top of the hut itself and the peepul tree.

It was a tall tree with many branches and it seemed unlikely that the water could ever go right over it. But how long would Sita have to remain there? She climbed a little higher, and as she did so, a jet-black jungle crow settled in the upper branches, and Sita saw that there was a nest in them—a crow's nest, an untidy platform of twigs wedged in the fork of a branch.

In the nest were four blue-green, speckled eggs. The crow sat on them and cawed disconsolately. But though the crow was miserable, its presence brought some cheer to Sita. At least she was not alone. Better to have a crow for company than no one at all.

Other things came floating out of the hut—a large pumpkin; a red turban belonging to Grandfather, unwinding in the water like a long snake; and then—Mumta! The doll, being filled with straw and wood shavings, moved quite swiftly on the water and passed close to the peepul tree. Sita saw it and wanted to call out, to urge her friend to make for the tree, but she knew that Mumta could not swim—the doll could only float, travel with the river and perhaps be washed ashore many miles downstream.

The tree shook in the wind and the rain. The crow cawed and flew up, circled the tree a few times and returned to the nest. Sita clung to her branch.

The tree trembled throughout its tall frame. To Sita it felt like an earthquake tremor; she felt the shudder of the tree in her own bones.

The river swirled all around her now. It was almost up to the roof of the hut. Soon the mud walls would crumble and vanish. Except for the big rock and some trees far, far away, there was only water to be seen.

For a moment or two Sita glimpsed a boat with several people in it moving sluggishly away from the ruins of a flooded village, and she thought she saw someone pointing towards her, but the river swept them on, and the boat was lost to view.

The river was very angry; it was like a wild beast, a dragon on the rampage, thundering down from the hills, and sweeping across the plain, bringing with it dead animals, uprooted trees, household goods and huge fish choked to death by the swirling mud.

The tall, old peepul tree groaned. Its long, winding roots clung tenaciously to the earth from which the tree had sprung many, many years ago. But the earth was softening; the stones were being washed away. The roots of the tree were rapidly losing their hold.

The crow must have known that something was wrong, because it kept flying up and circling the tree, reluctant to settle in it and reluctant to fly away. As long as the nest was there, the crow would remain, flapping about and cawing in alarm.

Sita's wet cotton dress clung to her thin body. The rain ran down from her long black hair. It poured from every leaf of the tree. The crow, too, was drenched and groggy.

The tree groaned and moved again. It had seen many monsoons. Once before, it had stood firm while the river had swirled around its massive trunk. But it had been young then. Now, old in years and tired of standing still, the tree was ready to join the river.

With a flurry of its beautiful leaves, and a surge of mud from below, the tree left its place in the earth, and, tilting, moved slowly forward, turning a little from side to side, dragging its roots along the ground. To Sita, it seemed as though the river was rising to meet the sky.

Then the tree moved into the main current of the river, and went a little faster, swinging Sita from side to side. Her feet were in the water but she clung tenaciously to her branch.

◆

The branches swayed, but Sita did not lose her grip. The water was very close now. Sita was frightened. She could not see the extent of the flood or the width of the river. She could only see the immediate danger—the water surrounding the tree.

The crow kept flying around the tree. The bird was in a terrible rage. The nest was still in the branches, but not for long… The tree lurched and twisted slightly to one side, and the nest fell into the water. Sita saw the eggs go one by one.

The crow swooped low over the water, but there was nothing it could do. In a few moments, the nest had disappeared.

The bird followed the tree for about fifty yards, as though hoping that something still remained in the tree. Then, flapping its wings, it rose high into the air and flew across the river until it was out of sight.

Sita was alone once more. But there was no time for feeling lonely. Everything was in motion—up and down and sideways and forwards. 'Any moment,' thought Sita, 'the tree will turn right over and I'll be in the water!'

She saw a turtle swimming past—a great river turtle, the kind that feeds on decaying flesh. Sita turned her face away. In the distance she saw a flooded village and people in flat-bottomed boats but they were very far away.

Because of its great size, the tree did not move very swiftly on the river. Sometimes, when it passed into shallow water, it stopped, its roots catching in the rocks; but not for long—the river's momentum soon swept it on. At one place, where there was a bend in the river, the tree struck a sandbank and was still.

Sita felt very tired. Her arms were aching and she was no longer upright. With the tree almost on its side, she had to cling tightly to her branch to avoid falling off.

The grey weeping sky was like a great shifting dome. She knew she could not remain much longer in that position. It might be better to try swimming to some distant rooftop or tree. Then she heard someone calling.

Craning her neck to look upriver, she was able to make out a small boat coming directly towards her.

The boat approached the tree. There was a boy in the boat who held on to one of the branches to steady himself, giving his free hand to Sita. She grasped it, and slipped into the boat beside him. The boy placed his bare foot against the tree trunk and pushed away. The little boat moved swiftly down the river. The big tree was left far behind. Sita would never see it again.

◆

She lay stretched out in the boat, too frightened to talk. The boy looked at her, but he did not say anything, he did not even smile. He lay on his two small oars, stroking smoothly, rhythmically, trying to keep from going into the middle of the river. He wasn't strong enough to get the boat right out of the swift current, but he kept trying.

A small boat on a big river—a river that had no boundaries but that reached across the plains in all directions. The boat moved swiftly on the wild waters, and Sita's home was left far behind.

The boy wore only a loincloth. A sheathed knife was knotted into his waistband. He was a slim, wiry boy, with a hard, flat belly; he had high cheekbones, strong white teeth. He was a little darker than Sita.

'You live on the island,' he said at last, resting on his oars, and allowing the boat to drift a little, for he had reached a broader, more placid stretch of the river.

'I have seen you sometimes. But where are the others?'

'My grandmother was sick,' said Sita, 'so Grandfather took her to the hospital in Shahganj.'

'When did they leave?'

'Early this morning.'

Only that morning—and yet it seemed to Sita as though it had been many mornings ago.

'Where have you come from?' she asked. She had never seen the boy before.

'I come from...' he hesitated, '...near the foothills. I was in my boat, trying to get across the river with the news that one of the villages was badly flooded, but the current was too strong. I was swept down past your island. We cannot fight the river, we must go wherever it takes us.'

'You must be tired. Give me the oars.'

'No. There is not much to do now, except keep the boat steady.'

He brought in one oar, and with his free hand he felt under the seat where there was a small basket. He produced two mangoes, and gave one to Sita.

They bit deep into the ripe, fleshy mangoes, using their teeth to tear the skin away. The sweet juice trickled down their chins. The flavour of the fruit was heavenly—truly this was the nectar of the gods!

Sita hadn't tasted a mango for over a year. For a few moments she forgot about the flood—all that mattered was the mango!

The boat drifted, but not so swiftly now, for as they went further away across the plains, the river lost much of its tremendous force.

'My name is Krishan,' said the boy. 'My father has many cows and buffaloes, but several have been lost in the flood.'

'I suppose you go to school,' said Sita.

'Yes, I am supposed to go to school. There is one not far from our village. Do you have to go to school?'

'No—there is too much work at home.'

It was no use wishing she was at home—home wouldn't be there any more—but she wished, at that moment, that she had another mango.

Towards evening, the river changed colour. The sun, low in the sky, emerged from behind the clouds, and the river changed slowly from grey to gold, from gold to a deep orange, and then, as the sun went down, all these colours were drowned in the river, and the river took on the colour of the night.

The moon was almost at the full and Sita could see across the river, to where the trees grew on its banks.

'I will try to reach the trees,' said the boy, Krishan. 'We do not want to spend the night on the water, do we?'

And so he pulled for the trees. After ten minutes of strenuous rowing, he reached a turn in the river and was able to escape the pull of the main current. Soon they were in a forest, rowing between tall evergreens.

◆

They moved slowly now, paddling between the trees, and the moon lighted their way, making a crooked silver path over the water.

'We will tie the boat to one of these trees,' said Krishan. 'Then we can rest. Tomorrow we will have to find our way out of the forest.'

He produced a length of rope from the bottom of the boat, tied one end to the boat's stern, and threw the other end over a stout branch which hung only a few feet above the water. The boat came to rest against the trunk of the tree.

It was a tall, sturdy toon tree—the Indian mahogany—and it was quite safe, for there was no rush of water here; besides, the trees grew close together, making the earth firm and unyielding.

But the denizens of the forest were on the move.

The animals had been flooded out of their holes, caves and lairs, and were looking for shelter and dry ground.

Sita and Krishan had barely finished tying the boat to the tree when they saw a huge python gliding over the water towards them. Sita was afraid that it might try to get into the boat; but it went past them, its head above water, its great awesome length trailing behind, until it was lost in the shadows.

Krishan had more mangoes in the basket, and he and Sita sucked hungrily on them while they sat in the boat.

A big sambar stag came thrashing through the water. He did not have to swim; he was so tall that his head and shoulders remained well above the water. His antlers were big and beautiful.

'There will be other animals,' said Sita. 'Should we climb into the tree?'

'We are quite safe in the boat,' said Krishan. 'The animals are interested only in reaching dry land. They will not even hunt each other. Tonight, the deer are safe from the panther and the tiger. So lie down and sleep, and I will keep watch.'

Sita stretched herself out in the boat and closed her eyes, and the sound of the water lapping against the sides of the boat soon lulled her to sleep. She woke once, when a strange bird called overhead. She raised herself on one elbow, but Krishan was awake, sitting in the prow, and he smiled reassuringly at her.

He looked blue in the moonlight, the colour of the young god Krishna, and for a few moments Sita was confused and wondered if the boy was indeed Krishna; but when she thought about it, she decided that it wasn't possible. He was just a village boy and she had seen hundreds like him—well, not exactly like him; he was different, in a way she couldn't explain to herself…

And when she slept again, she dreamt that the boy and Krishna were one, and that she was sitting beside him on a great white bird which flew over mountains, over the snow peaks of the Himalaya, into the cloudland of the gods. There was a great rumbling sound, as though the gods were angry about the whole thing, and she woke up to this terrible sound and looked about her, and there in the moonlit glade, up to his belly in water, stood a young elephant, his trunk raised as he trumpeted his predicament to the forest—for he was a young elephant, and he was lost, and he was looking for his mother.

He trumpeted again, and then lowered his head and listened. And presently, from far away, came the shrill trumpeting of another elephant. It must have been the young one's mother, because he gave several excited trumpet calls, and then went stamping and churning through the flood water towards a gap in the trees. The boat rocked in the waves made by his passing.

'It's all right now,' said Krishan. 'You can go to sleep again.'

'I don't think I will sleep now,' said Sita.

'Then I will play my flute for you,' said the boy, 'and the time will pass more quickly.'

From the bottom of the boat he took a flute, and putting it to his lips, he began to play. The sweetest music that Sita had ever heard came pouring from the little flute, and it seemed to fill the forest with its beautiful sound. And the music carried her away again, into the land of dreams, and they were riding on the bird once more, Sita and the blue god, and they were passing through clouds and mist, until suddenly the sun shot out through the clouds. And at the same moment, Sita opened her eyes and saw the sun streaming through the branches of the toon tree, its bright green leaves making a dark pattern against the blinding blue of the sky.

Sita sat up with a start, rocking the boat. There were hardly any clouds left. The trees were drenched with sunshine.

The boy Krishan was fast asleep at the bottom of the boat. His flute lay in the palm of his half-opened hand. The sun came slanting across his bare brown legs. A leaf had fallen on his upturned face, but it had not woken him; it lay on his cheek as though it had grown there.

Sita did not move again. She did not want to wake the boy. It didn't look as though the water had gone down, but it hadn't risen, and that meant the flood had spent itself.

The warmth of the sun, as it crept up Krishan's body, woke him at last. He yawned, stretched his limbs, and sat up beside Sita.

'I'm hungry,' he said with a smile.

'So am I,' said Sita.

'The last mangoes,' he said, and emptied the basket of its last two mangoes.

After they had finished the fruit, they sucked the big seeds until they were quite dry. The discarded seeds floated well on the water. Sita had always preferred them to paper boats.

'We had better move on,' said Krishan.

He rowed the boat through the trees, and then for about an hour they were passing through the flooded forest, under the dripping branches of rain-washed trees.

Sometimes they had to use the oars to push away vines and creepers. Sometimes drowned bushes hampered them. But they were out of the forest before noon.

Now the water was not very deep and they were gliding over flooded fields. In the distance they saw a village. It was on high ground. In the old days, people had built their villages on hilltops, which gave them a better defence against bandits and invading armies.

This was an old village, and though its inhabitants had long ago exchanged their swords for pruning forks, the hill on which it stood now protected it from the flood.

The people of the village—long-limbed, sturdy Jats—were generous, and gave the stranded children food and shelter. Sita was anxious to find her grandparents, and an old farmer who had business in Shahganj offered to take her there. She was hoping that Krishan would accompany her, but he said he would wait in the village, where he knew others would soon be arriving, his own people among them.

'You will be all right now,' said Krishan. 'Your grandfather will be anxious for you, so it is best that you go to him as soon as you can. And in two or three days, the water will go down and you will be able to return to the island.'

'Perhaps the island has gone forever,' said Sita.

As she climbed into the farmer's bullock cart, Krishan handed her his flute.

'Please keep it for me,' he said. 'I will come for it one day.'

And when he saw her hesitate, he added, his eyes twinkling, 'It is a good flute!'

◆

It was slow going in the bullock cart. The road was awash, the wheels got stuck in the mud, and the farmer, his grown son and Sita had to keep getting down to heave and push in order to free the big, wooden wheels.

They were still in a foot or two of water. The bullocks were bespattered with mud, and Sita's legs were caked with it. They were a day and a night in the bullock cart before they reached Shahganj; by that time, Sita, walking down the narrow bazaar of the busy market town, was hardly recognizable.

Grandfather did not recognize her. He was walking stiffly down the road, looking straight ahead of him, and would have walked right past the dusty, dishevelled girl if she had not charged straight at his thin, shaky legs and clasped him around the waist.

'Sita!' he cried, when he had recovered his wind and his balance. 'But how are you here? How did you get off the island? I was so worried—it has been very bad these last two days…'

'Is Grandmother all right?' asked Sita.

But even as she spoke, she knew that Grandmother was no longer with them. The dazed look in the old man's eyes told her as much. She wanted to cry, not for Grandmother, who could suffer no more, but for Grandfather, who looked so helpless and bewildered; she did not want him to be unhappy. She forced back her tears, took his gnarled and trembling hand, and led him down the crowded street. And she knew, then, that it would be on her shoulder that Grandfather would have to lean in the years to come.

They returned to the island after a few days, when the river was no longer in spate. There was more rain, but the worst was over. Grandfather still had two of the goats; it had not been necessary to sell more than one.

He could hardly believe his eyes when he saw that the tree had disappeared from the island—the tree that had seemed as permanent as the island, as much a part of his life as the river itself. He marvelled at Sita's escape.

'It was the tree that saved you,' he said.

'And the boy,' said Sita.

Yes, and the boy.

She thought about the boy, and wondered if she would ever see him again. But she did not think too much, because there was so much to do.

For three nights they slept under a crude shelter made out of jute bags. During the day she helped Grandfather rebuild the mud hut. Once again, they used the big rock as a support.

The trunk, which Sita had packed so carefully, had not been swept off the island, but the water had got into it, and the food and clothing had been spoilt. But Grandfather's hookah had been saved, and, in the evenings, after their work was done and they had eaten the light meal that Sita prepared, he would smoke with a little of his old contentment, and tell Sita about other floods and storms that he had experienced as a boy.

Sita planted a mango seed in the same spot where the peepul tree had stood. It would be many years before it grew into a big tree, but Sita liked to imagine sitting in its branches one day, picking the mangoes straight from the tree and feasting on them all day. Grandfather was more particular about making a vegetable garden and putting down peas, carrots, gram and mustard.

One day, when most of the hard work had been done and the new hut was almost ready, Sita took the flute which had been given to her by the boy, and walked down to the water's edge and tried to play it.

But all she could produce were a few broken notes, and even the goats paid no attention to her music.

Sometimes Sita thought she saw a boat coming down the river and she would run to meet it; but usually there was no boat, or if there was, it belonged to a stranger or to another fisherman. And so she stopped looking out for boats. Sometimes she thought she heard the music of a flute, but it seemed very distant and she could never tell where the music came from.

Slowly, the rains came to an end. The flood waters had receded, and in the villages people were beginning to till the land again, and sow crops for the winter months. There were cattle fairs and wrestling matches. The days were warm and sultry. The water in the river was no longer muddy, and one evening Grandfather brought home a huge mahseer fish and Sita made it into a delicious curry.

◆

Grandfather sat outside the hut, smoking his hookah. Sita was at the far end of the island, spreading clothes on the rocks to dry.

One of the goats had followed her. It was the friendlier of the two, and often followed Sita about the island. She had made it a necklace of coloured beads.

She sat down on a smooth rock, and, as she did so, she noticed a small, bright object in the sand near her feet. She stooped and picked it up. It was a little wooden toy—a coloured peacock—that must have come down on the river and been swept ashore on the island. Some of the paint had rubbed off, but for Sita, who had no toys, it was a great find. Perhaps it would speak to her, as Mumta had spoken to her.

As she held the toy peacock in the palm of her hand, she thought she heard the flute music again, but she did not look up. She had heard it before, and she was sure that it was all in her mind. But this time the music sounded nearer, much nearer. There was a soft footfall in the sand. And, looking up, she saw the boy, Krishan, standing over her.

'I thought you would never come,' said Sita.

'I had to wait until the rains were over. Now that I am free, I will come more often. Did you keep my flute?'

'Yes, but I cannot play it properly. Sometimes it plays by itself, I think, but it will not play for me!'

'I will teach you to play it,' said Krishan.

He sat down beside her, and they cooled their feet in the water, which was clear now, reflecting the blue of the sky. You could see the sand and the pebbles of the riverbed.

'Sometimes the river is angry, and sometimes it is kind,' said Sita.

'We are part of the river,' said the boy. 'We cannot live without it.'

It was a good river, deep and strong, beginning in the mountains and ending in the sea. Along its banks, for hundreds of miles, lived millions of people, and Sita was only one small girl among them, and no one had ever heard of her, no one knew her—except for the old man, the boy and the river.

HOME

'The boy's useless,' said Mr Kapoor, speaking to his wife but making sure his son could hear. 'I don't know what he'll do with himself when he grows up. He takes no interest in his studies.'

Suraj's father had returned from a business trip and was seeing his son's school report for the first time. 'Good at cricket,' said the report. 'Poor in studies. Does not pay attention in class.'

Suraj's mother, a quiet, dignified woman, said nothing. Suraj stood at the window, refusing to speak. He stared out at the light drizzle that whispered across the garden. He had angry black eyes and bushy eyebrows, and he was feeling rebellious.

His father was doing all the talking. 'What's the use of spending money on his education if he can't show anything for it? He comes home, eats as much as three boys, asks for money, and then goes out to loaf with his friends!'

Mr Kapoor paused, expecting Suraj to reply and give cause for further scolding; but Suraj knew that silence would irritate his father even more, and there were times when he enjoyed watching his father get irritated.

'Well, I won't stand for it,' said Mr Kapoor finally. 'If you don't make some effort, my boy, you can leave this house!' And having at last addressed Suraj directly, he stormed out of the room.

Suraj remained a few moments at the window. Then he went to the front door, opened it, stepped out into the rain, and banged the door behind him.

His mother made as if to call out after him, but she thought better of it, and turned and walked into the kitchen.

Suraj stood in the drizzle, looking back at the house.

'I'll never go back,' he said fiercely. 'I can manage without them. If they want me back, they can come and ask me to return!'

And he thrust his hands into his pockets and walked down the road with an independent air.

His fingers came into contact with a familiar crispness, a five rupee note. It was all the money he had in the world. He clutched it tight. He had meant to spend it at the cinema, but now it would have to serve more urgent needs. He wasn't sure what these needs would be because just now he was angry and his mind wasn't running on practical lines. He walked blindly, unconscious of the rain, until he reached the maidan.

When he reached the maidan, the sun came out.

Though there was still a drizzle, the sun seemed to raise Suraj's spirits at once. He remembered his friend Ranji and decided he would stay with Ranji until he found some sort of work. He knew that if he didn't find work, he wouldn't be able to stay away from home for long. He wondered what kind of work a thirteen-year-old could get. He did not fancy delivering newspapers or serving tea in a small tea shop in the bazaar; it was much better being a customer.

The drizzle ceased altogether, and Suraj hurried across the maidan and down a quiet road until he reached Ranji's house. When he went in at the gate, his spirits sank.

The house was shut. There was a lock on the front door.

Suraj went round the house three times but he couldn't find an open door or window. Perhaps, he thought, the family have gone out for the morning—a picnic or birthday treat; they were sure to be back for lunch. With spirits mounting once again, he strolled leisurely down the road, in the direction of the bazaar.

Suraj had a weakness for the bazaar, for its crowded variety of goods, its smells and colours and the music playing over the loudspeakers. He lingered now at a tea-and-pakora shop, tempted by the appetizing smells that came from inside; but decided that he would eat at Ranji's house and spend his money on something other than food. He couldn't resist the big yellow yo-yo in the toy-seller's glass case; it was set with pieces of different coloured glass which shone and twinkled in the sunshine.

'How much?' asked Suraj.

'Two rupees,' said the shop-keeper. 'But to a regular customer like you I give it for one rupee.'

'It must be an old one,' said Suraj, but he paid the rupee and took possession of the yo-yo. He immediately began working it, strolling through the bazaar with the yo-yo swinging up and down from his index finger.

Fingering the four remaining notes in his pocket, he decided that he was thirsty. Not tap-water, nor a fizzy drink, but only a vanilla milkshake would meet his need. He sat at a table and sucked milkshake through a straw. One eye caught sight of the clock on the wall. It was nearly one o'clock. Ranji and his family should be home by now.

Suraj slipped off his chair, paid for the drink—that left him with two rupees—and went sauntering down the bazaar road, the yo-yo making soothing sounds beside him.

Ranji's house was still shut.

This was something Suraj hadn't anticipated. He walked quickly round the house, but it was locked as before. On his second round he met the gardener, an old man over sixty.

'Where is everybody?' asked Suraj.

'They have gone to Delhi for a week,' said the gardener, looking sharply at Suraj. 'Why, is anything the matter?'

Suraj had never seen the old man before, but he did not hesitate to confide in him. 'I've left home. I was going to stay with Ranji. Now there's nowhere to go.'

The old man thought this over for a minute. His face was wrinkled like a walnut, his hands and feet hard and cracked; but his eyes were bright and almost youthful.

He was a part-time gardener who worked for several families along the road; there were no big gardens in this part of the town.

'Why don't you go home again?' he suggested.

'It's too soon,' said Suraj. 'I haven't really run away as yet. They must know I've run away. Then they'll feel sorry!'

The gardener smiled. 'You should have planned it better,' he said. 'Have you saved any money?'

'I had five rupees this morning. Now there are two rupees left.' He looked down at his yo-yo. 'Would you like to buy it?'

'I wouldn't know how to work it,' said the gardener. 'The best thing for you to do is to go home, wait till Ranji gets back, and then run away.'

Suraj considered this interesting advice, and decided that there was something in it. But he didn't make up his mind right away. A little suspense at home would be a good thing for his parents.

He returned to the maidan and sat down on the grass. As soon as he sat down, he felt hungry.

He had never felt so hungry before. Visions of tandoori

chickens and dripping spangled sweets danced before him. He wondered if the toy-seller would take back the yo-yo. He probably would, for half the price; but, as much as Suraj wanted food, he did not want to give up the yo-yo.

There was nothing to do but go home. His mother, he was sure, would be worried by now. His father (he hoped) would be pacing up and down the verandah, glancing at his watch every few seconds. It would be a lesson to them. He would walk back into the house as if doing them a favour.

He only hoped they had kept his lunch.

Suraj walked into the sitting-room and threw his yoyo on the sofa.

Mr Kapoor was sitting in his favourite armchair, reading a newspaper prior to going back to his office. He stood up for a moment as Suraj came into the room, said, 'You're very late,' and returned to his newspaper.

Suraj found his mother and his food in the kitchen. She did not speak to him, but was smiling to herself.

'Feeling hungry?' she asked.

'No,' said Suraj, and seized the tray and tucked into his food.

When he returned to the sitting-room he was surprised to see his father fumbling with the yo-yo.

'How do you work this stupid thing?' said Mr Kapoor.

Suraj didn't reply. He just stood there gloating over his father's clumsiness. At last he couldn't help bursting into laughter.

'It's easy,' he said. 'I'll show you.' And he took the yo-yo from his father and gave a demonstration.

When Mrs Kapoor came into the room she did not appear at all surprised to find her husband and son deeply absorbed in the working of a cheap bazaar toy. She was used to such absurdities. Men never really grew up.

Mr Kapoor had forgotten he was supposed to be returning to his office, and Suraj had forgotten about running away. They had both forgotten the morning's unpleasantness. That had been a long, long time ago.

WHEN THE GUAVAS ARE RIPE

Guava trees are easy to climb. And guavas are good to eat. So it's little wonder that an orchard of guava trees is a popular place with boys and girls.

Just across the road from Ranji's house, on the other side of a low wall, was a large guava orchard. The monsoon rains were almost over. It was a warm, humid day in September, and the guavas were ripening, turning from green to gold; no longer hard, but growing soft and sweet and juicy.

The schools were closed because of a religious festival. Ranji's father was at work in his office. Ranji's mother was enjoying an afternoon siesta on a cot in the backyard. His grandmother was busy teaching her pet parrot to recite a prayer.

'I feel like getting into those guava trees,' said Ranji to himself. 'It's months since I climbed a tree.'

He was soon across the road and over the wall and among the trees. He chose a tree that grew in the middle of the orchard, where it was unlikely that he would be disturbed; then he climbed swiftly into its branches. A cluster of guavas swung just above him. He reached up for one of them, but to his surprise he found himself clutching a small, bare foot which had suddenly been thrust through the foliage.

Having caught the foot, Ranji did not let go. Instead he pulled hard on it. There was a squeal and someone came toppling down on him. Ranji found himself clutching at arms and legs. Together they crashed through a couple of branches and landed with a thud on the soft ground beneath the tree.

Ranji and the intruder struggled fiercely. They rolled about on the grass. Ranji tried a judo hold—without any success. Then he saw that his opponent was a girl. It was his friend and neighbour, Koki.

'It's you!' he gasped.

'It's me,' said Koki. 'And what are *you* doing here?'

'Get your knee out of my stomach and I'll tell you.'

When he had recovered his breath, he said, 'I just felt like climbing a tree.'

'So did I.'

He stared at her. There was guava juice at the corners of her mouth and on her chin.

'Are the guavas good?' he asked.

'Quite sweet, in this tree,' said Koki. 'You find another tree for yourself, Ranji. There must be thirty or forty trees to choose from.'

'And all going to waste,' said Ranji. 'Look, some of the guavas have been spoilt by the birds.'

'Nobody wants them, it seems.'

Koki climbed back onto her tree, and Ranji obligingly walked a little further and climbed another tree. After a few polite exchanges they fell silent, their attention given over entirely to the eating of guavas.

'I've eaten five,' said Koki after some time.

'You'd better stop.'

'You're only saying that because you've just started.'

'Well, three's enough for me.'

'I'm getting a tummy ache, I think.'

'I warned you. Come on, I'll take you home. We can come back tomorrow. There are still lots of guavas left.'

'I don't think I want to eat any more,' said Koki.

◆

She felt better the next day—so well, in fact, that Ranji found her leaning on the gate, waiting for him to join her. She was accompanied by her small brother, Teju, who was only six and very mischievous.

'How are you feeling today?' asked Ranji.

'Hungry,' said Koki.

'Why did you bring your brother?'

'He wants to start climbing trees.'

Soon they were in the orchard. Ranji and Koki helped Teju onto the branches of one of the smaller trees and then made for other trees, disturbing a party of parrots who flew in circles around the orchard, screaming their protests.

Two boys and a girl talking to each other from three different trees can make quite a lot of noise, and it wasn't only the birds who were disturbed. Though they did not know it, the orchard belonged to a wealthy property dealer and he employed a watchman, whose duty it was to keep away birds, children, monkeys, flying foxes, and other fruit-eating pests. But on a hot, sultry afternoon, Gopal, the watchman, could not resist taking a nap. He was stretched out under a shady jackfruit tree, snoring so loudly that the flies who had been buzzing around him felt that a storm was brewing and kept their distance.

He woke to the sound of voices raised high in glee. Sitting up, he brushed a ladybird from his long moustache, then seized his lathi, a long, stout stick usually carried by watchmen.

'Who's there?' he shouted, struggling to his feet.

There was a sudden silence on the trees.

'Who's there?' he called again.

No answer.

'I must have been dreaming,' he muttered, and was preparing to lie down and take another nap when Teju, who had been watching him, burst into laughter.

'Ho!' shouted the watchman, coming to life again. 'Thieves! I'll settle you!' And he began striding towards the centre of the orchard, boasting all the time of his physical prowess. 'I'm not afraid of thieves, bandits, or wild beasts! I'll have you know that I was once the wrestling champion of the entire district of Dehra. Come on out and fight me if you dare!'

'Run!' hissed Koki, scrambling down from her tree.

'Run!' shouted Ranji, as though it were a cricket match.

Teju was so startled by the sudden activity that he tumbled out of his tree and began crying and Ranji and Koki had to go to his aid.

The sight of an enormous ex-wrestler bearing down on them was enough to make Teju stop crying and get to his feet. Then all three were fleeing across the grove, the watchman a little way behind them, waving his lathi and shouting at the top of his voice. Although he was an ex-wrestler (or perhaps because of it) he could not run very fast and was still huffing and puffing some twenty metres behind them when they climbed up and over the wall. He could not climb walls either. They ran off in different directions before returning home.

◆

Next day, Ranji met Koki and Teju at the far end of the road.

'Is he there?' asked Koki.

'I haven't seen him. But he must be around somewhere.'

'Maybe he's gone for his lunch. We'll just walk past and take a quick look.'

The three of them strolled casually down the road. Koki said the gardens were looking very pretty. Teju gazed admiringly at a boy flying a kite from a rooftop. Ranji kept one eye on the road and one eye on the orchard wall. A squirrel ran along the top of the wall; the parrots were back in the guava trees.

They moved closer to the wall. Ranji leaned casually against it and Koki began to pick little daisies growing at the edge of the road. Teju, unable to hide his curiosity, pulled himself up on the wall and looked over. At the same time, Gopal, the watchman, who had been hiding behind the wall waiting for them, stood up slowly and glared fiercely at Teju.

Teju gulped, but he did not flinch. He was looking straight into the watchman's red angry eyes.

'And what can I do for you?' growled Gopal.

'I was just looking,' said Teju.

'At what?'

'At the view.'

Gopal was a little baffled. They looked just like the children he'd chased away yesterday, but he couldn't be sure. They didn't *look* guilty. But did children ever look guilty?

'There's a better view from the other side of the road,' he said gruffly. 'Now be off!'

'What lovely guavas,' said Koki, smiling sweetly. There weren't many people who could resist that smile!

'True,' said Ranji, with the air of one who was an expert on guavas and all things good to eat. 'They are just the right size and colour. I don't think I've seen better. But they'll be spoilt by the birds if you don't gather them soon.'

'It's none of your business,' said the watchman.

'Just look at his muscles,' said Teju, trying a different approach. 'He's really strong!'

Gopal looked pleased for once. He was proud of his former prowess, even though he was now rather flabby around the waist.

'You look like a wrestler,' said Ranji.

'I *am* a wrestler,' said Gopal.

'I told you so,' said Koki. 'What else could he be?'

'I'm a retired wrestler,' said Gopal.

'You don't look retired,' said Teju, fast learning that flattery can get you almost anywhere.

Gopal swelled with pride; such admiration hadn't come his way for a long time. To Koki he looked like a bullfrog swelling up, but she thought it better not to say so.

'Do you want to see my muscles?' he asked.

'Yes, yes!' they cried. 'Do show us!'

Gopal peeled off his shirt and thumped his chest. It sounded like a drum. They were really impressed. Then he bent his elbow and his biceps bulged like cricket balls.

'You can touch them,' he said generously.

Teju poked a finger into Gopal's biceps.

'Mister Universe!' he exclaimed.

Gopal glowed all over. He liked these children. How intelligent they were! Not everyone had the sense to appreciate his strength, his manliness, his magnificent physique!

'Climb over the wall and join me,' he said. 'Come sit on the grass and I'll tell you about the time when I was a wrestling champion.'

Over the wall they came and sat politely on the grass. Gopal told them about some of his exploits: how he had vanquished a world-famous wrestler in five seconds flat, and how he had saved a carload of travellers from drowning by single-handedly dragging their car out of a river. They listened patiently. Then Teju mentioned that he was feeling hungry.

'Hungry?' said Gopal. 'Why didn't you tell me before? I'll bring you some guavas, that's all there is to eat here. I know which tree has the best ones. And they're all going to rot if no one eats them—no one's buying the crop this year, the owner's price is too high!'

Gopal hurried off and soon returned with a basket full of guavas.

'Help yourselves,' he said. 'But don't eat too many, you'll get sick.'

So they munched guavas and listened to Gopal tell them about the time he was waylaid by three bandits and how he threw them all into the village pond.

'Will you come again tomorrow?' asked Gopal eagerly, when the guavas were finished and the children got up to leave. 'Come tomorrow and I'll tell you another story.'

'We'll come tomorrow,' said Teju, looking at all the guava trees still laden with fruit.

Somehow it seemed very important to Gopal that they should come again. It was lonely in the orchard. Koki sensed this and said, 'We like your stories.'

'They are good stories,' said Ranji, even if they were not entirely true, he thought...

They climbed over the wall and waved goodbye to Gopal.

They came again the next day.

And even when the guava season was over and Gopal had nothing to offer them but his stories, they went to see him because by that time they had grown to like him.

ALL CREATURES GREAT AND SMALL

Instead of having brothers and sisters to grow up with in India, I had as my companions an odd assortment of pets, which included a monkey, a tortoise, a python and a Great Indian Hornbill. The person responsible for all this wildlife in the home was my grandfather. As the house was his own, other members of the family could not prevent him from keeping a large variety of pets, though they could certainly voice their objections; and as most of the household consisted of women—my grandmother, visiting aunts and occasional in-laws (my parents were in Burma at the time)—Grandfather and I had to be alert and resourceful in dealing with them. We saw eye to eye on the subject of pets, and whenever Grandmother decided it was time to get rid of a tame white rat or a squirrel, I would conceal them in a hole in the jackfruit tree; but unlike my aunts, she was generally tolerant of Grandfather's hobby, and even took a liking to some of our pets.

Grandfather's house and menagerie were in Dehra and I remember travelling there in a horse-drawn buggy. There were cars in those days—it was just over twenty years ago—but in the foothills a tonga was just as good, almost as fast, and certainly more dependable when it came to getting across the swift little Tons River.

During the rains, when the river flowed strong and deep, it was impossible to get across except on a hand-operated ropeway; but in the dry months, the horse went splashing through, the carriage wheels churning through clear mountain water. If the horse found the going difficult, we removed our shoes, rolled up our skirts or trousers, and waded across.

When Grandfather first went to stay in Dehra, early in the century, the only way of getting there was by the night mail coach. Mail ponies, he told me, were difficult animals, always attempting to turn around and get into the coach with the passengers. It was only when the coachman used his whip liberally, and reviled the ponies' ancestors as far back as their third and fourth generations, that the beasts could be persuaded to move. And once they started, there was no stopping them. It was a gallop all the way to the first stage, where the ponies were changed to the accompaniment of a bugle blown by the coachman.

At one stage of the journey, drums were beaten; and if it was night, torches were lit to keep away the wild elephants who, resenting the approach of this clumsy caravan, would sometimes trumpet a challenge and throw the ponies into confusion.

◆

Grandfather disliked dressing up and going out, and was only too glad to send everyone shopping or to the pictures—Harold Lloyd and Eddie Cantor were the favourites at Dehra's small cinema—so that he could be left alone to feed his pets and potter about in the garden. There were a lot of animals to be fed, including, for a time, a pair of Great Danes who had such enormous appetites that we were forced to give them away to a more affluent family.

The Great Danes were gentle creatures, and I would sit astride one of them and go for rides round the garden. Inspite of their size, they were very sure-footed and never knocked over people or chairs. A little monkey, like Toto, did much more damage.

Grandfather bought Toto from a tonga-owner for the sum of five rupees. The tonga-man used to keep the little red monkey tied to a feed-trough, and Toto looked so out of place there—almost conscious of his own incongruity—that Grandfather immediately decided to add him to our menagerie.

Toto was really a pretty little monkey. His bright eyes sparkled with mischief beneath deep-set eyebrows, and his teeth, a pearly-white, were often on display in a smile that frightened the life out of elderly Ango-Indian ladies. His hands were not those of a Tallulah Bankhead (Grandfather's only favourite actress), but were shrivelled and dried-up, as though they had been pickled in the sun for many years. But his fingers were quick and restless; and his tail, while adding to his good looks—Grandfather maintained that a tail would add to anyone's good looks—often performed the service of a third hand. He could use it to hang from a branch; and it was capable of scooping up any delicacy that might be out of the reach of his hands.

Grandmother, anticipating an outcry from other relatives, always raised objections when Grandfather brought home some new bird or animal; and so for a while we managed to keep Toto's presence a secret by lodging him in a little closet opening into my bedroom wall. But in a few hours he managed to dispose of Grandmother's ornamental wallpaper and the better part of my school blazer. He was transferred to the stables for a day or two, and then Grandfather had to make a trip to neighbouring Saharanpur to collect his railway pension. Anxious to keep Toto out of trouble, he decided to take the monkey along with him.

Unfortunately I could not accompany Grandfather on this trip, but he told me about it afterwards.

A black kitbag was provided for Toto. When the strings of the bag were tied, there was no means of escape from within, and the canvas was too strong for Toto to bite his way through. His initial efforts to get out only had the effect of making the bag roll about on the floor, or occasionally jump in the air—an exhibition that attracted a curious crowd of onlookers on the Dehra railway platform.

Toto remained in the bag as far as Saharanpur, but while Grandfather was producing his ticket at the railway turnstile, Toto managed to get his hands through the aperture where the bag was tied, loosened the strings, and suddenly thrust his head through the opening.

The poor ticket-collector was visibly alarmed; but with great presence of mind, and much to the annoyance of Grandfather, he said, 'Sir, you have a dog with you. You'll have to pay for it accordingly.'

In vain did Grandfather take Toto out of the bag to prove that a monkey was not a dog or even a quadruped. The ticket-collector, now thoroughly annoyed, insisted on categorizing Toto as a dog; and three rupees and four annas had to be handed over as his fare. Then Grandfather, out of sheer spite, took out from his pocket a live tortoise that he happened to have with him, and said, 'What must I pay for this, since you charge for all animals?'

The ticket-collector retreated a pace or two; then advancing again with caution, he subjected the tortoise to a grave and knowledgeable stare.

'No ticket is necessary, sir,' he finally declared. 'There is no charge for insects.'

◆

When we discovered that Toto's favourite pastime was catching mice, we were able to persuade Grandmother to let us keep him. The unsuspecting mice would emerge from their holes at night to pick up any corn left over by our pony; and to get at it they had to run the gauntlet of Toto's section of the stable. He knew this, and would pretend to be asleep, keeping, however, one eye open. A mouse would make a rush—in vain; Toto, as swift as a cat, would have his paws upon him… Grandmother decided to put his talents to constructive use by tying him up one night in the larder, where a guerrilla-band of mice were playing havoc with our food supplies.

Toto was removed from his comfortable bed of straw in the stable, and chained up in the larder, beneath shelves of jam pots and other delicacies. The night was a long and miserable one for Toto, who must have wondered what he had done to deserve such treatment. The mice scampered about the place, while he, most uncatlike, lay curled up in a soup tureen, trying to snatch some sleep. At dawn, the mice returned to their holes; Toto awoke, scratched himself, emerged from the soup tureen, and looked about for something to eat. The jam pots attracted his notice, and it did not take him long to prise open the covers. Grandmother's treasured jams—she had made most of them herself—disappeared in an amazingly short time. I was present when she opened the door to see how many mice Toto had caught. Even the rain-god Indra could not have looked more terrible when planning a thunderstorm; and the imprecations Grandmother hurled at Toto were surprising coming from someone who had been brought up in the genteel Victorian manner.

The monkey was later reinstated in Grandmother's favour. A great treat for him on cold winter evenings was the large bowl of warm water provided by Grandmother for his bath. He would bathe himself, first of all gingerly testing the temperature of the water with his fingers. Leisurely he would step into the bath, first one foot, then the other, as he had seen me doing, until he was completely sitting down in it. Once comfortable, he would take the soap in his hands or feet, and rub himself all over. When he found the water becoming cold, he would get out and run as quickly as he could to the fire, where his coat soon dried. If anyone laughed at him during this performance, he would look extremely hurt, and refuse to go on with his ablutions.

One day Toto nearly succeeded in boiling himself to death.

The large kitchen kettle had been left on the fire to boil for tea; and Toto, finding himself for a few minutes alone with it, decided to take the lid off. On discovering that the water inside was warm, he got into the kettle with the intention of having a bath, and sat down with his head protruding from the opening. This was very pleasant for some time, until the water began to simmer. Toto raised himself a little, but finding it cold outside, sat down again. He continued standing and sitting for some time, not having the courage to face the cold air. Had it not been for the timely arrival of Grandmother, he would have been cooked alive.

If there is a part of the brain especially devoted to mischief, that part must have been largely developed in Toto. He was always tearing things to bits, and whenever one of my aunts came near him, he made every effort to get hold of her dress and tear a hole in it. A variety of aunts frequently came to stay with my grandparents, but during Toto's stay they limited their visits to a day or two, much to Grandfather's relief and Grandmother's annoyance.

Toto, however, took a liking to Grandmother, inspite of the beatings he often received from her. Whenever she allowed him the liberty, he would lie quietly in her lap instead of scrambling all over her as he did on most people.

Toto lived with us for over a year, but the following winter, after too much bathing, he caught pneumonia. Grandmother wrapped him in flannel, and Grandfather gave him a diet of chicken soup and Irish stew; but Toto did not recover. He was buried in the garden, under his favourite mango tree.

◆

Perhaps it was just as well that Toto was no longer with us when Grandfather brought home the python, or his demise might have been less conventional. Small monkeys are a favourite delicacy with pythons.

Grandmother was tolerant of most birds and animals, but she drew the line at reptiles. She said they made her blood run cold. Even a handsome, sweet-tempered chameleon had to be given up. Grandfather should have known that there was little chance of his being allowed to keep the python. It was about four feet long, a young one, when Grandfather bought it from a snake charmer for six rupees, impressing the bazaar crowd by slinging it across his shoulders and walking home with it. Grandmother nearly fainted at the sight of the python curled round Grandfather's throat.

'You'll be strangled!' she cried. 'Get rid of it at once!'

'Nonsense,' said Grandfather. 'He's only a young fellow. He'll soon get used to us.'

'Will he, indeed?' said Grandmother. But I have no intention of getting used to him. You know quite well that your cousin Mabel is coming to stay with us tomorrow. She'll leave us the minute she knows there's a snake in the house.'

'Well, perhaps we ought to show it to her as soon as she

arrives,' said Grandfather, who did not look forward to fussy Aunt Mabel's visits any more than I did.

'You'll do no such thing,' said Grandmother.

'Well, I can't let it loose in the garden,' said Grandfather with an innocent expression. 'It might find its way into the poultry house, and then where would we be?'

'How exasperating you are!' grumbled Grandmother. 'Lock the creature in the bathroom, go back to the bazaar and find the man you bought it from, and get him to come and take it back.'

In my awestruck presence, Grandfather had to take the python into the bathroom, where he placed it in a steep-sided tin tub. Then he hurried off to the bazaar to look for the snake charmer, while Grandmother paced anxiously up and down the verandah. When he returned looking crestfallen, we knew he hadn't been able to find the man.

'You had better take it away yourself,' said Grandmother, in a relentless mood. 'Leave it in the jungle across the riverbed.'

'All right, but let me give it a feed first,' said Grandfather; and producing a plucked chicken, he took it into the bathroom, followed, in single file, by me, Grandmother and a curious cook and gardener.

Grandfather threw open the door and stepped into the bathroom. I peeped round his legs, while the others remained well behind. We couldn't see the python anywhere.

'He's gone,' announced Grandfather. 'He must have felt hungry.'

'I hope he isn't too hungry,' I said.

'We left the window open,' said Grandfather, looking embarrassed.

A careful search was made of the house, the kitchen, the

garden, the stable and the poultry shed; but the python couldn't be found anywhere.

'He'll be well away by now,' said Grandfather reassuringly.

'I certainly hope so,' said Grandmother, who was halfway between anxiety and relief.

Aunt Mabel arrived next day for a three-week visit, and for a couple of days Grandfather and I were a little apprehensive in case the python made a sudden reappearance; but on the third day, when he didn't show up, we felt confident that he had gone for good.

And then, towards evening, we were startled by a scream from the garden. Seconds later, Aunt Mabel came flying up the verandah steps, looking as though she had seen a ghost.

'In the guava tree!' she gasped. 'I was reaching for a guava, when I saw it staring at me. The *look* in its eyes! As though it would *devour* me—'

'Calm down, my dear,' urged Grandmother, sprinkling her with eau de cologne. 'Calm down and tell us what you saw.'

'A snake!' sobbed Aunt Mabel. 'A great boa constrictor. It must have been twenty feet long! In the guava tree. Its eyes were terrible. It looked at me in such a *queer* way...'

My grandparents looked significantly at each other, and Grandfather said, 'I'll go out and kill it,' and sheepishly taking hold of an umbrella, sallied out into the garden. But when he reached the guava tree, the python had disappeared.

'Aunt Mabel must have frightened it away,' I said.

'Hush,' said Grandfather. 'We mustn't speak of your aunt in that way.' But his eyes were alive with laughter.

After this incident, the python began to make a series of appearances, often in the most unexpected places. Aunt Mabel had another fit of hysterics when she saw him admiring her from under a cushion. She packed her bags, and Grandmother made us intensify the hunt.

Next morning I saw the python curled up on the dressing-table, gazing at his reflection in the mirror. I went for Grandfather, but by the time we returned the python had moved elsewhere. A little later he was seen in the garden again. Then he was back on the dressing-table, admiring himself in the mirror. Evidently he had become enamoured with his own reflection. Grandfather observed that perhaps the attention he was receiving from everyone had made him a little conceited.

'He's trying to look better for Aunt Mabel,' I said; a remark that I instantly regretted, because Grandmother overheard it, and brought the flat of her broad hand down on my head.

'Well, now we know his weakness,' said Grandfather.

'Are you trying to be funny too?' demanded Grandmother, looking her most threatening.

'I only meant he was becoming very vain,' said Grandfather hastily. 'It should be easier to catch him now.'

He set about preparing a large cage with a mirror at one end. In the cage he left a juicy chicken and various other delicacies, and fitted up the opening with a trapdoor. Aunt Mabel had already left by the time we had this trap ready, but we had to go on with the project because we couldn't have the python prowling about the house indefinitely.

For a few days nothing happened, and then, as I was leaving for school one morning, I saw the python curled up in the cage. He had eaten everything left out for him, and was relaxing in front of the mirror with something resembling a smile on his face—if you can imagine a python smiling… I lowered the trapdoor gently, but the python took no notice; he was in raptures over his handsome reflection. Grandfather and the gardener put the cage in the pony trap, and made a journey to the other side of the riverbed. They left the cage in the jungle, with the trapdoor open.

'He made no attempt to get out,' said Grandfather later. 'And I didn't have the heart to take the mirror away. It's the first time I've seen a snake fall in love.'

◆

'And the frogs have sung their old song in the mud…' This was Grandfather's favourite quotation from Virgil, and he used it whenever we visited the rainwater pond behind the house where there were quantities of mud and frogs and the occasional water buffalo. Grandfather had once brought a number of frogs into the house. He had put them in a glass jar, left them on a windowsill, and then forgotten all about them. At about four o'clock in the morning the entire household was awakened by a loud and fearful noise, and Grandmother and several nervous relatives gathered in their nightclothes on the verandah. Their timidity changed to fury when they discovered that the ghastly sounds had come from Grandfather's frogs. Seeing the dawn breaking, the frogs had with one accord begun their morning song.

Grandmother wanted to throw the frogs, jar and all, out of the window; but Grandfather said that if he gave the jar a good shaking, the frogs would remain quiet. He was obliged to keep awake, in order to shake the bottle whenever the frogs showed any inclination to break into song. Fortunately for all concerned, the next day a servant took the top off the bottle to see what was inside. The sight of several big frogs so startled him that he ran off without replacing the cover; the frogs jumped out and presumably found their way back to the pond.

It became a habit with me to visit the pond on my own, in order to explore its banks and shallows. Taking off my shoes, I would wade into the muddy water up to my knees, to pluck the water lilies that floated on the surface.

One day I found the pond already occupied by several buffaloes. Their keeper, a boy a little older than me, was swimming about in the middle. Instead of climbing out on to the bank, he would pull himself up on the back of one of his buffaloes, stretch his naked brown body out on the animal's glistening wet hide, and start singing to himself.

When he saw me staring at him from across the pond, he smiled, showing gleaming white teeth in a dark, sun-burnished face. He invited me to join him in a swim. I told him I couldn't swim, and he offered to teach me. I hesitated, knowing that Grandmother held strict and old-fashioned views about mixing with village children; but, deciding that Grandfather—who sometimes smoked a hookah on the sly—would get me out of any trouble that might occur, I took the bold step of accepting the boy's offer. Once taken, the step did not seem so bold.

He dived off the back of his buffalo, and swam across to me. And I, having removed my clothes, followed his instructions until I was floundering about among the water lilies. His name was Ramu, and he promised to give me swimming lessons every afternoon; and so it was during the afternoons—especially summer afternoons when everyone was asleep—that we usually met. Before long I was able to swim across the pond to sit with Ramu astride a contented buffalo, the great beast standing like an island in the middle of a muddy ocean.

Sometimes we would try racing the buffaloes, Ramu and I sitting on different mounts. But they were lazy creatures, and would leave one comfortable spot only to look for another; or, if they were in no mood for games, would roll over on their backs, taking us with them into the mud and green slime of the pond. Emerging in shades of green and khaki, I would slip into the house through the bathroom, bathing under the tap before getting into my clothes.

One afternoon Ramu and I found a small tortoise in the mud, sitting over a hole in which it had laid several eggs. Ramu kept the eggs for his dinner, and I presented the tortoise to Grandfather. He had a weakness for tortoises, and was pleased with this addition to his menagerie, giving it a large tub of water all to itself, with an island of rocks in the middle. The tortoise, however, was always getting out of the tub and wandering about the house. As it seemed able to look after itself quite well, we did not interfere. If one of the dogs bothered it too much, it would draw its head and legs into its shell, and defy all their attempts at rough play.

Ramu came from a family of bonded labourers, and had received no schooling. But he was well-versed in folklore, and knew a great deal about birds and animals.

'Many birds are sacred,' said Ramu, as we watched a bluejay swoop down from a peepul tree and carry off a grasshopper. He told me that both the bluejay and Lord Shiva were called 'Nilkanth'. Shiva had a blue throat, like the bird, because out of compassion for the human race he had swallowed a deadly poison which was intended to destroy the world. Keeping the poison in his throat, he did not let it go any further.

'Are squirrels sacred?' I asked, seeing one sprint down the trunk of the peepul tree.

'Oh yes, Lord Krishna loved squirrels,' said Ramu. 'He would take them in his arms and stroke them with his long fingers. That is why they have four dark lines down their backs from head to tail. Krishna was very dark, and the lines are the marks of his fingers.'

Both Ramu and Grandfather were of the opinion that we should be more gentle with birds and animals, and should not kill so many of them.

'It is also important that we respect them,' said Grandfather. 'We must acknowledge their rights. Everywhere, birds and animals are finding it more difficult to survive, because we are trying to destroy both them and their forests. They have to keep moving as the trees disappear.'

This was especially true of the forests near Dehra, where the tiger and the pheasant and the spotted deer were beginning to disappear.

Ramu and I spent many long summer afternoons at the pond. I still remember him with affection, though we never saw each other again after I left Dehra. He could not read or write, so we were unable to keep in touch. And neither his people, nor mine, knew of our friendship. The buffaloes and frogs had been our only confidants. They had accepted us as part of their own world, their muddy but comfortable pond. And when I left Dehra, both they and Ramu must have assumed that I would return again like the birds.

THE LOST RUBY

Once upon a time there lived a king, who was a great and powerful monarch. One day he was very sad, and as he sat in his council hall surrounded by his ministers, the chief minister, who was a good and wise man, asked him, 'Defender of the World! Why is your spirit sad today? Your Majesty ought not to allow grief to trouble your mind.'

The king would not tell him his grief. On the contrary, he resented his good minister's concern for him. 'It is all very well for you to talk,' he said. 'But if you had reason to be sad, I am sure you would find it impossible to practise what you have just suggested.' And the king decided to put his chief minister to the test, and told him to wait at the royal palace after the council was dismissed.

The minister accordingly made his way to the royal apartments and awaited further orders. The king took out a ruby of great price from a beautiful ivory casket and, placing it in the minister's hand, told him to look after it with great care.

When the minister got home, he found his wife reclining on cushions, chewing scented paan. He gave her the ruby to keep. She dropped it in a partition of her cash box and thought no more about it.

No sooner had the wily king delivered the ruby to his minister than he employed female spies to follow him up and mark where he kept the jewel. After a few days he bribed the steward of the minister's household to steal it for him. The king was sitting on the balcony of his palace overlooking the river when the jewel was brought to him. Taking it from the hands of the steward, he deliberately threw it into the river.

The next morning, after dismissing his court, he asked the chief minister, 'Where is the ruby that I gave you to keep the other day?' The minister replied, 'I have got it, Defender of the World.'

'Well then,' said the king, 'go and fetch it, for I want it right now.'

Imagine the poor minister's amazement when, on going home, he understood that the ruby was nowhere to be found. He hurried back to the king and reported the loss. 'Your Majesty,' he said, 'if you will allow me a few days' grace, I hope to find it and bring it back to you.'

'Very well,' said the king, laughing to himself. 'I give you three days in which to find the ruby. If, at the end of that time, you fail to find it, your life and the lives of all who are dear to you will be forfeit. And your house will be razed to the ground and ploughed up by donkeys!'

The minister left the palace with a heavy heart. He searched everywhere for the lost jewel, but because of its mysterious disappearance, he did not have much hope of finding it.

I have no one, he thought, to whom I can leave my riches and possessions. My wife is the only soul on earth who is dear to me, and it seems we must both die after three days. What could be better than for us to enjoy ourselves during this period? We'll make the most of the time that's left to us.

In this mood he reached home and told his wife about the king's decision.

'Let us spend our wealth liberally and freely,' he said, 'for soon we must die.'

His wife sighed deeply and only said, 'As you wish. Fate has dealt us a cruel blow. Let us take it with dignity and good cheer.'

That day saw the commencement of a period of great revelry in the chief minister's house. Musicians of all kinds were engaged, and the halls were filled with guests, who came wondering what great luck had come the way of the chief minister. Rich food was served, and night and day the sound of music and laughter filled the house.

In addition, large quantities of food were prepared and given to the poor. No one who came to the house was allowed to leave empty-handed. Tradesmen, when they brought their customary presents of fresh fruit, were rewarded with gold coins, and went away rejoicing.

In a village near by, there lived a poor flower seller and a fisherwoman—the two women were neighbours and close friends. The flower seller happened to be visiting the bazaar, where she heard of the grand doings at the minister's house. So she hurried there with a present of vegetables and garlands, and received a gold coin. Then she walked across to her friend's house and advised her to take a present of fish to the minister, who would reward her in the same manner.

The fisherwoman was very poor. Her husband used to go fishing daily, but he seldom was able to catch large fish; those that he caught were so small that they rarely fetched more than a few pice in the bazaar. So the fisherwoman said to herself: 'Those miserable fish that my husband brings home are hardly worth presenting to the minister—he'll only feel insulted,' and she thought no more about it.

But the following morning, as good luck would have it, her husband caught a large Rohu, the most delicious of Indian fresh-water fish. Delighted at his good fortune, he took it home to show his wife, who immediately placed the fish in a basket, covered it with a clean cloth, and hurried to the minister's house. The minister was really pleased to see such a fine large Rohu fish, and instead of giving her one gold coin, he gave her two. The fisherwoman was overjoyed. She ran home with her prize, which was enough to keep herself and her husband in comfort for many a month.

This happened on the third and last day of the minister's life; the next day he and his wife were to be executed. Being very fond of fish curry, he said to his wife, 'Let's have one of your delightful fish curries for lunch today. We will never be able to enjoy it again. Now here's a fine Rohu. Let's take it to the kitchen and have it cleaned.'

He and his wife sat together to see the fish cut. The cook took out his kitchen knife and set to work.

As the cook thrust his knife into the fish's belly, out dropped the ruby which had been thrown into the river.

The minister and his wife were overcome with astonishment and joy. They washed the ruby in perfumed water, and then the minister hastened to restore it to the king.

The king was equally amazed to see the ruby that he had thrown into the river. He at once demanded an explanation for its recovery. The minister told him how he had decided to spend all his riches, and how he had received the present of a fish which, when it was cut, gave up the lost ruby.

The king then acknowledged the part he had played in the loss of the ruby. 'But I see that you took your own advice to me,' he said. 'Endure sorrow cheerfully!' He bestowed high honours on his minister, and commended his wisdom and understanding before all his courtiers and ministers.

And so the minister's evil fortune was changed to good.

'And may the Eternal Dispenser of all Good thus deal with his servants'.

THE WINDOW

When Amir was thirteen, he decided that he was old enough to have a room of his own.

'What for?' asked his mother.

'The kids make too much noise,' he said, referring to his younger brothers and sisters. 'I can't study.'

'Well, if you really want to study, you can have your own room,' said his grandfather, who owned the old building. 'There's the room on the roof.'

So Amir took the room on the roof. It was a long, low building with large cracks in the walls from which peepul trees were growing. Amir's grandfather said he couldn't afford to have it repaired. There were a number of tenants in the building and they were paying rents that had been fixed forty years back, when rents were very low, so there wasn't much money coming in. Amir's father had a tailor's shop in the bazaar, but that didn't make much money either. The building had a flat roof, with just the one small room—called a *barsati*—opening on to it. From the window of his room Amir looked out upon a world quite different from the world below.

The banyan tree, just opposite, was his, and its inhabitants his subjects. There were two squirrels, several mynahs, a crow and, at night, a pair of flying foxes. The squirrels were busy in the afternoon, the birds in the morning and evening, the flying foxes at night. Amir wasn't very busy. He'd look at his books now and then, but decided that it wasn't a very good year for studying. There was much more to learn from looking out of his window.

At first he felt lonely in the room. But then he discovered the power of the window. It looked out on the banyan tree and the mango grove, on the rather untidy garden, on the broad path running past the building, and out over the roofs of other houses, over roads and fields, as far as the horizon. The path was a busy one: fruit and vegetable vendors came and went, as did the toy seller and the balloon man, their wares strung on poles; there were boys on cycles, babies in prams, schoolgirls chattering, housewives quarrelling, old men gossiping…all passed his way, the way of his window.

Early that summer a tonga came rattling and jingling down the path and stopped in front of the building. A girl and an elderly lady got down, while a servant unloaded their luggage. They went into the house and the tonga moved off.

The next day the girl looked up from the garden and saw Amir at the window.

She had black hair that came to her shoulders. Her eyes were black, like her hair, and just as shiny. She must have been about eleven years old.

'Hello,' said Amir.

She looked up at him suspiciously. 'Who are you?' she asked.

'I am a ghost.'

She laughed, and her laugh had a gay, mocking quality, 'You look like one!'

Amir didn't think her remark was very funny, but he had asked for it.

'What are you doing up there?' she asked.

'Practising magic,' he said.

She laughed again but this time without the mockery. 'I don't believe you,' she said.

'Why don't you come up and see for yourself?'

She came round to the steps and began climbing them slowly, cautiously. When she entered the room, she stared at Amir and said: 'Where's your magic?'

'Come here,' he said, and he took her to the window and showed her his world.

She said nothing, just stared out of the window. Then she turned and smiled at Amir, and they were friends.

He only knew that she was called Chummo, and that she had come with her aunt for the summer months. He did not need to know any more about her, and she did not need to know any more about him except that he wasn't really a ghost.

She came up the steps nearly every day and joined Amir at the window. There was a lot of excitement to be had in the world of the window, especially when the monsoon rains arrived.

At the first rumblings, women would rush outside to retrieve their washing from the clothesline and, if there was a breeze, to chase a few garments across the compound. When the rain came, it came with a vengeance, making a bog of the garden and a river of the path.

A cyclist would come riding furiously down the path, an elderly gentleman would be having difficulty with his umbrella, naked toddlers would be frisking about in the rain. Sometimes Amir would run out on the roof and shout and dance in the rain. And the rain would come through the open door and window of the room, flooding the floor and making an island of the bed.

But the window was more fun than anything else.

'It's like a film,' said Chummo. 'The window is the screen, the world outside is the picture.'

Soon the mangoes were ripe and Chummo was in the branches of the mango tree as often as she was at Amir's window. Amir was supposed to be deep in study, so any forays into the mango tree on his part would not have pleased his grandfather. But from the window he had a good view of the tree, and he could speak to Chummo from about the same level. She brought him unripe mangoes, and they ate far too many of them and had tummy aches for the rest of the day.

'Let's make a garden on the roof,' said Chummo.

'How do we do that?' asked Amir.

'It's easy. We bring up mud and bricks and make the flower beds. Then we plant the seeds. We'll grow all sorts of flowers.'

'The roof will fall in,' said Amir.

'Never mind,' said Chummo.

They spent two days carrying buckets of mud up the steps to the roof and laying out the flower beds. It was hard work, but Chummo did most of it. When the beds were ready, they had a planting ceremony. But apart from a few small plants collected from the garden below, they had only one kind of seed—pumpkin.

'I can't eat pumpkins,' said Amir.

'Have you ever met anyone who likes pumpkins?' asked Chummo.

'No. Everyone hates them.'

'True. And yet people keep on growing them, and selling them, and forcing children to eat them.'

'They just do it to make us suffer,' said Amir.

'True. We'll present our pumpkins to our enemies.'

So they planted the pumpkin seeds in the mud and felt proud of themselves.

But the following night it rained very heavily, and in the morning they discovered that everything—except the bricks—had been washed away.

So they returned to the window.

A mynah had been in a fight and the feathers had been knocked off its head. A bougainvillaea creeper that had been climbing the wall had sent a long green shoot in through the window.

Chummo said, 'Now we can't shut the window without spoiling the creeper.'

'Then we won't close the window,' said Amir.

And they let the creeper into the room.

◆

The rains passed and an autumn wind came whispering through the branches of the banyan tree. There were red leaves on the ground and the wind picked them up and blew them about so that they looked like butterflies. Amir would watch the sunrise, the sky all red until the first rays splashed the windowsill and crept up the walls of the room. And in the evening Chummo and Amir would watch the sun go down in a sea of fluffy clouds. Sometimes the clouds were pink, sometimes orange; they were nearly always coloured clouds, framed in the window.

'I'm going tomorrow,' said Chummo one evening.

Amir was too surprised to say anything.

'You stay here all the time, don't you?' she said.

Amir nodded.

'When I come again next year, you'll still be here, won't you?'

'I suppose so,' said Amir.

In the morning the tonga was at the door, and the servant, the aunt, and Chummo were in it. Amir was at his window.

Chummo waved up to him. Then the driver flicked the pony's reins, the tonga creaked and rattled, the bell jingled. Down the path and through the compound gate went the tonga, and all the time Chummo waved.

When the tonga was out of sight, Amir took the spray of bougainvillaea and pushed it out of the room. Then he closed the window. It would be opened only when the spring and Chummo came again.

THOSE THREE BEARS

Most Himalayan villages lie in the valleys where there are small streams, some farmland, and protection from the biting winds that come through the mountain passes in winter. The houses are usually made of large stones and have sloping slate roofs so the heavy monsoon rain can run off easily. During the sunny autumn months, the roofs are often covered with pumpkins, left there to ripen in the sun.

One October night, when I was sleeping at a friend's house in a village in these hills, I was awakened by a rumbling and thumping on the roof. I woke my friend and asked him what was happening.

'It's only a bear,' he said.

'Is it trying to get in?'

'No. It's after the pumpkins.'

A little later, when we looked out a window, we saw a black bear making off through a field, leaving a trail of half-eaten pumpkins.

Face to Face

In winter, when snow covers the higher ranges, the Himalayan bears come to lower altitudes in search of food. Sometimes they forage in fields and, because they are short-sighted and suspicious of anything that moves, they can be dangerous. But, like most wild animals, they avoid humans as much as possible.

Village folk always advise me to run downhill if chased by a bear. They say bears find it easier to run uphill than down. I am yet to be chased by a bear, and will happily skip the experience. But I have seen a few of these mountain bears in India, and they are always fascinating to watch.

Himalayan bears enjoy pumpkins, corn, plums and apricots. Once, while I was sitting in an oak tree hoping to see a pair of pine martens that lived nearby, I heard the whining grumble of a bear, and presently, a small bear ambled into the clearing beneath the tree.

He was little more than a cub, and I was not alarmed. I sat very still, waiting to see what he would do.

He put his nose to the ground and sniffed his way along until he came to a large anthill. Here he began huffing and puffing, blowing rapidly in and out of his nostrils, so that the dust from the anthill flew in all directions. But the anthill had been deserted, and so, grumbling, the bear made his way up a nearby plum tree. Soon he was perched high in the branches. It was then that he saw me.

The bear at once scrambled several feet higher up the tree and lay flat on a branch. Since it wasn't a very big branch, there was a lot of bear showing on either side. He tucked his head behind another branch. He could no longer see me, so he apparently was satisfied that he was hidden, although he couldn't help grumbling.

Like all bears, this one was full of curiosity. So, slowly, inch by inch, his black snout appeared over the edge of the branch. As soon as he saw me, he drew his head back and hid his face.

He did this several times. I waited until he wasn't looking, then moved some way down my tree. When the bear looked over and saw that I was missing, he was so pleased that he stretched right across to another branch and helped himself to a plum. I couldn't help bursting into laughter.

The startled young bear tumbled out of the tree, dropped through the branches some fifteen feet, and landed with a thump in a pile of dried leaves. He was unhurt, but fled from the clearing, grunting and squealing all the way.

The Flag 'Bearer'

Another time, my friend Prem told me, a bear had been active in his cornfield. We took up a post at night in an old cattle shed, which gave a clear view of the moonlit field.

A little after midnight, a female bear came down to the edge of the field. She seemed to sense that we had been about. She was hungry, however. So, after standing on her hind legs and peering around to make sure the field was empty, she came cautiously out of the forest.

Her attention was soon distracted by some Tibetan prayer flags, which had been strung between two trees. She gave a grunt of disapproval and began to back away, but the fluttering of the flags was a puzzle that she wanted to solve. So she stopped and watched them.

Soon the bear advanced to within a few feet of the flags, examining them from various angles. Then, seeing that they posed no danger, she went right up to the flags and pulled them down. Grunting with apparent satisfaction, she moved into the field of corn.

Prem had decided that he didn't want to lose any more of

his crop, so he started shouting. His children woke up and soon came running from the house, banging on empty kerosene tins.

Deprived of her dinner, the bear made off in a bad temper. She ran downhill at a good speed, and I was glad that I was not in her way.

Uphill or downhill, an angry bear is best given a very wide berth.

THE ELEPHANT AND THE CASSOWARY BIRD

The baby elephant wasn't out of place in our home in north India because India is where elephants belong, and in any case, our house was full of pets brought home by Grandfather, who was in the Forest Service. But the cassowary bird was different. No one had ever seen such a bird before—not in India, that is. Grandfather had picked it up on a voyage to Singapore, where he'd been given the bird by a rubber planter who'd got it from a Dutch trader who'd got it from a man in Indonesia.

Anyway, it ended up at our home in Dehra, and seemed to do quite well in the subtropical climate. It looked like a cross between a turkey and an ostrich, but bigger than the former and smaller than the latter—about five feet in height. It was not a beautiful bird, nor even a friendly one, but it had come to stay, and everyone was curious about it, especially the baby elephant.

Right from the start, the baby elephant took a great interest in the cassowary, a bird unlike any found in the Indian jungles. He would circle round the odd creature, and diffidently examine with his trunk the texture of its stumpy wings. Of course he suspected no evil, and his childlike curiosity encouraged him to take liberties, which resulted in an unpleasant experience.

Noticing the baby elephant's attempts to make friends with the rather morose cassowary, we felt a bit apprehensive. Self-contained and sullen, the big bird responded only by slowly and slyly raising one of its powerful legs, in the meantime gazing into space with an innocent air. We knew what the gesture meant; we had seen that treacherous leg raised on many an occasion, and suddenly shooting out with a force that would have done credit to a vicious camel. In fact, camel and cassowary kicks are delivered on the same plan, except that the camel kicks backward like a horse and the bird forward.

We wished to spare our baby elephant a painful experience, and led him away from the bird. But he persisted in his friendly overtures, and one morning, he received an ugly reward. Rapid as lightning, the cassowary hit straight from the hip and knee joints, and the elephant ran squealing to Grandfather.

For several days he avoided the cassowary, and we thought he had learnt his lesson. He crossed and recrossed the compound and the garden, swinging his trunk, thinking furiously. Then, a week later, he appeared on the verandah at breakfast time in his usual cheery, childlike fashion, sidling up to the cassowary as if nothing had happened.

We were struck with amazement at this and so, it seemed, was the bird. Had the painful lesson already been forgotten, and by a member of the elephant tribe noted for its ability to never forget? Another dose of the same medicine would serve the booby right.

The cassowary once more began to draw up its fighting leg with sinister determination. It was nearing the true position for the master kick, kung fu style, when all of a sudden the baby elephant seized with his trunk the cassowary's other leg and pulled it down. There was a clumsy flapping of wings, a tremendous swelling of the bird's wattle, and an undignified getting up, as if it were a floored boxer doing his best to beat the count of ten. The bird then marched off with an attempt to look stately and unconcerned, while we at the breakfast table were convulsed with laughter.

After this, the cassowary bird gave the baby elephant as wide a berth as possible. But they were not forced to coexist for very long. The baby elephant, getting bulky and cumbersome, was sold and now lives in a zoo where he is a favourite with young visitors who love to take rides on his back.

As for the cassowary, he continued to grace our verandah for many years, gaped at but not made much of, while entering on a rather friendless old age.

THE LAST TIGER

On the left bank of the Ganga, where it emerges from the Himalayan foothills, there is a long stretch of heavy forest. There are villages on the fringe of the forest, inhabited by bamboo cutters and farmers, but there are few signs of commerce or religion. Hunters, however, have found it an ideal hunting ground over the last seventy years, and as a result the animals are not as numerous as they used to be. The trees, too, have been disappearing slowly; and, as the forest recedes, the animals lose their food and shelter and move on, further into the foothills. Slowly, they are being denied the right to live.

Only the elephants could cross the river. And two years ago, when a large area of forest was cleared to make way for a refugee resettlement camp, a herd of elephants—finding their favourite food, the green shoots of the bamboo, in short supply—waded across the river. They crashed through the suburbs of Haridwar, knocked down a factory wall, plucked away several tin roofs, held up a train, and left a trail of devastation in their wake until they reached a new forest, still untouched, where they settled down to a new life—but an unsettled, wary life. Because, they did not know when men would appear again, with tractors and bulldozers and dynamite.

There was a time when this forest provided food and shelter for some thirty or forty tigers; but men in search of trophies shot them all, and today there remains only one old tiger in the jungle. Many hunters have tried to get him. But he is a wise and crafty old tiger who knows the ways of men, and he has so far survived all attempts on his life.

This is his story. It is also the story of the jungle.

◆

Although the tiger has passed the prime of his life, he has lost none of his majesty; his muscles ripple beneath the golden yellow of his coat, and he walks through the long grass with the confidence of one who knows that he is still king, even though his subjects are fewer. His great head pushes through the foliage, and it is only his tail, swinging high, that shows occasionally above the sea of grass.

He is heading for water, the only water in the forest (if you don't count the river, which is several miles away)—the water of a large *jheel*, which is almost a lake during the rainy season, but just a muddy marsh at this time of the year, in the late spring.

Here, at different times of the day and night, all the animals come to drink—the long-horned sambar deer, the delicate spotted chital, the swamp deer, the wolves and jackals, the wild boar, the panthers—and the tiger. Since the elephants have gone, the water is usually clear except when buffaloes from the nearest village come to wallow, and then it is very muddy. These buffaloes, though they are not wild, are not afraid of the panther or even of the tiger. They know the panther is afraid of their long horns and they know the tiger prefers the flesh of the deer.

Today, there are several sambar at the water's edge, but they do not stay long. The tiger is coming with the breeze, and there is no mistaking its strong feline odour. The deer hold their heads high for a few moments, their nostrils twitching, and then scatter into the forest, disappearing behind screens of leaf and bamboo.

When the tiger arrives, there is no other animal near the water. But the birds are still there. The egrets continue to wade in the shallows, and a kingfisher darts low over the water, dives suddenly, a flash of blue and gold, and makes off with a slim silver fish, which glistens in the sun like a polished gem. A long brown snake glides in amongst the water lilies and disappears beneath a fallen tree which lies rotting in the shallows.

The tiger waits in the shelter of a rock, his ears pricked up for the least unfamiliar sound; for he knows that it is often at this place that men lie up for him with guns; for they covet his beauty—they covet his stripes, and the gold of his body, and his fine teeth and his whiskers and his noble head. They would like to hang his pelt on a wall, and stick glass eyes in his head, and boast of their conquest over the king of the jungle.

The old tiger has been hunted before, and he does not usually show himself in the open during the day, but of late he has heard no guns, and if there were hunters around, you would have heard their guns (for a man with a gun cannot resist letting it off, even if it is only at a rabbit—or at another man). And, besides, the tiger is thirsty.

He is also feeling quite hot. It is March, and the shimmering dust-haze of summer has come early this year. Tigers—unlike other cats—are fond of water, and on a hot day will wallow for hours.

He walks into the water, in amongst the water lilies, and drinks slowly. He is seldom in a hurry when he eats or drinks. Other animals might bolt their food, but they are only other animals. A tiger has his dignity to preserve!

He raises his head and listens. One paw remains suspended

in the air. A strange sound has come to him on the breeze, and he is wary of strange sounds. So he moves swiftly through the grass that borders the jheel, and climbs a hillock until he reaches his favourite rock. This rock is big enough to hide him and to give him shade. Anyone looking up from the jheel might think it strange that the rock has a round bump on the top. The bump is the tiger's head. He keeps it very still.

The sound he has heard is only the sound of a flute, sounding thin and reedy in the forest. It belongs to a boy, a slim brown boy who rides a buffalo. The boy blows vigorously on the flute, while another, slightly smaller boy, riding another buffalo, brings up the rear of the herd.

There are about eight buffaloes in the herd, and they belong to the families of Ramu and Shyam, the two Gujjar boys who are friends. The Gujjars are a caste who possess herds of buffaloes and earn their livelihood from the sale of milk and butter. The boys are about twelve years old, but they cannot tell you how many months past twelve, because in their village nobody thinks birthdays are important. They are almost the same age as the tiger, but he is old and experienced while they are still cubs.

◆

The tiger has often seen them at the tank, and he is not worried. He knows the village people will bring him no harm as long as he leaves their buffaloes alone. Once, when he was younger and full of bravado, he had killed a buffalo—not because he was hungry but because he was young and wanted to test his strength—and after that the villagers had hunted him for days, with spears, bows and arrows, and an old muzzle-loader. Now he left the buffaloes alone, even though the deer in the forest were not as numerous as before.

The boys know that a tiger lives in the jungle, for they have often heard him roar, but they do not know that today he is so near to them.

The tiger gazes down from his rock, and the sight of eight fat black buffaloes does make him give a low, throaty moan. But the boys are there, and besides—a buffalo is not easy to kill.

He decides to move on and find a cool shady place in the heart of the jungle, where he can rest during the warm afternoon and be free of the flies and mosquitoes that swarm around in the vicinity of the tank. At night he will hunt.

With a lazy, half-humorous roar—'A—oonh!'—he gets up from his haunches and saunters off into the jungle.

Even the gentlest of a tiger's roars can be heard half a mile away, and the boys, who are barely fifty yards off, look up immediately.

'There he goes!' calls Ramu, taking the flute from his lips and pointing with it towards the hillock. He is not afraid, for he knows that an un-hunted and uninjured tiger is not aggressive. 'Did you see him?'

'I saw his tail, just before he disappeared. He's a big tiger!'

'Do not call him tiger. Call him Uncle, or Maharaj.'

'Oh, why?'

'Don't you know that it's unlucky to call a tiger a tiger? My father always told me so. But if you meet a tiger, and call him Uncle, he will leave you alone.'

'I'll try and remember that,' says Shyam.

◆

The buffaloes are now well into the water, and some of them are lying down in the mud. Buffaloes love soft, wet mud and will wallow in it for hours. The more mud the better. Ramu, to avoid being dragged down into the mud with his buffalo, slips off its back and plunges into the water. Using an easy breaststroke, he swims across to a small islet covered with reeds and water lilies. Shyam is close behind him.

They lie down on their hard, flat stomachs, on a patch of grass, and allow the warm sun to beat down on their bare brown bodies. Ramu is the more knowledgeable boy, because he has been to Haridwar several times with his father. Shyam has never been out of the village.

Shyam says, 'The pool is not so deep this year.'

'We have had no rain since January,' says Ramu. 'If we do not get rain soon, the tank may dry up altogether.'

'And then what will we do?'

'We? There is a well in the village. But even that may dry up. My father told me that it failed once, just about the time I was born, and everyone had to walk ten miles to the river for water.'

'And what about the animals?'

'Some will stay here and die. Others will go to the river. But there are too many people near the river now—not only temples, but houses and factories—and the animals stay away. And the trees have been cut, so that between the jungle and the river there is no place to hide. Animals are afraid of the open—they are afraid of men with guns.'

'Even at night?'

'At night men come in jeeps, with searchlights. They kill the deer for meat, and sell the skins of tigers and panthers.'

'I didn't know a tiger's skin was worth anything.'

'It is worth more than our skins,' says Ramu knowingly. 'It will fetch six hundred rupees. Who would pay that much for our skins?'

'Our fathers would.'

'True—if they had the money.'

'If my father sold his fields, he would get more than six hundred rupees.'

'True—but if he sold his fields, none of you would have anything to eat. A man needs land as much as a tiger needs a jungle.'

'True,' says Shyam. 'And that reminds me—my mother asked me to take some roots home.'

'I will help you.'

They wade into the jheel until the water is up to their waists, and begin pulling up water lilies by the root. The flower is beautiful but the villagers value the root more. When it is cooked, it makes a delicious and nourishing dish. The plant multiplies rapidly and is always in good supply. In the year when famine hit the village, it was only the root of the water lily that saved many from starvation.

When Shyam and Ramu have finished gathering roots, they emerge from the water and pass the time in wrestling with each other, slipping about in the soft mud, which soon covers them from head to toe.

To get rid of the mud, they dive into the water again and swim across to their buffaloes. Then, digging their heels into the thick hides of the buffaloes, the boys race them across the jheel, shouting and hollering so much that all the birds fly away in disgust, and the monkeys set up a shrill chattering of their own in the dhak trees.

In March, the twisted, leafless flame of the forest or dhak trees are ablaze with flaming scarlet and orange flowers.

It is evening, and the twilight is fading fast, when the buffalo herd finally wends its way homewards, to be greeted outside the village by the barking of dogs, the gurgle of hookah pipes, and the homely smell of cowdung smoke.

◆

The tiger makes a kill that night. He approaches with the wind against him, and the unsuspecting spotted deer does not see him until it is too late. A blow on the deer's haunches from the tiger's paw brings it down, and then the great beast fastens onto the struggling deer's throat. It is all over in a few minutes. The tiger is too quick and strong, and the deer does not struggle for long.

The deer's life is over, but he has not lived in fear of death. It is only man's imagination and fear of the hereafter that makes him afraid of meeting death. In the jungle, sudden death appears at intervals. Wild creatures do not have to think about it, and so the sudden passing of one of their number due to the arrival of some flesh-eating animal is only a fleeting incident soon forgotten by the survivors.

The tiger feasts well, growling with pleasure as he eats, and then leaves the carcass in the jungle for the vultures and jackals. The old tiger never returns to the same deer's carcass, even if there is still some flesh on it. In the past, when he has done that, he has often found a man sitting in a tree over the kill, waiting for him with a rifle.

His belly full, the tiger comes to the edge of the forest, looks out across the wasteland out over the deep, singing river, at the twinkling lights of Haridwar on the opposite bank, and raises his head and roars his defiance at the world.

He is a lonesome bachelor. It is five or six years since he had a mate. She was shot by trophy-hunters, and the cubs, two of them, were trapped by men who trade in wild animals:

one went to a circus, where it had to learn undignified tricks and respond to the flick of a whip, the other, more fortunate, went first to a zoo in Delhi and was later transferred to a zoo in America.

Sometimes, when the old tiger is very lonely, he gives a great roar, which can be heard throughout the forest. The villagers think he is roaring in anger, but the animals know that he is really roaring out of loneliness. When the sound of his roar has died away, he pauses, standing still, waiting for an answering roar, but it never comes. It is taken up instead by the shrill scream of a barbet high up in a sal tree.

It is dawn now, dew-fresh and cool, and the jungle dwellers are on the move. The black, beady little eyes of a jungle rat were fixed on a small brown hen who was returning cautiously to her nest. He had a large family to feed, and he knew that in the hen's nest was a clutch of delicious fawn-coloured eggs. He waited patiently for nearly an hour before he had the satisfaction of seeing the hen leave her nest and go off in search of food.

As soon as she had gone, the rat lost no time in making his raid. Slipping quietly out of his hole, he slithered along among the leaves, but, clever as he was, he did not realize that his own movements were being watched.

A pair of grey mongooses were scouting about in the dry grass. They, too, were hungry, and eggs usually figured large on their menu. Now, lying still on an outcrop of rock, they watched the rat sneaking along, occasionally sniffing at the air, and finally vanishing behind a boulder. When he reappeared, he was struggling to roll an egg uphill towards his hole.

The rat was in difficulties, pushing the egg sometimes with his paws, sometimes with his nose. The ground was rough, and the egg wouldn't go straight. Deciding that he must have help, he scuttled off to call his spouse. Even now the mongoose did not descend on that tantalizing egg. He waited until the rat returned with his wife, and then watched as the male rat took the egg firmly between his forepaws and rolled over on to his back. The female rat then grabbed her mate's tail and began to drag him along.

Totally absorbed in their struggle with the egg, the rats did not hear the approach of the mongooses. When these two large furry visitors suddenly bobbed up from behind a stone, the rats squealed with fright, abandoned the egg, and fled for their lives.

The mongooses wasted no time in breaking open the egg and making a meal of it. But just as, a few minutes ago, the rat had not noticed their approach, so now they did not notice the village boy, carrying a small bright axe and a net bag in his hands, creeping along.

Ramu too was searching for eggs, and when he saw the mongooses busy with one, he stood still to watch them, his eyes roving in search of the nest. He was hoping the mongooses would lead him to the nest, but, when they had finished their meal, the breeze took them in another direction, and Ramu had to do his own searching. He failed to find the nest, and moved further into the forest. The rat's hopes were just reviving when, to his disgust, the mother hen returned.

Ramu now made his way to a mahua tree.

The flowers of the mahua tree can be eaten by animals as well as men. Bears are particularly fond of them and will eat large quantities of its flowers, which gradually start fermenting in their stomachs with the result that the animals get quite drunk. Ramu had often seen a couple of bears stumbling home to their cave, bumping into each other or into the trunks of trees—they are short-sighted to begin with, and when drunk can hardly see at all—but their sense of smell and hearing are so good that they finally find their way home.

Ramu decided he would gather some mahua flowers, and climbed swiftly into the tree, which is leafless when it blossoms. He began breaking the white flowers and throwing them to the ground. He had been in the tree for about five minutes when he heard the whining grumble of a bear, and presently a young sloth bear ambled into the clearing beneath the tree.

He was a small bear, little more than a cub, and Ramu was not frightened, but, because he thought the mother might be in the vicinity, he decided to take no chances, and sat very still, waiting to see what the bear would do. He hoped it wouldn't choose the same mahua tree for a meal.

At first the young bear put his nose to the ground and sniffed his way along until he came to a large white anthill. Here he began huffing and puffing, blowing rapidly in and out of his nostrils, so that the dust from the anthill flew in all directions. But he was a disappointed bear, because the anthill had been deserted long ago. And so, grumbling, he made his way across to a wild plum—a tall tree, the wild plum—and shinning rapidly up the smooth trunk, was soon perched in its topmost branches. It was only then that he saw Ramu.

The bear at once scrambled several feet higher up the tree, and laid himself out flat on a branch. It wasn't a very thick branch and left a large expanse of bear showing on either side of it. The bear tucked his head away behind another branch, and, so long as he could not see Ramu, seemed quite satisfied that he was well hidden, though he couldn't help grumbling with anxiety, for a bear, like most animals, is afraid of man—until he discovers that man is afraid of him.

Bears, however, are also very curious—and curiosity has often led them into trouble. Slowly, inch by inch, the young bear's black snout appeared over the edge of the branch, but, immediately, the eyes came into view and met Ramu's. He drew back with a jerk and the head was once more hidden. The bear did this two or three times, and Ramu, highly amused, waited until it wasn't looking, then moved some way down the tree. When the bear looked up again and saw that the boy was missing, he was so pleased with himself that he stretched right across to the next branch, to get at a plum. Ramu chose this moment to burst into loud laughter. The startled bear tumbled out of the tree, dropped through the branches for a distance of some fifteen feet, and landed with a thud in a heap of dry leaves.

And then several things happened almost at the same time.

The mother bear came charging into the clearing. Spotting Ramu in the tree, she reared up on her hind legs, grunting fiercely. It was Ramu's turn to be startled. There are few animals as dangerous as a rampaging mother bear, and the boy knew that one blow from her clawed forepaws could rip his skull open.

But before the bear could approach the tree, there was a tremendous roar, and the tiger bounded into the clearing. He had been asleep in the bushes not far away—he liked a good sleep after a heavy meal—and the noise in the clearing had woken him.

He was in a very bad temper, and his loud 'A—oonh!' made his displeasure quite clear. The bears turned and ran from the clearing, the youngster squealing with fright.

The tiger then came into the centre of the clearing, looked up at the trembling boy, and roared again.

Ramu nearly fell out of the tree.

'Good day to you, Uncle,' he stammered, showing his teeth in a nervous grin.

Perhaps this was too much for the tiger. With a low growl, he turned his back on the mahua tree and padded off into the jungle, his tail twitching in disgust.

◆

That night, when Ramu told his parents and grandfather about the tiger and how it had saved him from a female bear, a number of stories were told about tigers, some of whom had been gentlemen, others rogues. Sooner or later the conversation came round to man-eaters, and Grandfather told two stories, which he swore were true, though the others only half believed him.

The first story concerned the belief that a man-eating tiger is guided towards his next victim by the spirit of a human being previously killed and eaten by the tiger. Grandfather said that he actually knew three hunters who sat up in a *machan* over a human kill, and when the tiger came, the corpse sat up and pointed with his right hand at the men in the tree. The tiger then went away. But the hunters knew he would return, and one man was brave enough to get down from the tree and tie the right arm of the corpse to the body. Later, when the tiger returned, the corpse sat up and pointed out the men with his left hand. The enraged tiger sprang into the tree and killed his enemies in the machan.

'And then there was a bania,' said Grandfather, beginning another story,. 'who lived in a village in the jungle. He wanted to visit a neighbouring village to collect some money that was owed him, but as the road lay through heavy forest, in which lived a terrible man-eating tiger, he did not know what to do. Finally, he went to a sadhu who gave him two powders. By eating the first powder, he could turn into a huge tiger, capable of dealing with any other tiger in the jungle, and by eating the second he could become a bania again.

'Armed with his two powders, and accompanied by his pretty young wife, the bania set out on his journey. They had not gone far into the forest when they came upon the man-eater sitting in the middle of the road. Before swallowing the first powder, the bania told his wife to stay where she was, so that when he returned after killing the tiger, she could at once give him the second powder and enable him to resume his old shape.

'Well, the bania's plan worked, but only up to a point. He swallowed the first powder and immediately became a magnificent tiger. With a great roar, he bounded towards the man-eater, and after a brief, furious fight, killed his opponent. Then, with his jaws still dripping blood, he returned to his wife.

'The poor girl was terrified and spilt the second powder on the ground. The bania was so angry that he pounced on his wife and killed and ate her. And afterwards this terrible tiger was so enraged at not being able to become a human again that he killed and ate hundreds of people all over the country.'

'The only people he spared,' said Grandfather, with a twinkle in his eye, 'were those who owed him money. A bania never gives up a loan as lost, and the tiger still hoped that one day he might become a human again and be able to collect his dues.'

Next morning, when Ramu came back from the well that was used to irrigate his father's fields, he found a crowd of curious children surrounding a jeep and three strangers with guns. Each of the strangers had a gun, and they were accompanied by two bearers and a vast amount of provisions.

They had heard that there was a tiger in the area, and they wanted to shoot it.

One of the hunters, who looked even stranger than the others, had come all the way to India for tiger, and he had vowed that he would not leave the country without a tiger's skin in his baggage. One of his companions had said that he could buy a tiger's skin in Delhi, but the hunter did not like the idea and said he'd have nothing to do with a tiger that he hadn't shot.

These men had money to spend, and, as most of the villagers needed money badly, they were only too willing to construct a machan for the hunters. The platform, big enough to take the three men, was put up in the branches of a tall toon, or mahogany tree.

It was the only night the hunters used the machan. At the end of March, though the days are warm, the nights are still cold. The hunters had neglected to bring blankets, and by midnight their teeth were chattering. Ramu, having tied up a goat for them at the foot of the tree, made as if to go home but instead circled the area, hanging up bits and pieces of old clothing on small trees and bushes. He thought he owed that much to the tiger. He knew the wily old king of the jungle would keep well away from the goat if he thought there were humans in the vicinity. And where there are men's clothes, there will be men.

As soon as it was dark, the goat began bleating, loud enough for any self-respecting tiger to hear it, but perhaps the ruse was too obvious, or perhaps the clothes Ramu had hung out were warning enough, because the tiger did not come near the toon tree. In any case, the men in the tree soon gave themselves away.

The cold was really too much for them. A flask of brandy was produced, and passed round, and it was not long before there was more purpose to finishing the brandy than to finishing off a tiger. Silent at first, the men soon began talking in whispers, and to jungle creatures a human whisper is as telling as a trumpet call. Soon the men were quite merry, talking in loud voices. And when the first morning light crept over the forest, and Ramu and his friends came by to see if the goat still lived, they found the hunters fast asleep in the machan.

The shikaris looked surly and embarrassed when they trudged back to the village.

'No game left in these parts,' said one.

'The wrong time of the year for tiger,' said another.

'I don't know what the country's coming to,' said the third.

And complaining about the weather, the quality of cartridges, the quality of rum, and the perversity of tigers, they drove away in disgust.

It was not until the onset of summer that an event occurred which altered the hunting habits of the tiger and brought him into conflict with the villagers.

◆

There had been no rain for almost two months, and the grass had become a dry yellow. Some refugee settlers, living in an area where the forest had been cleared, were careless in putting out a fire. The tiger sniffed at the acrid smell of smoke in the air, and, wandering to the edge of the jungle, saw in the distance the dancing lights of a forest fire. As night came on, the flames grew more vivid, the smell stronger. The tiger turned and made for the jheel, where he knew he would be safe, provided he swam across to the little island in the centre.

Next morning he was on the island, which was untouched by the fire. But his surroundings had changed. The slopes of the hills were black with burnt grass, and most of the tall bamboo had disappeared. The deer and the wild pig, finding that their natural cover had gone, fled further east.

The tiger prowled throughout the smoking forest but he found no game. Once he came across the body of a burnt rabbit, but he could not eat it. He drank at the jheel and settled down in a shady spot to sleep the day away. Perhaps, by evening, some of the animals would return. If not, he too would have to look for new hunting grounds—or new game.

The tiger had not eaten for five days and he was so hungry that he had been forced to scratch about in the grass and leaves for worms and beetles. This was a sad comedown for the king of the jungle. But even now he hesitated to leave the area, for he had a deep suspicion and fear of the forests further south and east—forests that were fast being swallowed up by human habitation. He could have gone north, into the hills, but they did not provide him with the long grass he needed. A panther could manage quite well in the hills, but not a tiger who loved the natural privacy of heavy jungle. In the hills, he would have to hide all the time.

At break of day, the tiger came to the jheel. The water was now shallow and muddy, and a green scum had spread over the top. But the water was still drinkable, and the tiger had quenched his thirst.

He lay down across his favourite rock, hoping for a deer, but none approached. He was about to get up and go away when he heard the warning chatter of a lone langur. Some animal was definitely approaching.

The tiger at once dropped flat on the ground, his tawny skin merging with the dry grass. A heavy animal was moving through the bushes, and the tiger waited patiently until a buffalo emerged and came to the water. The buffalo was alone.

He was a big male buffalo, and his long curved horns lay right back across his shoulders. He moved leisurely towards the water, completely unaware of the tiger's presence.

The tiger hesitated before making his charge. It was a long time—many years—since he had killed a buffalo, and he knew the villagers would not like it. But hunger helped him to overcome his caution. There was no morning breeze, everything was still, and the smell of the tiger did not carry to the buffalo. The monkey still chattered in a nearby tree, but his warning went unheeded.

Moving at a crouch, the tiger skirted the edge of the jheel and approached the buffalo from the rear. The water birds, who were used to the presence of both animals, did not raise an alarm.

Getting closer, the tiger glanced around to see if there were men, or other buffaloes, in the vicinity. Then, satisfied that he was alone, he crept forward. The buffalo was drinking, standing in shallow water at the edge of the tank, when the tiger charged from the side and bit deep into the animal's thigh.

The buffalo turned to fight, but the tendons of his right hind leg had been snapped, and he could only stagger forward a few paces. But he was not afraid. He bellowed, and lowered his horns at the tiger, but the great cat was too fast and, circling the buffalo, bit into the other hind leg.

The buffalo crashed to the ground, both hind legs crippled, and then the tiger dashed in, using both tooth and claw, biting deep into the buffalo's throat until the blood gushed out from the jugular vein.

The buffalo gave one long last bellow before dying.

The tiger, having rested, now began to gorge himself, but, even though he had been starving for days, he could not finish the buffalo. At least one good meal still remained when, satisfied and feeling his strength return, he quenched his thirst at the jheel. Then he dragged the remains of the buffalo into the bushes and went off to find a place to sleep. He would return to the kill when he was hungry.

The villagers were upset when they discovered that a buffalo was missing, and next day, when Ramu and Shyam came running home to say that they had found the carcass near the jheel, half-eaten by the tiger, the men were disturbed and angry. They felt that the tiger had tricked and deceived them. And they knew that once he found he could kill buffaloes quite easily, he would make a habit of it.

Kundan Singh, Shyam's father, and the owner of the dead buffalo, said he would go after the tiger himself.

'It is all very well to talk about what you will do to the tiger,' said his wife, 'but you should never have let the buffalo go off on its own.'

'He had been out on his own before,' said Kundan. 'This is the first time the tiger has attacked one of our beasts. A shaitan—a devil—has entered the Maharaj.'

'He must have been very hungry,' said Shyam.

'Well, we are hungry too,' said Kundan. 'Our best buffalo—the only male in our herd—'

'The tiger will kill again,' said Ramu's father.

'If we let him,' said Kundan. 'Should we send for the shikaris?'

'No. They were not clever. The tiger will escape them easily. And, besides, there is no time. The tiger will return for another meal tonight. We must finish him off ourselves!'

'But how?'

Kundan Singh smiled secretively, played with the ends of his moustache for a few moments, and then, with great pride, produced from under his cot a double-barrelled gun of ancient vintage.

'My father bought it from an Englishman,' he said.

'How long ago was that?'

'At the time I was born.'

'And have you ever used it?' asked Ramu's father, who was not sure that the gun would work.

'Well, some years back, I let it off at some bandits. You remember the time when those dacoits raided our village? They chose the wrong village, and were severely beaten for their pains. As they left, I fired my gun off at them, and as a result they didn't stop running until they had crossed the Ganga!'

'Yes, but did you hit anyone?'

'I would have, if someone's goat hadn't got in the way at the last moment. But we had roast mutton that night! Don't worry, brother, I know how the thing works. It takes a fistful of powder and bullets the size of pigeon's eggs!'

Accompanied by Ramu's father and some others, Kundan set out for the jheel, where, without shifting the buffalo's carcass—for they knew the tiger would not come near them if it suspected a trap—they made another machan in a tall tree some thirty feet from the kill.

Later that evening—at the 'hour of cow-dust', Kundan Singh and Ramu's father settled down for the night on their crude tree platform.

Several hours passed, and nothing but a jackal was seen by the watchers. And then, just as the moon came up over the distant hills, Kundan and his companion were startled by a low 'A—oonh', followed by a suppressed, rumbling growl.

Kundan grasped his old gun, while his friend drew closer to him for comfort. There was complete silence for a minute or two—a time that was an agony of suspense for the watchers—and then there was the sound of a stealthy footfall on some dead leaves under the tree.

A moment later the tiger walked out into the moonlight and stood over his kill.

At first Kundan could do nothing. He was completely overawed by the size of this magnificent tiger. Ramu's father had to nudge him, and then Kundan quickly put the gun to his shoulder, aimed at the tiger's head, and pressed the trigger.

The gun went off with a flash and a tremendous roar, but the bullet only singed the tiger's shoulder.

The enraged animal rushed at the tree and tried to leap into its branches. Fortunately the machan had been built at a safe height, and the tiger, unable to reach it, roared twice, and then bounded off into the forest.

'What a tiger!' exclaimed Kundan, half in fear and half in admiration. 'I feel as though my liver has turned to water.'

'You missed him completely,' said Ramu's father. 'Your gun makes a big noise, but an arrow would have been more accurate.'

'I did not miss him,' said Kundan, feeling offended. 'You heard him roar, didn't you? He would not have been so angry if he had not been hit. If I have wounded him badly, he will die.'

'And if you have wounded him slightly, he may turn into a man-eater, and then where will we be?'

'I don't think he will come back,' said Kundan. 'He will leave these forests.'

They waited until the sun was up before coming down from the tree. They found a few drops of blood on the dry grass, but no trail led into the forest, and Ramu's father was convinced that the wound was only a slight one.

The bullet, missing the fatal spot behind the ear, had only grazed the back of the skull and cut a deep groove at its base.

It took a few days to heal, and during this time the tiger

lay low and did not go near the jheel except when it was very dark and he was very thirsty. The villagers thought the tiger had gone away, and Ramu and Shyam—accompanied by some other youths, and always carrying sticks and axes—began bringing the buffaloes to the tank again during the day; but they were careful not to let any of them stray far from the herd, and they returned home while it was still daylight.

While the buffaloes wallowed in the muddy water, and the boys wrestled on their grassy islet, a tawny eagle circled high above them, looking for a meal—a sure sign that some of the animals were beginning to return to the forest. It was not long before his keen eyes detected a movement in the glade below.

What the eagle saw was a baby hare, a small fluffy thing, its long pink-tinted ears laid flat along its sides. Had it not been creeping along between two large stones, it would have escaped notice. The eagle waited to see if the mother was about, and even as he waited he realized that he was not the only one who coveted this juicy hare. From the bushes there had appeared a sinuous yellow creature, pressed low to the ground and moving rapidly towards the hare. It was a yellow jungle cat, hardly noticeable in the scorched grass. With great stealth and artistry the jungle cat stalked the baby hare.

He pounced. The hare's squeal was cut short by the cat's cruel claws, but it had been heard by the mother hare, who now bounded into the glade and without the slightest hesitation attacked the surprised cat.

There was nothing haphazard about the hare's attack. She flashed around behind the cat and jumped clean over it. As she landed, she kicked back, sending a stinging jet of dust shooting into the cat's face. She did this again and again.

The bewildered cat, crouching and snarling, picked up the

kill and tried to run away with it. But the hare would not permit this. She continued her leaping and buffeting till eventually the cat, out of sheer frustration, dropped the kill and attacked the mother.

The cat sprang at the hare a score of times, lashing out with its claws, but the mother hare was both clever and agile enough to keep just out of reach of those terrible claws, and drew the cat further and further away from her baby—for she did not as yet know that it was dead.

The tawny eagle saw his chance. Swift and true, he swooped.

For a brief moment, as his wings overspread the furry little hare and his talons sank deep into it, he caught a glimpse of the cat racing towards him and the mother hare fleeing into the bushes. And then, with a shrill 'kee-ee-ee' of triumph, he rose and whirled away with his dinner.

The boys had heard this shrill cry and looked up just in time to see the eagle flying over the jheel with the small hare held firmly in its talons.

'Poor hare,' said Shyam. 'Its life was short.'

'That's the law of the jungle,' said Ramu. 'The eagle has a family too, and must feed it.'

'I wonder if we are any better than animals,' said Shyam.

'Perhaps we are a little better,' said Ramu. 'Grandfather always says, "To be able to laugh and to be merciful are the only things that make man better than the beast".'

◆

The next day, while the boys were taking the herd home, one of the buffaloes lagged behind. Ramu did not know the animal was missing until he heard her agonized bellow. He glanced over his shoulder just in time to see the big striped tiger dragging the buffalo into a clump of young bamboo. At the same time the herd became aware of the danger, and the buffaloes snorted with fear as they hurried along the forest path. To urge them forward, and to warn his friends, Ramu cupped his hands to his mouth and gave vent to a yodelling call.

The buffaloes bellowed, the boys shouted, and the birds flew shrieking from the trees. It was almost a stampede by the time the herd emerged from the forest. The villagers heard the thunder of hoofs, and saw the herd coming home in dust and confusion, and knew that something was wrong. 'The tiger!' shouted Ramu. 'He is here! He has killed one of the buffaloes.'

'He is afraid of us no longer,' said Shyam.

'Did you see where he went?' asked Kundan Singh, hurrying up to them.

'I remember the place,' said Ramu. 'He dragged the buffalo in amongst the bamboo.'

'Then there is no time to lose,' said his father.

'Kundan, you take your gun and two men, and wait near the suspension bridge, where the Garur stream joins the Ganga. The jungle narrows there. We will beat the jungle from our side, and drive the tiger towards you. He will not escape us, unless he swims the river!'

'Good!' said Kundan, running into his house for his gun, with Shyam close at his heels. 'Was it one of our buffaloes again?' he asked.

'It was Ramu's buffalo this time,' said Shyam, 'A good milk buffalo.'

'Then Ramu's father will beat the jungle thoroughly. You boys had better come with me. It will not be safe for you to accompany the beaters.'

◆

And so, Kundan Singh carrying his gun and accompanied by Ramu, Shyam and two men, headed for the river junction, while Ramu's father collected about twenty men from the village and, guided by one of the boys who had been with Ramu, made for the spot where the tiger had killed the buffalo.

The tiger was still eating when he heard the men coming. He had not expected to be disturbed so soon. With an angry 'Whoof!' he bounded into the bamboo thicket and watched the men through a screen of leaves and tall grass.

The men did not seem to take much notice of the dead buffalo, but gathered round their leader and held a consultation. Most of them carried hand drums which hung down to their waists by shoulder-straps. They also carried sticks, spears and axes.

After a hurried conversation, they turned to face the jungle and began beating their drums with the palms of their hands.

Some of the men banged empty kerosene tins. These made even more noise than the drums.

The tiger did not like the noise and retreated further into the jungle. But he was surprised to find that the men, instead of going away, came after him into the jungle, banging away on their drums and tins, and shouting at the top of their voices. They had separated now, and advanced singly or in pairs, but nowhere were they more than fifteen yards apart. The tiger could easily have broken through this slowly advancing semicircle of men—one swift blow from his paw would have felled the strongest of them—but his main aim was to get away from the noise. He hated and feared the noise made by men.

He was not a man-eater and he would not attack a man unless he was very angry or very frightened or very desperate; and he was none of these things as yet. He had eaten well, and he would like to rest in peace—but there would be no rest for any animal until the men had gone with their tremendous clatter and din.

For an hour Ramu's father and the others beat the jungle, calling, drumming and trampling the undergrowth. The tiger had no rest. Whenever he was able to put some distance between himself and the men, he would sink down in some shady spot to rest, but, within five or ten minutes, the trampling and drumming would sound nearer, and the tiger, with an angry snarl, would get up and pad silently north along the narrowing strip of jungle, towards the junction of the Garur stream and the Ganga. Ten years back, he would have had the jungle on his right in which to hide; but the trees had been felled long ago, to make way for more humans, and now he could only move to the left, towards the river.

It was about noon when the tiger finally appeared in the open. He longed for the darkness and security of the night, for the sun was his enemy. Kundan and the boys had a clear view of him as he stalked slowly along, now in the open with the sun glinting on his glossy side, now in the shade, or passing through the shorter reeds. He was still out of range of Kundan's gun, but there was no fear of his getting out of the beat, as the 'stops' were all picked men from the village. He disappeared among some bushes but soon reappeared to retrace his steps, the beaters having done their work well. He was now only one hundred and fifty yards from the rocks where Kundan Singh waited, and he looked very big.

◆

The beat had closed in, and his exit along the bank downstream was completely blocked; so the tiger turned into a belt of reeds, and Kundan Singh expected that his head would soon peer out of the cover a few yards away. The beaters were now making a great noise, shouting and beating their drums, but nothing moved, and Ramu, watching from a distance, wondered, 'Has he slipped through the beaters?' And hoped he had.

Tins clashed, drums beat, and some of the men poked into the reeds with their spears or long bamboos. Perhaps one of these thrusts found a mark, because at last the tiger was roused, and with an angry, desperate snarl he charged out of the reeds, splashing his way through an inlet of mud and water.

Kundan Singh fired, and his bullet struck the tiger on the thigh.

The mighty animal stumbled; but he was up in a minute, and, rushing through a gap in the narrowing line of beaters, he made straight for the only way across the river—the suspension bridge that passed over the Ganga here, providing a route into the high hills beyond.

'We'll get him now,' said Kundan, priming his gun again. 'He's right in the open!'

The suspension bridge swayed and trembled as the wounded tiger lurched across it. Kundan fired, and this time the bullet hit the tiger on the shoulder. The animal bounded forward, lost his footing on the unfamiliar, slippery planks of the swaying bridge, and went over the side, falling headlong into the strong, swirling waters of the river.

He rose to the surface once, but the current took him under and away, and only a thin streak of blood remained on the river's surface.

Kundan and the others hurried downstream to see if the dead tiger had been washed up on the river's banks; but though they searched the riverside for several miles, they did not find the tiger. The river had taken him to its bosom. He had not provided anyone with a trophy. His skin would not be spread on a couch, nor would his head be hung upon a wall. No claw of his would be hung as a charm around the neck of a child. No villager would use his fat as a cure for rheumatism.

◆

At first the villagers were glad because they felt their buffaloes were safe. Then the men began to feel that something had gone out of their lives, out of the life of the forest; they began to feel that the forest was no longer a forest. It had been shrinking year after year, but, as long as the tiger had been there and the villagers had heard it roar at night, they had known that they were still secure from the intruders and newcomers who came to fell the trees and eat up the land and let the floodwaters into the village. But, now that the tiger had gone, it was as though a protector had gone, leaving the forest open and vulnerable, easily destroyable. And, once the forest was destroyed, they too would be in danger…

There was another thing that had gone with the tiger, another thing that had been lost, a thing that was being lost everywhere—something called 'nobility'.

Ramu remembered something that his grandfather had once said, 'The tiger is the very soul of India, and when the last tiger has gone, so will the soul of the country.'

The boys lay flat on their stomachs on their little mud island and watched the monsoon clouds gathering overhead.

'The king of our forest is dead,' said Shyam. 'There are no more tigers.'

'There must be tigers,' said Ramu. 'How can there be an India without tigers?'

The river had carried the tiger many miles away from its

home, from the forest it had always known, and brought it ashore on a strip of warm yellow sand, where it lay in the sun, quite still but breathing.

Vultures gathered and waited at a distance, some of them perching on the branches of nearby trees.

But the tiger was more drowned than hurt, and as the river water oozed out of his mouth, and the warm sun made new life throb through his body, he stirred and stretched, and his glazed eyes came into focus. Raising his head, he saw trees and tall grass.

Slowly he heaved himself off the ground and moved at a crouch to where the grass waved in the afternoon breeze. Would he be harried again, and shot at? There was no smell of Man. The tiger moved forward with greater confidence.

There was, however, another smell in the air—a smell that reached back to the time when he was young and fresh and full of vigour—a smell that he had almost forgotten but could never quite forget—the smell of a tigress!

He raised his head high, and new life surged through his tired limbs. He gave a full-throated roar and moved purposefully through the tall grass. And the roar came back to him, calling him, calling him forward—a roar that meant there would be more tigers in the land.

WILD FRUIT

It was a long walk to school. Down the hill, through the rhododendron trees, across a small stream, around a bare, brown hill, and then through the narrow little bazaar, past fruit stalls piled high with oranges, guavas, bananas and apples.

The boy's gaze often lingered on those heaps of golden oranges—oranges grown in the plains, now challenging the pale winter sunshine in the hills. His nose twitched at the sharp smell of melons in summer; his fingers would sometimes touch for a moment the soft down on the skin of a peach. But these were forbidden fruit. The boy hadn't the money for them.

He took one meal at seven in the morning when he left home; another at seven in the evening when he returned from school. There were times— especially when he was at school, and his teacher droned on and on, lecturing on honesty, courage, duty and self-sacrifice—when he felt very hungry; but on the way to school, or on the way home, there was nearly always the prospect of some wild fruit.

The boy's name was Vijay, and he belonged to a village near Mussoorie. His parents tilled a few narrow terraces on the hill slopes. They grew potatoes, onions, barley, maize; barely enough to feed themselves. When greens were scarce, they boiled the tops of the stinging-nettle and made them into a dish resembling spinach.

Vijay's parents realized the importance of sending him to school, and it didn't cost them much, except for the books. But it was all of four miles to the town, and a long walk makes a boy hungry.

But there was nearly always the wild fruit. The purple berries of the thorny bilberry bushes, ripening in May and June. Wild strawberries, growing in shady places like spots of blood on the deep green monsoon grass. Small, sour cherries, and tough medlars. Vijay's strong teeth and probing tongue extracted whatever tang or sweetness lay hidden in them. And in March there were the rhododendron flowers.

His mother made them into jam. But Vijay liked them as they were. He placed the petals on his tongue and chewed them till the sweet juice trickled down his throat. But in November, there was no wild fruit. Only acorns on the oak trees, and they were bitter, fit only for the monkeys.

He walked confidently through the bazaar, strong in the legs. He looked a healthy boy, until you came up close and saw the patches on his skin and the dullness in his eyes.

He passed the fruit stalls, wondering who ate all that fruit, and what happened to the fruit that went bad; he passed the sweet shop, where hot, newly-fried *jelabies* lay protected like twisted orange jewels in a glass case, and where a fat, oily man raised a knife and plunged it deep into a thick slab of rich amber-coloured *halwa*.

The saliva built up in Vijay's mouth; there was a dull ache in his stomach. But his eyes gave away nothing of the sharp pangs he felt.

And now, a confectioner's shop. Glass jars filled with chocolates, peppermints, toffees—sweets he didn't know the names of, English sweets—wrapped up in bits of coloured paper.

A boy had just bought a bag of sweets. He had one in his mouth. He was a well-dressed boy; coins jingled in his pocket. The sweet moved from one cheek to the other. He bit deep into it, and Vijay heard the crunch and looked up. The boy smiled at Vijay, but moved away.

They met again, further along the road. Once again the boy smiled, even looked as though he was about to offer Vijay a sweet; but this time, Vijay shyly looked away. He did not want it to appear that he had noticed the sweets, or that he hungered for one.

But he kept meeting the boy, who always managed to reappear at some corner, sucking a sweet, moving it about in his mouth, letting it show between his wet lips—a sticky green thing, temptingly, lusciously beautiful.

The bag of sweets was nearly empty.

Reluctantly, Vijay decided that he must overtake the boy, forget all about the sweets, and hurry home. Otherwise, he would be tempted to grab the bag and run!

And then, he saw the boy leave the bag on a bench, look at him once, and smile—smile shyly and invitingly—before moving away.

Was the bag empty? Vijay wondered with mounting excitement. It couldn't be, or it would have blown away almost immediately. Obviously, there were still a few sweets in it. The boy had disappeared. He had gone for his tea, and Vijay could have the rest of the sweets.

Vijay took the bag and jammed it into a pocket of his shirt. Then he hurried homewards. It was getting late, and he wanted to be home before dark.

As soon as he was out of the town, he opened the bag and shook the sweets out. Their red wrappers glowed like rubies in the palm of his hand.

Carefully, he undid a wrapper.

There was no sweet inside, only a smooth, round stone.

Vijay found stones in all the wrappers. In his mind's eye, Vijay saw the smiling face of the boy in the bazaar: a boy who smiled sweetly but exchanged stones for sweets.

Forcing back angry tears, Vijay flung the stones down the hillside. Then he shouldered his bag of books and began the long walk home.

There were patches of snow on the ground. The grass was a dirty brown, the bushes were bare.

There is no wild fruit in November.

RANJI'S WONDERFUL BAT

'How's that!' shouted the wicketkeeper, holding the ball up in his gloves.

'How's that!' echoed the slip fielders.

'How?' growled the fast bowler, glaring at the umpire.

'Out!' said the umpire.

And Suraj, the captain of the school team, was walking slowly back to the pavilion—which was really a toolshed at the end of the field.

The score stood at 53 runs for 4 wickets. Another 60 runs had to be made for victory, and only one good batsman remained. All the rest were bowlers who couldn't be expected to make many runs.

It was Ranji's turn to bat.

He was the youngest member of the team, only eleven, but sturdy and full of pluck. As he walked briskly to the wicket, his unruly black hair was blown about by a cool breeze that came down from the hills.

Ranji had a good eye and strong wrists, and had made lots of runs in some of the minor matches. But in the last two inter-school games, his scores had been poor, the highest being 12 runs. Today he was determined to make enough runs to take his side to victory.

Ranji took his guard and prepared to face the bowler.

The fielders moved closer, in anticipation of another catch. The tall fast bowler scowled and began his long run. His arm whirled over, and the hard, shiny red ball came hurtling towards Ranji.

Ranji was going to lunge forward and play the ball back to the bowler, but at the last moment he changed his mind and stepped back, intending to push the ball through the ring of fielders on his right or offside.

'How's that!' screamed the bowler, hopping about like a kangaroo.

'How?' shouted the wicketkeeper.

The umpire slowly raised a finger.

'Out,' he said.

'Never mind,' said Suraj, patting Ranji on the back. 'You'll do better next time. You're out of form just now, that's all.'

'You'll have to make more runs in the next game,' he told Ranji, 'or you'll lose your place in the side!'

Avoiding the other players, Ranji slowly walked homewards, his head down, his hands in his pockets. He was very upset. He had been trying so hard and practising so regularly, but when an important game came along he failed to make a big score. It seemed that there was nothing he could do about it. But he loved playing cricket, and he couldn't bear the thought of being out of the school team.

On his way home he had to pass the clock tower, where he often stopped at Mr Kumar's Sports Shop, to chat with the owner or look at all the things on the shelves: footballs, cricket balls, badminton rackets, hockey sticks, balls of various shapes and sizes—it was a wonderland where Ranji liked to linger every day.

But this was one day when he didn't feel like stopping. He

looked the other way and was about to cross the road when Mr Kumar's voice stopped him.

'Hello, Ranji! Off in a hurry today? And why are you looking so sad?'

So Ranji had to stop and say namaste. He couldn't ignore Mr Kumar, who had always been so kind and helpful, often giving him advice on how to bowl in different styles. Mr Kumar had been a state-level player once, and had scored a century in a match against Tanzania. Now he liked encouraging young players and he thought Ranji would make a good cricketer.

'What's the trouble?' he asked as Ranji stepped into the shop. Because Mr Kumar was so friendly, the sports merchandise also seemed friendly. The bats and balls and shuttlecocks all seemed to want to be helpful.

'We lost the match,' said Ranji.

'Never mind,' said Mr Kumar. 'Where would we be without losers? There wouldn't be any games without them—no cricket or football or hockey or tennis! No carom or marbles. No sports shop for me! Anyway, how many runs did you make?'

'None, I made a big, round egg.'

Mr Kumar rested his hand on Ranji's shoulder. 'Never mind. All good players have a bad day now and then.'

'But I haven't made a good score in my last three matches,' said Ranji. 'I'll be dropped from the team if I don't do something in the next game.'

'Well, we can't have that happening,' mused Mr Kumar. 'Something will have to be done about it.'

'I'm just unlucky,' said Ranji.

'Maybe, maybe... But in that case, it's time your luck changed.'

'It's too late now,' said Ranji.

'Nonsense. It's never too late. Now, you just come with me to the back of the shop and I'll see if I can do something about your luck.'

Puzzled, Ranji followed Mr Kumar through the curtained partition at the back of the shop. He found himself in a badly-lit room stacked to the ceiling with all kinds of old and second-hand sporting goods—torn football bladders, broken bats, rackets without strings, broken darts, and tattered badminton nets. Mr Kumar began examining a number of old cricket bats, and after a few minutes he said, 'Ah!' Picking up one of the bats, he held it out to Ranji.

'This is it!' he said. 'This is the luckiest of all my old bats. This is the bat I made a century with!' He gave it a twirl and started hitting an imaginary ball to all corners of the room.

'Of course it's an old bat, but it hasn't lost any of its magic,' said Mr Kumar, pausing in his stroke-making to recover his breath. He held it out to Ranji. 'Here, take it!' I'll lend it to you for the rest of the cricket season. You won't fail with this with you.'

Ranji took the bat and looked at it with awe and delight.

'Is it really the bat you made a century with?' he asked.

'It is,' said Mr Kumar. 'And it may get you a hundred runs too!'

Ranji spent a nervous week waiting for Saturday's match. His school team would be playing against a strong side from another town. There was a lot of classwork that week, so Ranji did not get much time to practise with the other boys. As he had no brothers or sisters he asked Koki, the girl next door, to bowl to him in the garden. Koki bowled quite well, but Ranji liked to hit the ball hard—'just to get used to the bat,' he told her—and she soon got tired of chasing the ball all over the garden.

At last Saturday arrived, bright and sunny and just right for cricket.

Suraj won the toss for the school and chose batting first.

The opening batsmen put on 30 runs without being separated. The visiting fast bowlers couldn't do much. Then the spin bowlers came on, and immediately there was a change in the game. Two wickets fell in one over, and the score was 33 for 2. Suraj made a few quick runs, then he too was out to one of the spinners, caught behind the wicket. The next batsman was clean bowled—46 for 4—and it was Ranji's turn to bat.

He walked slowly to the wicket. The fielders crowded around him. He took guard and prepared for the first ball.

The bowler took a short run and then the ball was twirling towards Ranji, looking as though it would spin away from his bat as he leaned forward into his stroke.

And then a thrill ran through Ranji's arm as he felt the ball meet the springy willow of the bat.

Crack!

The ball, hit firmly with the middle of Ranji's bat, streaked past the helpless bowler and sped towards the boundary. Four runs!

The bowler was annoyed, with the result that his next ball was a loose full toss. Ranji swung it to the onside boundary for another four.

And that was only the beginning. Now, Ranji began to play all the strokes he knew: late cuts and square cuts, straight drives, on drives and off drives. The rival captain tried all his bowlers, fast and spin, but none of them could remove Ranji. Instead, he sent the fielders scampering to all corners of the field.

By the lunch break he had scored 40 runs. And twenty minutes after lunch, when Suraj closed the innings, Ranji was not out with 58.

The rival team was bowled out for a poor score, and Ranji's school won the match.

On his way home, Ranji stopped at Mr Kumar's shop to give him the good news.

'We won!' he said. 'And I made 58—my highest score so far. It really is a lucky bat!'

'I told you so,' said Mr Kumar, giving Ranji a warm handshake. 'There will be bigger scores yet.'

Ranji went home in high spirits. He was so pleased that he stopped at the Jumma Sweet Shop and bought two laddus for Koki. She was crazy about laddus.

Mr Kumar was right. It was only the beginning of Ranji's success with the bat. In the next game he scored 40, and was out when he grew careless and allowed himself to be stumped by the wicketkeeper. The game that followed was a two-day match, and Ranji, who was now batting at Number 3, made 45 runs. He hit a number of boundaries before being caught. In the second innings, when the school team needed only 6 runs for victory, Ranji was batting at 25 when the winning runs were hit.

Everyone was pleased with him—his coach, his captain, Suraj, and Mr Kumar—but only one knew about the lucky bat. That was a secret between Ranji and Mr Kumar.

One evening, during an informal game on the maidan, Ranji's friend Bhim slipped while running after the ball, and cut his hand on a sharp stone. Ranji took him to a doctor near the clock tower, where the wound was washed and bandaged. As it was getting late, he decided to go straight home. Usually he walked, but that evening he caught a bus near the clock tower.

When he got home, his mother brought him a cup of tea, and while he was drinking it, Koki walked in, and the first thing she said was, 'Ranji, where's your bat?'

'Oh, I must have left it at the maidan when Bhim got hurt,' said Ranji, starting up and spilling his tea. 'I'd better go and get it now, or it will disappear.'

'You can fetch it tomorrow,' said his mother. 'It's getting dark.'

'I'll take a torch,' said Ranji.

He was worried about the bat.

Without it, his luck might desert him.

He hadn't the patience to wait for a bus, and ran all the way to the maidan.

The maidan was deserted, and there was no sign of the bat. And then Ranji remembered that he'd had it with him on the bus, after saying goodbye to Bhim at the clock tower. He must have left it on the bus!

Well, he'd never find it now. The bat was lost forever. And on Saturday Ranji's school would be playing their last and most important match of the cricket season against a public school team from Delhi.

Next day he was at Mr Kumar's shop, looking very sorry for himself.

'What's the matter?' asked Mr Kumar.

'I've lost the bat,' said Ranji. 'Your lucky bat. The one I made all my runs with! I left it in the bus. And the day after tomorrow we are playing the Delhi school, and I'll be out for a duck, and we'll lose our chance of being the champion school.'

Mr Kumar looked a little anxious at first; then he smiled and said, 'You can still make all the runs you want.'

'But I don't have the bat any more,' said Ranji.

'Any bat will do,' said Mr Kumar.

'What do you mean?'

'I mean it's the batsman and not the bat that matters. Shall I tell you something? That old bat I gave you was no different from any other bat I've used. True, I made a lot of runs with it, but I made runs with other bats too. A bat has magic only when the batsman has magic! What you needed was confidence, not a bat. And by believing in the bat, you got your confidence back!'

'What's confidence?' asked Ranji. It was a new word for him.

'Confidence,' said Mr Kumar slowly, 'confidence is knowing you are good.'

'And I can be good without the bat?'

'Of course. You have always been good. You are good now. You will be good the day after tomorrow. Remember that. If you remember it, you'll make the runs.'

On Saturday, Ranji walked to the wicket with a bat borrowed from Bhim.

The school team had lost its first wicket with only two runs on the board. Ranji went in at this stage. The Delhi school's opening bowler was sending down some really fast ones. Ranji faced up to him.

The first ball was very fast but it wasn't on a good length. Quick on his feet, Ranji stepped back and pulled it hard to the onside boundary. The ball soared over the heads of the fielders and landed with a crash in a crate full of cold drink bottles.

A six! Everyone stood up and cheered.

And it was only the beginning of Ranji's wonderful innings.

The match ended in a draw, but Ranji's 75 was the talk of the school.

On his way home he bought a dozen laddus. Six for Koki and six for Mr Kumar.

AND NOW WE ARE TWELVE

People often ask me why I've chosen to live in Mussoorie for so long—almost forty years without any significant breaks.

'I forgot to go away,' I tell them, but of course, that isn't the real reason.

The people here are friendly, but then people are friendly in a great many other places. The hills, the valleys are beautiful; but they are just as beautiful in Kulu or Kumaon.

'This is where the family has grown up and where we all live,' I say, and those who don't know me are puzzled because the general impression of the writer is of a reclusive old bachelor.

Unmarried I may be, but single I am not. Not since Prem came to live and work with me in 1970. A year later, he was married. Then his children came along and stole my heart; and when they grew up, their children came along and stole my wits. So now I'm an enchanted bachelor, head of a family of twelve. Sometimes I go out to bat, sometimes to bowl, but generally I prefer to be twelfth man, carrying out the drinks!

In the old days, when I was a solitary writer living on baked beans, the prospect of my suffering from obesity was very remote. Now there is a little more of author than there used to be, and the other day five-year-old Gautam patted me on my tummy (or balcony, as I prefer to call it) and remarked: 'Dada, you should join the WWF.'

'I'm already a member,' I said. 'I joined the World Wildlife Fund years ago.'

'Not that,' he said. 'I mean the World Wrestling Federation.'

If I have a tummy today, it's thanks to Gautam's grandfather and now his mother who, over the years, has made sure that I am well-fed and well-proportioned.

Forty years ago, when I was a lean young man, people would look at me and say, 'Poor chap, he's definitely undernourished. What on earth made him take up writing as a profession?' Now they look at me and say, 'You wouldn't think he was a writer, would you? Too well nourished!'

It was a cold, wet and windy March evening when Prem came back from the village with his wife and first-born child, then just four months old. In those days, they had to walk to the house from the bus stand; it was a half-hour walk in the cold rain, and the baby was all wrapped up when they entered the front room. Finally, I got a glimpse of him, and he of me, and it was friendship at first sight. Little Rakesh (as he was to be called) grabbed me by the nose and held on. He did not have much of a nose to grab, but he had a dimpled chin and I played with it until he smiled.

The little chap spent a good deal of his time with me during those first two years of his in Maplewood—learning to crawl, to toddle and then to walk unsteadily about the little sitting room. I would carry him into the garden, and later, up the steep gravel path to the main road. Rakesh enjoyed these little excursions, and so did I, because in pointing out trees, flowers, birds, butterflies, beetles, grasshoppers, et al., I was giving myself a chance to observe them better instead of just taking them for granted.

In particular, there was a pair of squirrels that lived in the big oak tree outside the cottage. Squirrels are rare in Mussoorie though common enough down in the valley. This couple must have come up for the summer. They became quite friendly, and although they never got around to taking food from our hands, they were soon entering the house quite freely. The sitting room window opened directly on to the oak tree whose various denizens—ranging from stag beetles to small birds and even an acrobatic bat—took to darting in and out of the cottage at various times of the day or night.

Life at Maplewood was quite idyllic, and when Rakesh's baby brother, Suresh, came into the world, it seemed we were all set for a long period of domestic bliss; but at such times tragedy is often lurking just around the corner. Suresh was just over a year old when he contracted tetanus. Doctors and hospitals were of no avail. He suffered—as any child would from this terrible affliction—and left this world before he had a chance of getting to know it. His parents were broken-hearted. And I feared for Rakesh, for he wasn't a very healthy boy, and two of his cousins in the village had already succumbed to tuberculosis.

It was to be a difficult year for me. A criminal charge was brought against me for a slightly risque story I'd written for a Bombay magazine. I had to face trial in Bombay and this involved three journeys there over a period of a year and a half, before an irate but perceptive judge found the charges baseless and gave me an honourable acquittal.

It's the only time I've been involved with the law and I sincerely hope it is the last. Most cases drag on interminably, and the main beneficiaries are the lawyers. My trial would have been much longer had not the prosecutor died of a heart attack in the middle of the proceedings. His successor did not pursue it with the same vigour. His heart was not in it. The whole issue had started with a complaint by a local politician, and when he lost interest so did the prosecution. Nevertheless the trial, once begun, had to be seen through. The defence (organized by the concerned magazine) marshalled its witnesses (which included Nissim Ezekiel and the Marathi playwright Vijay Tendulkar). I made a short speech which couldn't have been very memorable as I have forgotten it! And everyone, including the judge, was bored with the whole business. After that, I steered clear of controversy publications. I have never set out to shock the world. Telling a meaningful story was all that really mattered. And that is still the case.

I was looking forward to continuing our idyllic existence in Maplewood, but it was not to be. The powers-that-be, in the shape of the Public Works Department (PWD), had decided to build a 'strategic' road just below the cottage and without any warning to us, all the trees in the vicinity were felled (including the friendly old oak) and the hillside was rocked by explosives and bludgeoned by bulldozers. I decided it was time to move. Prem and Chandra (Rakesh's mother) wanted to move too; not because of the road, but because they associated the house with the death of little Suresh, whose presence seemed to haunt every room, every corner of the cottage. His little cries of pain and suffering still echoed through the still hours of the night.

I rented rooms at the top of Landour, a good thousand feet higher up the mountain. Rakesh was now old enough to go to school, and every morning I would walk with him down to the little convent school near the clock tower. Prem would go to fetch him in the afternoon. The walk took us about half an hour, and on the way Rakesh would ask for a story and I would have to rack my brains in order to invent one. I am not the most inventive of writers, and fantastical plots are beyond me. My forte is observation, recollection and reflection. Small boys prefer action. So I invented a leopard who suffered from acute indigestion because he'd eaten one human too many and a belt buckle was causing an obstruction.

This went down quite well until Rakesh asked me how the leopard got around the problem of the victim's clothes.

'The secret,' I said, 'is to pounce on them when their trousers are off!'

Not the stuff of which great picture books are made, but then, I've never attempted to write stories for beginners. Red Riding Hood's granny-eating wolf always scared me as a small boy, and yet parents have always found it acceptable for toddlers. Possibly they feel grannies are expendable.

Mukesh was born around this time and Savitri (Dolly) a couple of years later. When Dolly grew older, she was annoyed at having been named Savitri (my choice), which is now considered very old fashioned; so we settled for Dolly. I can understand a child's dissatisfaction with given names.

My first name was Owen, which in Welsh means 'brave'. As I am not in the least brave, I have preferred not to use it. One given name and one surname should be enough.

When my granny said, 'But you should try to be brave, otherwise how will you survive in this cruel world?' I replied: 'Don't worry, I can run very fast.'

Not that I've ever had to do much running, except when I was pursued by a lissome Australian lady who thought I'd make a good obedient husband. It wasn't so much the lady I was running from, but the prospect of spending the rest of my life in some remote cattle station in the Australian outback. Anyone who has tried to drag me away from India has always met with stout resistance.

Up on the heights of Landour lived a motley crowd. My immediate neighbours included a Frenchwoman who played the sitar (very badly) all through the night; a Spanish lady with two husbands, one of whom practised acupuncture—rather ineffectively as far as he was concerned, for he seemed to be dying of some mysterious debilitating disease. The other came and went rather mysteriously, and finally ended up in Tihar Jail, having been apprehended at Delhi airport carrying a large amount of contraband hashish.

Apart from these and a few other colourful characters, the area was inhabitated by some very respectable people, retired brigadiers, air marshals and rear admirals, almost all of whom were busy writing their memoirs. I had to read or listen to extracts from their literary efforts. This was slow torture. A few years before, I had done a stint of editing for a magazine called *Imprint.* It had involved going through hundreds of badly written manuscripts, and in some cases (friends of the owner!) rewriting some of them for publication. One of life's joys had been to throw up that particular job, and now here I was, besieged by all the top brass of the Army, Navy and Air Force, each one determined that I should read, inwardly digest, improve, and if possible find a publisher for their outpourings. Thank goodness they were all retired. I could not be shot or court-martialled. But at least two of them set their wives upon me, and these intrepid ladies would turn up around noon with my 'homework'—typescripts to read and edit! There was no escape. My own writing was of no consequence to them. I told them that I was taking sitar lessons, but they disapproved, saying I was more suited to the tabla.

When Prem discovered a set of vacant rooms further down the Landour slope, close to the school and bazaar, I rented them without hesitation. This was Ivy Cottage. Come up and see me sometimes, but leave your manuscripts behind.

When we came to Ivy Cottage in 1980, we were six, Dolly having just been born. Now, twenty-four years later, we are twelve. I think that's a reasonable expansion. The increase has been brought about by Rakesh's marriage twelve years ago, and Mukesh's marriage two years ago. Both precipitated themselves into marriage when they were barely twenty, and both were lucky. Beena and Binita, who happen to be real sisters, have brightened and enlivened our lives with their happy, positive natures and the wonderful children they have brought into the world. More about them later.

Ivy Cottage has, on the whole, been kind to us, and particularly kind to me. Some houses like their occupants, others don't. Maplewood, set in the shadow of the hill, lacked a natural cheerfulness; there was a settled gloom about the place. The house at the top of Landour was too exposed to the elements to have any sort of character. The wind moaning in the deodars may have inspired the sitar player but it did nothing for my writing. I produced very little up there.

On the other hand, Ivy Cottage—especially my little room facing the sunrise—has been conducive to creative work. Novellas, poems, essays, children's stories, anthologies, have all come tumbling on to whatever sheets of paper happen to be nearest me. As I write by hand, I have only to grab for the nearest pad, loose sheet, page-proof or envelope whenever the muse takes hold of me; which is surprisingly often.

I came here when I was nearing fifty. Now I'm seventy, and instead of drying up, as some writers do in their later years, I find myself writing with as much ease and assurance as when I was twenty. And I enjoy writing. It's not a burdensome task.

I may not have anything of earth-shattering significance to convey to the world, but in conveying my sentiments to you, dear readers, and in telling you something about my relationship with people and the natural world, I hope to bring a little pleasure and sunshine into your life.

Life isn't a bed of roses, not for any of us, and I have never had the comforts or luxuries that wealth can provide. But here I am, doing my own thing, in my own time and my own way. What more can I ask of life? Give me a big cash prize and I'd still be here. I happen to like the view from my window. And I like to have Gautam coming up to me, patting me on the tummy, and telling me that I'll make a good goalkeeper one day.

It's a Sunday morning, as I come to the conclusion of this chapter. There's bedlam in the house. Siddharth's football keeps smashing against the front door. Shrishti is practising her dance routine in the back verandah. Gautam has cut his finger and is trying his best to bandage it with Sellotape. He is, of course, the youngest of Rakesh's three musketeers, and probably the most independent-minded. Siddharth, now ten, is restless, never quite able to expend all his energy. 'Does not pay enough attention,' says his teacher. It must be hard for anyone to pay attention in a class of sixty! How does the poor teacher pay attention?

If you, dear reader, have any ambitions to be a writer, you must first rid yourself of any notion that perfect peace and quiet is the first requirement. There is no such thing as perfect peace and quiet except perhaps in a monastery or a cave in the mountains. And what would you write about, living in a cave? One should be able to write in a train, a bus, a bullock cart, in good weather or bad, on a park bench or in the middle of a noisy classroom.

Of course, the best place is the sun-drenched desk right next to my bed. It isn't always sunny here, but on a good day like this, it's ideal. The children are getting ready for school, dogs are barking in the street, and down near the water tap there's an altercation between two women with empty buckets, the tap having dried up. But these are all background noises and will subside in due course. They are not directed at me.

Hello! Here's Atish, Mukesh's little ten-month old infant, crawling over the rug, curious to know why I'm sitting on the edge of my bed scribbling away, when I should be playing with him. So I shall play with him for five minutes and then come back to this page. Giving him my time is important. After all, I won't be around when he grows up.

Half an hour later. Atish soon tired of playing with me, but meanwhile Gautam had absconded with my pen. When I asked him to return it, he asked, 'Why don't you get a computer? Then we can play games on it.'

'My pen is faster than any computer,' I tell him, 'I wrote three pages this morning without getting out of bed. And yesterday I wrote two pages sitting under Billoo's chestnut tree.'

'Until a chestnut fell on your head,' says Gautam, 'Did it hurt?'

'Only a little,' I said, putting on a brave front.

He had saved the chestnut and now he showed it to me. The smooth brown horse-chestnut shone in the sunlight.

'Let's stick it in the ground,' I said. 'Then in the spring a chestnut tree will come up.'

So we went outside and planted the chestnut on a plot of wasteland. Hopefully a small tree will burst through the earth at about the time this little book is published.

FOUR BOYS ON A GLACIER

On a day that promised rain we bundled ourselves into the bus that was to take us to Kapkote (where people lost their caps and coats, punned Anil), the starting-point of our Himalayan trek. I was seventeen at the time, and Anil and Somi were sixteen. Each of us carried a haversack, and we had also brought along a good-sized bedding-roll which, apart from blankets, contained bags of rice and flour, thoughtfully provided by Anil's mother. We had no idea how we would carry the bedding-roll once we started walking, but we didn't worry too much about details.

We were soon in the hills of Kumaon, on a winding road that took us up and up, until we saw the valley and our small town spread out beneath us, the river a silver ribbon across the plain. We took a sharp bend, the valley disappeared, and the mountains towered above us.

At Kapkote, we had refreshments and the shopkeeper told us we could spend the night in one of his rooms. The surroundings were pleasant, the hills wooded with deodars, the lower slopes planted with fresh green paddy. At night there was a wind moaning in the trees and it found its way through the cracks in the windows and eventually through our blankets.

Next morning we washed our faces at a small stream near the shop and filled our water bottles for the day's march. A boy from the nearby village approached us, and asked where we were going.

'To the glacier,' said Somi.

'I'll come with you,' said the boy. 'I know the way.'

'You're too small,' said Anil. 'We need someone who can carry our bedding-roll.'

'I'm small but I'm strong,' said the boy, who certainly looked sturdy. He had pink cheeks and a well-knit body.

'See!' he said, and, picking up a rock the size of a football, he heaved it across the stream.

'I think he can come with us,' I said.

And then, we were walking—at first above the little Sarayu River, then climbing higher along the rough mule track, always within sound of the water, which we glimpsed now and then, swift, green and bubbling.

We were at the forest rest-house by six in the evening, after covering fifteen miles. Anil found the watchman asleep in a patch of fading sunlight and roused him. The watchman, who hadn't been bothered by visitors for weeks, grumbled at our intrusion but opened a room for us. He also produced some potatoes from his store, and these were roasted for dinner.

Just as we were about to get into our beds we heard a thud on the corrugated tin roof, and then the sound of someone—or something—scrambling about on the roof. Anil, Somi and I were alarmed; but Bisnu, who was already under the blankets, merely yawned, and turned over on his side.

'It's only a bear,' he said. 'Didn't you see the pumpkins on the roof? Bears love pumpkins.'

For half an hour we had to listen to the bear as it clambered about on the roof, feasting on the watchman's ripe pumpkins. At last there was silence. Anil and I crawled out of our blankets and went to the window. And through the frosted glass we saw a black Himalayan bear ambling across the slope in front of the house.

Our next rest-house lay in a narrow valley, on the banks of the rushing Pindar River, which twisted its way through the mountains. We walked on, past terraced fields and small stone houses, until there were no more fields or houses, only forest and sun and silence.

It was different from the silence of a room or an empty street.

And then, the silence broke into sound—the sound of the river.

Far down in the valley, the Pindar tumbled over itself in its impatience to reach the plains. We began to run; slipped and stumbled, but continued running.

The rest-house stood on a ledge just above the river, and the sound of the water rushing down the mountain-defile could be heard at all times. The sound of the birds, which we had grown used to, was drowned by the sound of the water, but the birds themselves could be seen, many-coloured, standing out splendidly against the dark green forest foliage—the red crowned jay, the paradise flycatcher, the purple whistling thrush and others we could not recognize.

Higher up the mountain, above some terraced land where oats and barley were grown, stood a small cluster of huts. This, we were told by the watchman, was the last village on the way to the glacier. It was, in fact, one of the last villages in India, because if we crossed the difficult passes beyond the glacier, we would find ourselves in Tibet.

Anil asked the watchman about the Abominable Snowman. The Nepalese believe in the existence of the Snowman, and our watchman was Nepalese.

'Yes, I have seen the yeti,' he told us. 'A great shaggy, flat-footed creature. In the winter, when it snows heavily, he passes the bungalow at night. I have seen his tracks the next morning.'

'Does he come this way in the summer?' asked Somi, anxiously.

'No,' said the watchman. 'But sometimes I have seen the *lidini.* You have to be careful of her.'

'And who is the *lidini?*' asked Anil.

'She is the snow-woman, and far more dangerous. She has the same height as the yeti—about seven feet when her back is straight—and her hair is much longer. Also she has very long teeth. Her feet face inwards, but she can run very fast, especially downhill. If you see a lidini, and she chases you, always run in an uphill direction. She tires quickly because of her crooked feet. But when running downhill she has no trouble at all, and you want to be very fast to escape her!'

'Well, we are quite fast,' said Anil with a nervous laugh. 'But its just a fairy-story, I don't believe a word of it.'

The watchman was most offended, and refused to tell us anything more about snowmen and snow-women. But he helped Bisnu make a fire, and presented us with a black, sticky sweet, which we ate with relish.

It was a fine, sunny morning when we set out to cover the last seven miles to the glacier. We had expected a stiff climb, but the rest-house was 11,000 feet above sea-level, and the rest of the climb was fairly gradual.

Suddenly, abruptly, there were no more trees. As the bungalow dropped out of sight, the trees and bushes gave way to short grass and little pink and blue alpine flowers. The snow peaks were close now, ringing us in on every side. We passed white waterfalls, cascading hundreds of feet down precipitous rock faces, thundering into the little river. A great white eagle hovered over us.

The hill fell away, and there, confronting us, was a great white field of snow and ice, cradled between two shining peaks. We were speechless for several minutes. Then we proceeded cautiously on to the snow, supporting each other on the slippery surface. We could not go far, because we were quite unequipped for any high-altitude climbing. But it was a satisfying feeling to know that we were the only young men from our town who had walked so far and so high.

The sun was reflected sharply from the snow and we felt surprisingly warm. It was delicious to feel the sun crawling over our bodies, sinking deep into our bones. Meanwhile, almost imperceptibly, clouds had covered some of the peaks, and white mist drifted down the mountain slopes. It was time to return: we would barely make it to the bungalow before it grew dark.

We took our time returning to Kapkote; stopped by the Sarayu River; bathed with the village boys we had seen on the way up; collected strawberries and ferns and wild flowers; and finally said goodbye to Bisnu.

Anil wanted to take Bisnu along with us, but the boy's parents refused to let him go, saying that he was too young for the life of a city.

'Never mind,' said Somi. 'We'll go on another trek next year, and we'll take you with us, Bisnu.'

This promise pleased Bisnu, and he saw us off at the bus-stop, shouldering our bedding-roll to the end. Then he climbed a pine tree to have a better view of us leaving. We saw him waving to us from the tree as the bus went round the bend from Kapkote, and then the hills were left behind and the plains stretched out below.

OWLS IN THE FAMILY

One morning we found a full-fledged baby spotted owlet on the ground by the verandah steps. When Grandfather picked it up, it hissed and clacked its bill, but, after a meal of raw meat and water, settled down for the day under my bed.

The spotted owlet, even when full grown, is only the size of a myna, and has none of the sinister appearance of the larger owls. A pair of them may often be found in an old mango or tamarind tree, and by tapping on the tree trunk you may be able to persuade the bird to show an enquiring face at the entrance to its hole. The bird is not normally afraid of man, nor is it strictly a night-bird; but it prefers to stay at home during the day, as it is sometimes attacked by other birds, who consider all owls as their enemies.

The little owlet was quite happy under my bed. The following day a second owlet was found in almost the same place on the verandah, and only then did we realize that where the rainwater pipe emerged through the roof, there was a rough sort of nest, from which the birds had fallen. We took the second young owl to join the first, and fed them both. When I went to bed they were on the ledge just inside the mosquito netting, and later in the night their mother found them there. From outside she crooned and gurgled for a long time, and in the morning I found that she had left a mouse with its tail tucked through the mosquito net! Obviously, she placed no reliance on me as a foster-parent.

The young birds throve and, ten days later at dawn, Grandfather and I took them into the garden to release them. I had placed one on a branch of the mango tree, and was stooping to pick up the other, when I received quite a heavy blow on the back of my head. A second or two later, the mother owl swooped down at Grandfather, but he was agile enough to duck out of its way. Quickly, I placed the second owl under the mango tree. Then from a safe distance we watched the mother fly down and lead her offspring into the long grass at the edge of the garden.

We thought she would take her family away from the vicinity of our rather strange household; but next morning, on coming out of my room, I found two young owls standing on the wall just outside the door! I ran to tell Grandfather, and when we came back we found the mother sitting on the bird-bath ten yards away. She was evidently feeling sorry for her behaviour the previous day, because she greeted us with a soft 'whoo-whoo'.

'Now, there's an unselfish mother for you!' said Grandfather. 'It's obvious she'd like them to have a good home. And they're probably getting a bit too big for her to manage.'

So the two owlets became regular members of our household, and, strangely enough, were among the few pets that Grandmother took a liking to. She objected to all snakes, most monkeys, and some crows, but she took quite a fancy to the owls, and frequently fed them on spaghetti. They seemed quite fond of spaghetti. In fact, the owls became so attached to Grandmother that they began to show affection towards anyone in a petticoat, including Aunt Mabel, who was terrified of them. She would run shrieking from the room every time one of the birds sidled up to her in a friendly manner.

Forgetful of the fact that Grandfather and I had reared them, the owls would sometimes swell their feathers and snap at anyone in trousers. To avoid displeasing them, Grandfather wore a petticoat at feeding time. This mild form of transvestism appeared to satisfy them. I compromised by wearing an apron.

In response to Grandmother's voice, the owlets would make sounds as gentle and soothing as the purring of a cat; but when wild owls were around, ours would rend the night with blood-curdling shrieks. Their nightly occupation was catching beetles, with which the kitchen-quarters were infested at the time. With their sharp eyes and powerful beaks they were excellent pest destroyers.

The owls loved to sit and splash in a shallow dish, especially if cold water was poured over them from a jug at the same time. They would get thoroughly wet, jump out on to a perch, shake themselves, then return for a second splash and sometimes a third. During the day they dozed in large cages under the trees in the garden. They needed cages for protection against attacks from wild birds. At night they had the freedom of the house, where they exercised their wings as much as they liked. Superstitious folk, who dread the cry of the owl, may be interested to know that—mice excepted—there were no untoward deaths in the house during the owls' residence.

Looking back on those owlish days, I carry in my mind a picture of Grandmother with a contented look in her rockingchair. Once, on entering her room while she was having an afternoon nap, I saw that one of the owls had crawled up her pillow till its head was snuggled under her ear. Both Grandmother and the little owl were snoring.

BOY SCOUTS FOREVER!

I was a Boy Scout once, although I couldn't tell a slip knot from a granny knot, or a reef knot from a thief knot, except that a thief knot was supposed to be used to tie up a thief, should you happen to catch one. I have never caught a thief, and wouldn't know what to do with one since I can't tie a knot. Just let him go with a warning, I suppose. Tell him to become a Boy Scout.

'Be prepared!' That's the Boy Scout motto. And a good one, too. But I never seem to be well-prepared for anything, be it an exam or a journey or the roof blowing off my room. I get halfway through a speech and then forget what I have to say next. Or I get a new suit to attend a friend's wedding, and then turn up in my pyjamas.

So how did I, the most impractical of boys, become a Boy Scout? I was at boarding school in Simla when it happened.

Well, it seems a rumour had gone around the junior school (I was still a junior then) that I was a good cook. I had never cooked anything in my life, but of course I had spent a lot of time in the tuck shop making suggestions and advising Chippu, who ran the tuck shop, and encouraging him to make more and better samosas, jalebis, tikkees and pakoras. For my unwanted advice he would favour me with an occasional free samosa, so naturally I looked upon him as a friend and benefactor. With this qualification I was given a cookery badge and put in charge of our troop's supply of rations.

There were about twenty of us in our troop, and during the summer break our Scoutmaster, Mr Oliver, took us on a camping expedition to Tara Devi, a temple-crowned mountain a few miles outside Simla. That first night we were put to work, peeling potatoes, skinning onions, shelling peas and pounding masalas. These various ingredients being ready, I was asked—as the troop's cookery expert—what should be done with them.

'Put everything in that big degchi,' I ordered. 'Pour half a tin of ghee over the lot. Add some nettle leaves and cook for half an hour.'

When this was done, everyone had a taste, but the general opinion was that the dish lacked something.

'More salt,' I suggested.

More salt was added. It still lacked something.

'Add a cup of sugar,' I ordered.

Sugar was added to the concoction. But still it lacked something.

'We forgot to add tomatoes,' said Bimal, one of the Scouts.

'Never mind,' I said. 'We have tomato sauce. Add a bottle of tomato sauce!'

'How about some vinegar?' asked another boy.

'Just the thing,' I agreed. 'A cup of vinegar!'

'Now it's too sour,' said one of the tasters.

'What jam did we bring?' I asked.

'Gooseberry jam.'

'Just the thing. Empty the bottle!'

The dish was a great success. Everyone enjoyed it, including Mr Oliver, who had no idea what went into it.

'What's this called?' he asked.

'It's an all-Indian sweet-and-sour jam-potato curry,' I ventured.

'For short, just call it a Bond-bhujji,' said Bimal.

I had earned my cookery badge!

Poor Mr Oliver! He wasn't really cut out to be a Scoutmaster, any more than I was meant to be a Scout. The following day he announced that he would give us a lesson in tracking. He would take a half-hour start and walk into the forest, leaving behind him a trail of broken twigs, chicken feathers, pine cones and chestnuts, and we were to follow the trail until we found him.

Unfortunately, we were not very good trackers. We did follow Mr Oliver's trail some way into the forest, but were distracted by a pool of clear water which looked very inviting. Abandoning our uniforms, we jumped into the pool and had a great time romping around or just lying on the grassy banks and enjoying the sunshine. A couple of hours later, feeling hungry, we returned to our campsite and set about preparing the evening meal. Bond-bhujji again, but with further variations.

It was growing dark, and we were beginning to worry about Mr Oliver's whereabouts when he limped into camp, assisted by a couple of local villagers. Having waited for us at the far end of the forest for a couple of hours, he had decided to come back by following his own trail, but in the gathering gloom he was soon lost. Some locals returning from the temple took charge of him and escorted him back to camp. He was very angry and made us all return our good-conduct and other badges, which he stuffed into his haversack. I had to give up my cookery badge too.

An hour later, when we were all preparing to get into our sleeping bags for the night, Mr Oliver called out: 'Where's dinner?'

'We've had ours,' said Bimal. 'Everything is finished, sir.'

'Where's Bond? He's supposed to be the cook. Bond, get up and make me an omelette.'

'Can't, sir.'

'Why not?'

'You have my badge. Not allowed to cook without it. Scout rule, sir.'

'Never heard of such a rule. But you can have your badges back, all of you. We return to school tomorrow.'

Mr Oliver returned to his tent in a huff. But I relented and made him an elaborate omelette, garnishing it with dandelion leaves and an extra chilli.

'Never had such an omelette before,' confessed Mr Oliver, blowing out his cheeks. 'A little too hot, but otherwise quite interesting.'

'Would you like another, sir?'

'Tomorrow, Bond, tomorrow. We'll breakfast early tomorrow.'

But we had to break up our camp very early the next day. In the early hours, a bear had strayed into our camp, entered the tent where our stores were kept, and created havoc with all our provisions, even rolling our biggest degchi down the hillside.

In the confusion and uproar that followed, the bear entered Mr Oliver's tent (he was already outside, fortunately) and came out entangled in Mr Oliver's dressing gown. It then made off in the direction of the forest.

A bear in a dressing gown? It was a comical sight.

And though we were a troop of brave little Scouts, we thought it better to let the bear keep the gown.

THE BICYCLE RIDE WITH UNCLE KEN

Kissing a girl while sharing a bicycle with her is no easy task, but I managed it when I was thirteen and my cousin Melanie was fourteen. Of course, we both fell off in the process, and landed in one of Granny's flower beds where we were well-cushioned by her nasturtiums.

I was a clumsy boy, always falling off bicycles, and Cousin Melanie was teaching me to ride properly, making me sit on the front seat while she guided the infernal machine from the carrier seat. The kiss was purely experimental. I had not kissed a girl before, and as Cousin Melanie seemed eminently kissable, I thought I'd start with her. I waited until we were stationary, and she was instructing me on the intricacies of the cycle chain, and then I gave her a hurried kiss on the cheek. She was so started that she fell backwards, taking me and the bicycle with her.

Later, she reported me to Granny, who said, 'We'll have to keep an eye on that boy. He's showing signs of a dissolute nature.'

'What's dissolute, Uncle Ken?' I asked my favourite uncle.

'It means you're going to the dogs. You're not supposed to kiss your cousin.'

'Can I kiss other girls?'

'Only if they are willing.'

'Did you ever kiss a girl, Uncle Ken?'

Uncle Ken blushed. 'Er...well...a long time ago.'

'Tell me about it.'

'Another time.'

'No, tell me now. How old were you?'

'About twenty.'

'And how old was she?'

'A bit younger.'

'And what happened?'

'We went cycling together. I was staying in Agra, when your grandfather worked there with the railways. Daisy's father was an engine driver. But she didn't like engines; they left her covered with soot. Everyone had a bicycle in those days, only the very rich had cars. And the cars could not keep up with the bicycles.

'We lived in the cantonment, where the roads were straight and wide. Daisy and I went on cycle rides to Fatehpur Sikri and Sikandra and of course the Taj Mahal, and one evening we saw the Taj Mahal by moonlight and it made us very romantic, and when I saw her home we kissed under the Ashoka trees.'

'I didn't know you were so romantic, Uncle Ken. Why didn't you marry Daisy?'

'I didn't have a job. She said she'd wait until I got one, but after two years, she got tired of waiting. She married a ticket inspector.'

'Such a sad story,' I said. 'And you still don't have a job.'

Uncle Ken had been through various jobs—private tutor, salesman, shop assistant, hotel manager (until he brought about the closure of the hotel), and cricket coach, this last on the strength of bearing a close resemblance to Bruce Hallam—but at present he was unemployed, and only too ready to put his vast experience of life at my disposal.

Not only did he teach me to ride a bicycle but also accompanied me on cycle rides around Dehra and along the lanes and country roads outside the town.

A bicycle provides its rider with a great amount of freedom. A car will take you further but the fact that you're sitting in a confined space detracts from the freedom of the open spaces and unfamiliar roads. On a cycle you can feel the breeze on your face, smell the mango trees in blossom, slow down and gaze at the buffaloes wading in their ponds, or just stop anywhere and enjoy a cup of tea or a glass of sugar cane juice. Foot-slogging takes time, and cars are too fast—everything whizzes past you before you can take a second look—and car drivers hate having to stop; they are intent only on reaching their destinations in good time. But a bicycle is just right for someone who likes to take a leisurely look at the world as well as to give the world a chance to look at him.

Uncle Ken and I had some exhilarating bicycle rides during my winter holidays, and the most memorable of these was our unplanned visit to a certain 'Rest Home' situated on the outskirts of the town. It isn't there now, so don't go looking for it.

We had cycled quite far that day, and were tired and thirsty. There was no sign of a tea-shop on that particular road, but when we arrived at the open gate of an impressive building with a signboard saying 'Rest and Recuperation Centre', we presumed it was a hotel or hostelry of sorts and rode straight into the premises. There was an extensive lawn to one side, surrounded by neat hedges and flowering shrubs. A number of people were strolling about on the lawn; some were sitting on benches; one or two were straddling a wall, talking to themselves; another was standing alone singing to a non-existent audience. Some were Europeans; a few were Indians.

We left our cycles in the porch and went in search of refreshments. A lady in a white sari gave us cool water from a surahi and told us we could wait on a bench just outside their office. But Uncle Ken said we'd prefer to meet some of the guests, and led me across the lawn to where a singer was practising his notes. He was a florid gentleman, heavily built.

'Do you like my singing?' he asked, as we came up.

'Wonderful!' exclaimed Uncle Ken. 'You sing like Caruso.'

'I am Caruso!' affirmed the tenor, and let rip the opening notes of a famous operatic aria. 'Your tiny hand is frozen,' he sang, although it was an unusually warm day.

We hurried on, and met an elegant couple who were parading up and down the lawn, waving their hands to an invisible crowd.

'Good day to you, gentlemen,' said the flamboyant individual. 'You're the ambassadors from Sweden, I suppose.'

'If you so wish,' said Uncle Ken gallantly. 'And I have the honour of speaking to—?'

'The Emperor Napoleon, of course.'

'Of course. And this must be the Empress Josephine.' Uncle Ken bowed to the lady beside him.

'Actually, his Marie Waleska,' said Napoleon.

'Josephine is indisposed today.'

I was beginning to feel like Alice at the Mad Hatter's tea party, and began tugging at Uncle Ken's coat sleeve, whispering that we were getting late for lunch.

A turbaned warrior with a tremendous moustache loomed in front of us. 'I'm Prithviraj Chauhan,' he announced. 'And I invite you to dinner at my palace.'

'Everyone's royalty here,' observed Uncle Ken.

'It's such a privilege to be with you.'

'Me too,' I put in nervously.

'Come with me, boy, and I'll introduce you to the others.' Prithviraj Chauhan took me by the hand and began guiding me across the lawn. 'There are many famous men and women here. That's Marco Polo over there. He's just back from China. And if you don't care for Caruso's signing, there's Tansen under that tamarind tree. Tamarind leaves are good for the voice, you know that of course. And that fashionable gentleman there, he's Lord Curzon, who used to be a viceroy. He's talking to the Sultan of Marrakesh. Come along, I'll introduce you to them… You're the young prince of Denmark, aren't you?'

'Hamlet himself,' said Uncle Ken with a wink.

Before I could refute any claims to royalty, we were intercepted by a white-coated gentleman accompanied by a white-coated assistant. They looked as though they were in charge.

'And what are you doing here, young man?' asked the senior of the two.

'I'm with my uncle,' I said, gesturing towards Uncle Ken, who approached and gave the in charge an affable handshake.

'And you must be Dr Freud,' said Uncle Ken. 'I must say this is a jolly sort of place.'

'Actually, I'm Dr Goel. You must be the new patient we were expecting. But they should have sent you over with someone a little older than this boy. Never mind, come along to the office and we'll have you admitted.'

Uncle Ken and I both protested that we were not potential patients but had entered the grounds by mistake. We had our bicycles to prove it! But Dr Goel was having nothing of this deception. He and his assistant linked arms with Uncle Ken and marched him off to the office, while I trailed behind, wondering if I should get on my bicycle and rush back to Granny with the terrible news that Uncle Ken had been incarcerated in a lunatic asylum.

Just then an ambulance arrived with the real patient, a school principal suffering from a persecution complex. He kept shouting that he was perfectly sane, and that his entire staff had plotted to have him put away. This might well have been true, as the staff was there in force to make sure he did not escape.

Dr Goel apologized to Uncle Ken. Uncle Ken apologized to Dr Goel. The good doctor even accompanied us to the gate. He shook hands with Uncle Ken and said, 'I have a feeling we'll see you here again.' He looked hard at my uncle and added, 'I think I've seen you before, sir. What did you say your name was?'

'Bruce Hallam,' said Uncle Ken mischievously, and rode away before they changed their minds and kept him in their 'Rest Home'.

THE EYES HAVE IT

I had the train compartment to myself up to Rohana, then a girl got in. The couple who saw her off was probably her parents. They seemed very anxious about her comfort and the woman gave the girl detailed instructions as to where to keep her things, when not to lean out of windows and how to avoid speaking to strangers.

They said their goodbyes and the train pulled out of the station. As I was totally blind at the time, my eyes sensitive only to light and darkness, I was unable to tell what the girl looked like. But I knew she wore slippers from the way they slapped against her heels.

It would take me some time to discover something about her looks and perhaps I never would. But I liked the sound of her voice and even the sound of her slippers.

'Are you going all the way to Dehra?' I asked. I must have been sitting in a dark corner because my voice startled her. She gave a little exclamation and said, 'I didn't know anyone else was here.'

Well, it often happens that people with good eyesight fail to see what is right in front of them. They have too much to take in, I suppose. Whereas people who cannot see (or see very little) have to take in only the essentials, whatever registers tellingly on their remaining senses.

'I didn't see you either,' I said. 'But I heard you come in.'

I wondered if I would be able to prevent her from discovering that I was blind. Provided I keep to my seat, I thought, it shouldn't be too difficult.

The girl said, 'I'm getting off at Saharanpur. My aunt is meeting me there.'

'Then I had better not get too familiar,' I replied. 'Aunts are usually formidable creatures.'

'Where are you going?' she asked.

'To Dehra and then to Mussoorie.'

'Oh, how lucky you are. I wish I was going to Mussoorie. I love the hills. Especially in October.'

'Yes, this is the best time,' I said, calling on my memories. 'The hills are covered with wild dahlias, the sun is delicious, and at night you can sit in front of a log fire and drink a little brandy. Most of the tourists have gone and the roads are quiet and almost deserted. Yes, October is the best time.'

She was silent. I wondered if my words had touched her or whether she thought me a romantic fool. Then I made a mistake.

'What is it like outside?' I asked.

She seemed to find nothing strange in the question. Had she noticed already that I could not see? But her next question removed my doubts.

'Why don't you look out of the window?' she asked.

I moved easily along the berth and felt for the window ledge. The window was open and I faced it, making a pretence of studying the landscape. I heard the panting of the engine, the rumble of the wheels, and, in my mind's eye I could see telegraph posts flashing by.

'Have you noticed,' I ventured, 'that the trees seem to be moving while we seem to be standing still?'

'That always happens,' she said. 'Do you see any animals?'

'No,' I answered quite confidently. I knew that there were hardly any animals left in the forests near Dehra. I turned from the window and faced the girl, and for a while we sat in silence.

'You have an interesting face,' I remarked. I was becoming quite daring but it was a safe remark. Few girls can resist flattery. She laughed pleasantly—a clear, ringing laugh.

'It's nice to be told I have an interesting face. I'm tired of people telling me I have a pretty face.'

Oh, so you do have a pretty face, thought I. And aloud I said, 'Well, an interesting face can also be pretty.'

'You are a very gallant young man,' she said. 'But why are you so serious?'

I thought, then, that I would try to laugh for her, but the thought of laughter only made me feel troubled and lonely.

'We'll soon be at your station,' I said.

'Thank goodness it's a short journey. I can't bear to sit in a train for more than two or three hours.'

Yet, I was prepared to sit there for almost any length of time, just to listen to her talk. Her voice had the sparkle of a mountain stream. As soon as she left the train she would forget our brief encounter. But it would stay with me for the rest of the journey and for some time after.

The engine's whistle shrieked, the carriage wheels changed their sound and rhythm, the girl got up and began to collect her things.

I wondered if she wore her hair in a bun or if it was plaited. Perhaps it was hanging loose over her shoulders. Or was it cut very short?

The train drew slowly into the station. Outside, there was the shouting of porters and vendors and a high-pitched female voice near the carriage door. That voice must have belonged to the girl's aunt.

'Goodbye,' the girl said.

She was standing very close to me. So close that the perfume from her hair was tantalizing. I wanted to raise my hand and touch her hair but she moved away. Only the scent of perfume still lingered where she had stood.

There was some confusion in the doorway. A man, getting into the compartment, stammered an apology. Then the door banged and the world was shut out again. I returned to my berth. The guard blew his whistle and we moved off. Once again I had a game to play and a new fellow traveller.

The train gathered speed, the wheels took up their song, the carriage groaned and shook. I found the window and sat in front of it, staring into the daylight that was darkness for me.

So many things were happening outside the window. It could be a fascinating game guessing what went on out there.

The man who had entered the compartment broke into my reverie.

'You must be disappointed,' he said. 'I'm not nearly as attractive a travelling companion as the one who just left.'

'She was an interesting girl,' I said. 'Can you tell me—did she keep her hair long or short?'

'I don't remember,' he said sounding puzzled. 'It was her eyes I noticed, not her hair. She had beautiful eyes but they were of no use to her. She was completely blind. Didn't you notice?'

THE PARROT WHO WOULD NOT TALK

'You are no beauty! Can't talk, can't dance!' With these words, Aunt Ruby would tease the unfortunate parakeet who stared sourly at everyone from his ornamental cage at one end of the long verandah of granny's bungalow in North India.

In those distant days, almost everyone, Indian or European, kept a pet parrot or parakeet, or a lovebird, as some of the smaller ones were called. Sometimes these birds became great talkers, or rather imitators, and would learn to recite mantras (religious chants), or scoldings to the children of the house, such as 'Padho beta, padho.' (Study child, study.) Or for the benefit of boys like me, 'Don't be greedy, don't be greedy.'

These expressions were, of course, picked up by the parrot over a period of time, after many repetitions by whichever member of the household had taken on the task of teaching the bird to talk.

But our parrot refused to talk.

He'd been bought by Aunt Ruby from a bird-catcher who had visited all the houses on our road, selling caged birds ranging from colourful budgerigars to happy little mynas and even common sparrows that had been patted with paint and passed off as some rare species. Neither granny nor grandfather were keen on keeping caged birds as pets, but Aunt Ruby showed signs of throwing a tantrum if she did not get her way and Aunt Ruby's tantrums were dreadful to watch.

Anyway, she insisted on keeping the parrot and teaching it to talk. But the bird took an instant dislike to my aunt and resisted all the pleasant things she said.

'Kiss, kiss,' Aunt Ruby would coo, putting her face close to the bars of the cage. But the parrot would back away, its shady little eyes getting even smaller with anger at the prospect of being kissed by Aunt Ruby. And on one occasion, it suddenly dived forward without warning and knocked Aunt Ruby's spectacles off her nose.

After that, Aunt Ruby gave up her efforts to show her love for the parrot and became quite unfriendly towards the poor bird, making faces at it and calling out, 'Can't sing, can't dance!' and other nasty comments.

It fell upon me, then, ten years old, to feed the parrot, and it seemed quite happy to receive the green chillies and ripe tomatoes from my hands. These delicacies were supplemented by slices of mango, for it was then the mango season. It also gave me an opportunity to consume a couple of mangoes while feeding the parrot.

One afternoon, while everyone was indoors enjoying a short nap, I gave the parrot his lunch and then purposely left the cage door open. Seconds later, the bird was winging its way into the freedom of the mango orchard.

At the same time, grandfather came onto the verandah and remarked, 'I see your Aunt's parrot has escaped.'

'The door was quite loose,' I said with a shrug. 'Well, I don't suppose we'll see it again.'

Aunt Ruby was upset at first, and threatened to buy another

bird. We put her off by promising to buy her a bowl of goldfish.

'But goldfish don't talk!' she protested.

'Well, neither did your bird,' said grandfather. 'So we'll get you a gramophone. You can listen to Clara Buck all day. They say she sings like a nightingale.'

I thought we'd never see the parrot again, but it probably missed its green chillies, because a few days later, I found the bird sitting on the verandah railing, looking expectantly at me with its head cocked to one side. Unselfishly, I gave the parrot half of my mango.

While the bird was enjoying the mango, Aunt Ruby emerged from her room, and with a cry of surprise, called out, 'Look! There's my parrot! Come back! He must have missed me!' With a loud squawk, the parrot flew out of her reach and perching on the nearest rose bush, glared at Aunt Ruby and screamed at her in my Aunt's familiar tones: 'You're no beauty! Can't talk, can't sing, can't dance!'

Aunt Ruby went ruby-red and dashed indoors.

But that wasn't the end of the affair. The parrot became a regular visitor to the garden and verandah, and whenever it saw Aunt Ruby, it would call out, 'You're no beauty! Can't talk, can't sing, and can't dance!'

The parrot had learnt to talk after all.

GOODBYE, MISS MACKENZIE

The Oaks, Holly Mount, The Parsonage, The Pines, Dumbarnie, Mackinnon's Hall, and Windermere. These are names of some of the old houses that still stand on the outskirts of one of the larger Indian hill-stations. They were built over a hundred years ago by British settlers who sought relief from the searing heat of the plains. A few fell into decay and are now inhabited by wild cats, owls, goats, and the occasional mule-driver. Others survive.

Among these old mansions stands a neat, white-washed cottage, Mulberry Lodge. And in it lived an elderly British spinster named Miss Mackenzie. She was sprightly and wore old-fashioned but well-preserved dresses. Once a week, she walked up to town and bought butter, jam, soap and sometimes a bottle of eau-de-cologne.

Miss Mackenzie had lived there since her teens, before World War I. Her parents, brother, and sister were all dead. She had no relatives in India, and lived on a small pension and gift parcels sent by a childhood friend. She had few visitors—the local padre, the postman, the milkman. Like other lonely old people, she kept a pet, a large black cat with bright, yellow eyes.

In a small garden, she grew dahlias, chrysanthemums, gladioli and a few rare orchids. She knew a great deal about wild flowers, trees, birds, and insects. She never seriously studied them, but had an intimacy with all that grew and flourished around her.

It was September, and the rains were nearly over. Miss Mackenzie's African marigolds were blooming. She hoped the coming winter wouldn't be too severe because she found it increasingly difficult to bear the cold. One day, as she was puttering about in her garden, she saw a schoolboy plucking wild flowers on the slope above the cottage. 'What are you up to, young man?' she called.

Alarmed, the boy tried to dash up the hillside, but slipped on pine needles and slid down the slope into Miss Mackenzie's nasturtium bed. Finding no escape, he gave a bright smile and said, 'Good morning, Miss.'

'Good morning,' said Miss Mackenzie severely. 'Would you mind moving out of my flower bed?'

The boy stepped gingerly over the nasturtiums, and looked at Miss Mackenzie with appealing eyes.

'You ought to be in school,' she said. 'What are you doing here?'

'Picking flowers, Miss.' He held up a bunch of ferns and wild flowers.

'Oh,' Miss Mackenzie was disarmed. It had been a long time since she had seen a boy taking an interest in flowers.

'Do you like flowers?' she asked.

'Yes, Miss. I'm going to be a botan…a botanitist.'

'You mean a botanist?'

'Yes, Miss.'

'That's unusual. Do you know the names of these flowers?'

'This is a buttercup,' he said, showing her a small golden flower. 'But I don't know what this is,' he said, holding out a pale, pink flower with a heart-shaped leaf.

'It's a wild begonia,' said Miss Mackenzie. 'And that purple stuff is salvia. Do you have any books on flowers?'

'No, Miss.'

'Come in and I'll show you one.'

She led the boy into a small front room crowded with furniture, books, vases, and jam jars. He sat awkwardly on the edge of the chair. The cat jumped immediately on to his knees and settled down, purring softly.

'What's your name?' asked Miss Mackenzie, as she rummaged through her books.

'Anil, Miss.'

'And where do you live?'

'When school closes, I go to Delhi. My father has a business there.'

'Oh, and what's that?'

'Bulbs, Miss.'

'Flower bulbs?'

'No, electric bulbs.'

'Ah, here we are!' she said taking a heavy tome from the shelf. '*Flora Himaliensis*, published in 1892, and probably the only copy in India. This is a valuable book, Anil. No other naturalist has recorded as many wild Himalayan flowers. But there are still many plants unknown to the botanists who spend all their time at microscopes instead of in the mountains. Perhaps you'll do something about that one day.'

'Yes, Miss.'

She lit the stove and put the kettle on for tea. And then the old English lady and the small Indian boy sat side by side, absorbed in the book. Miss Mackenzie pointed out many flowers that grew around the hill-station, while the boy made notes of their names and seasons.

'May I come again?' asked Anil, when finally he rose to go.

'If you like,' said Miss Mackenzie. 'But not during school hours. You mustn't miss your classes.'

After that, Anil visited Miss Mackenzie about once a week, and nearly always brought a wild flower for her to identify. She looked forward to the boy's visits. Sometimes when more than a week passed and he didn't come, she would grumble at the cat.

By the middle of October, with only a fortnight left before school closed, snow fell on the distant mountains. One peak stood high above the others, a white pinnacle againt an azure sky. When the sun set, the peak turned from orange to pink to red.

'How high is that mountain?' asked Anil.

'It must be over 15,000 feet,' said Miss Mackenzie. 'I always wanted to go there, but there is no proper road. On the lower slopes, there'll be flowers that you don't get here: blue gentian, purple columbine.'

The day before school closed, Anil came to say goodbye. As he was about to leave, Miss Mackenzie thrust the *Flora Himaliensis* into his hands. 'It's a gift,' she said.

'But I'll be back next year, and I'll be able to look at it then,' he protested. 'Besides, it's so valuable!'

'That's why I'm giving it to you. Otherwise, it will fall into the hands of the junk dealers.'

'But, Miss...'

'Don't argue.'

The boy tucked the book under his arm, stood at attention, and said, 'Goodbye, Miss Mackenzie.' It was the first time he had spoken her name.

Strong winds soon brought rain and sleet, killing the flowers in the garden. The cat stayed indoors, curled up at the foot of the bed. Miss Mackenzie wrapped herself in old shawls and mufflers, but still felt cold. Her fingers grew so stiff that it took almost an hour to open a can of baked beans. Then it snowed, and for several days the milkman did not come.

Tired, she spent most of her time in bed. It was the warmest place. She kept a hot-water bottle against her back, and the cat kept her feet warm. She dreamed of spring and summer. In three months, the primroses would be out, and Anil would return.

One night the hot-water bottle burst, soaking the bed. The sun didn't shine for several days, and the blankets remained damp. Miss Mackenzie caught a chill and had to keep to her cold, uncomfortable bed.

A strong wind sprang up one night and blew the bedroom window open. Miss Mackenzie was too weak to get up and close it. The wind swept the rain and sleet into the room. The cat snuggled close to its mistress's body. Towards morning, the body lost its warmth, and the cat left the bed and started scratching about on the floor.

As sunlight streamed through the window, the milkman arrived. He poured some milk into the saucer on the doorstep, and the cat jumped down from the window-sill.

The milkman called out a greeting to Miss Mackenzie. There was no answer. Knowing she was always up before sunrise, he poked his head in the open window and called again.

Miss Mackenzie did not answer. She had gone to the mountain, where the blue gentian and purple columbine grow.

A SPECIAL TREE

One day, when Rakesh was six, he walked home from the Mussoorie bazaar eating cherries. They were a little sweet, a little sour; small, bright red cherries, which had come all the way from the Kashmir Valley.

Here in the Himalayan foothills where Rakesh lived, there were not many fruit trees. The soil was stony, and the dry cold winds stunted the growth of most plants. But on the more sheltered slopes there were forests of oak and deodar.

Rakesh lived with his grandfather on the outskirts of Mussoorie, just where the forest began. His father and mother lived in a small village fifty miles away, where they grew maize and rice and barley in narrow terraced fields on the lower slopes of the mountain. But there were no schools in the village, and Rakesh's parents were keen that he should go to school. As soon as he was of school-going age, they sent him to stay with his grandfather in Mussoorie.

He had a little cottage outside the town.

Rakesh was on his way home from school when he bought the cherries. He paid fifty paise for the bunch. It took him about half-an-hour to walk home, and by the time he reached the cottage there were only three cherries left.

'Have a cherry, Grandfather,' he said, as soon as he saw his grandfather in the garden.

Grandfather took one cherry and Rakesh promptly ate the other two. He kept the last seed in his mouth for some time, rolling it round and round on his tongue until all the tang had gone. Then he placed the seed on the palm of his hand and studied it.

'Are cherry seeds lucky?' asked Rakesh.

'Of course.'

'Then I'll keep it.'

'Nothing is lucky if you put it away. If you want luck, you must put it to some use.'

'What can I do with a seed?'

'Plant it.'

So Rakesh found a small space and began to dig up a flowerbed.

'Hey, not there,' said Grandfather, 'I've sown mustard in that bed. Plant it in that shady corner, where it won't be disturbed.'

Rakesh went to a corner of the garden where the earth was soft and yielding. He did not have to dig. He pressed the seed into the soil with his thumb and it went right in.

Then he had his lunch, and ran off to play cricket with his friends, and forgot all about the cherry seed.

When it was winter in the hills, a cold wind blew down from the snows and went *whoo-whoo-whoo* in the deodar trees, and the garden was dry and bare. In the evenings Grandfather and Rakesh sat over a charcoal fire, and Grandfather told Rakesh stories—stories about people who turned into animals, and ghosts who lived in trees, and beans that jumped and stones that wept—and in turn Rakesh would read to him from the newspaper, Grandfather's eyesight being rather weak. Rakesh found the newspaper very dull—especially after the stories—but Grandfather wanted all the news…

They knew it was spring when the wild duck flew north

again, to Siberia. Early in the morning, when he got up to chop wood and light a fire, Rakesh saw the V-shaped formation streaming northward, the calls of the birds carrying clearly through the thin mountain air.

One morning in the garden he bent to pick up what he thought was a small twig and found to his surprise that it was well rooted. He stared at it for a moment, then ran to fetch Grandfather, calling, 'Dada, come and look, the cherry tree has come up!'

'What cherry tree?' asked Grandfather, who had forgotten about it. 'The seed we planted last year—look, it's come up!'

Rakesh went down on his haunches, while Grandfather bent almost double and peered down at the tiny tree. It was about four inches high.

'Yes, it's a cherry tree,' said Grandfather. 'You should water it now and then.'

Rakesh ran indoors and came back with a bucket of water.

'Don't drown it!' said Grandfather.

Rakesh gave it a sprinkling and circled it with pebbles.

'What are the pebbles for?' asked Grandfather.

'For privacy,' said Rakesh.

He looked at the tree every morning but it did not seem to be growing very fast, so he stopped looking at it except quickly, out of the corner of his eye. And, after a week or two, when he allowed himself to look at it properly, he found that it had grown—at least an inch!

That year the monsoon rains came early and Rakesh plodded to and from school in raincoat and chappals. Ferns sprang from the trunks of trees, strange-looking lilies came up in the long grass, and even when it wasn't raining the trees dripped and mist came curling up the valley. The cherry tree grew quickly in this season.

It was about two feet high when a goat entered the garden and ate all the leaves. Only the main stem and two thin branches remained.

'Never mind,' said Grandfather, seeing that Rakesh was upset. 'It will grow again, cherry trees are tough.'

Towards the end of the rainy season new leaves appeared on the tree. Then a woman cutting grass scrambled down the hillside, her scythe swishing through the heavy monsoon foliage. She did not try to avoid the tree: one sweep, and the cherry tree was cut in two.

When Grandfather saw what had happened, he went after the woman and scolded her; but the damage could not be repaired.

'Maybe it will die now,' said Rakesh.

'Maybe,' said Grandfather.

But the cherry tree had no intention of dying.

By the time summer came round again, it had sent out several new shoots with tender green leaves. Rakesh had grown taller too. He was eight now, a sturdy boy with curly black hair and deep black eyes. 'Blackberry eyes,' Grandfather called them.

That monsoon Rakesh went home to his village, to help his father and mother with the planting and ploughing and sowing. He was thinner but stronger when he came back to Grandfather's house at the end of the rains to find that the cherry tree had grown another foot. It was now up to his chest.

Even when there was rain, Rakesh would sometimes water the tree. He wanted it to know that he was there.

One day he found a bright green praying-mantis perched on a branch, peering at him with bulging eyes. Rakesh let it remain there; it was the cherry tree's first visitor.

The next visitor was a hairy caterpillar, who started making a meal of the leaves. Rakesh removed it quickly and dropped it on a heap of dry leaves.

'Come back when you're a butterfly,' he said.

Winter came early. The cherry tree bent low with the weight of snow. Field-mice sought shelter in the roof of the cottage. The road from the valley was blocked, and for several days there was no newspaper, and this made Grandfather quite grumpy. His stories began to have unhappy endings.

In February it was Rakesh's birthday. He was nine—and the tree was four, but almost as tall as Rakesh.

One morning, when the sun came out, Grandfather came into the garden to 'let some warmth get into my bones,' as he put it. He stopped in front of the cherry tree, stared at it for a few moments, and then called out, 'Rakesh! Come and look! Come quickly before it falls!'

Rakesh and Grandfather gazed at the tree as though it had performed a miracle. There was a pale pink blossom at the end of a branch.

The following year there were more blossoms. And suddenly the tree was taller than Rakesh, even though it was less than half his age. And then it was taller than Grandfather, who was older than some of the oak trees.

But Rakesh had grown too. He could run and jump and climb trees as well as most boys, and he read a lot of books, although he still liked listening to Grandfather's tales.

In the cherry tree, bees came to feed on the nectar in the blossoms, and tiny birds pecked at the blossoms and broke them off. But the tree kept blossoming right through the spring, and there were always more blossoms than birds.

That summer there were small cherries on the tree. Rakesh tasted one and spat it out.

'It's too sour,' he said.

'They'll be better next year,' said Grandfather.

But the birds liked them—especially the bigger birds, such as the bulbuls and scarlet minivets—and they flitted in and out of the foliage, feasting on the cherries.

On a warm sunny afternoon, when even the bees looked sleepy, Rakesh was looking for Grandfather without finding him in any of his favourite places around the house. Then he looked out of the bedroom window and saw Grandfather reclining on a cane chair under the cherry tree.

'There's just the right amount of shade here,' said Grandfather. 'And I like looking at the leaves.'

'They're pretty leaves,' said Rakesh. 'And they are always ready to dance, if there's a breeze.'

After Grandfather had come indoors, Rakesh went into the garden and lay down on the grass beneath the tree. He gazed up through the leaves at the great blue sky; and turning on his side, he could see the mountains striding away into the clouds. He was still lying beneath the tree when the evening shadows crept across the garden. Grandfather came back and sat down beside Rakesh, and they waited in silence until the stars came out and the nightjar began to call. In the forest below, the crickets and cicadas began tuning up; and suddenly the trees were full of the sound of insects.

'There are so many trees in the forest,' said Rakesh. 'What's so special about this tree? Why do we like it so much?'

'We planted it ourselves,' said Grandfather. That's why it's special.'

'Just one small seed,' said Rakesh, and he touched the smooth bark of the tree that he had grown. He ran his hand along the trunk of the tree and put his finger to the tip of a leaf. 'I wonder,' he whispered. 'Is this what it feels to be God?'

RUNNING AWAY

Once, during my schooldays, my friend Daljit and I decided to run away. The main reason for running away was not to get back to the bazaars of Dehra, which we both missed, but to reach my uncle's ship in Jamnagar, Gujarat.

Uncle Jim was one of my father's cousins. He used to write to me off and on throughout the years. His letters came in envelopes that bore colourful stamps of different countries. They came from Valparaiso, San Diego, San Francisco, Buenos Aires, Dar-es-Salaam, Mombasa, Freetown, Singapore, Bombay, Marseilles, London…these were some of the places where Uncle Jim's ship called. He was seldom on the same route, and seemed to move leisurely across the oceans of the earth, calling at ports that had only the most romantic associations for me, for I had already read Stevenson, Captain Marryat, some Conrad and W.W. Jacobs.

In his letters, Uncle Jim often spoke of my joining him at sea—'When you are a little older, Ruskin.'

But I felt I was old enough then. I was sick of school and sick of my guardian. But that was not all. I was in love with the world. I wanted to see the world, every corner of it, the places I had read about in books—the junks and sampans of Hong Kong, the palm-fringed lagoons of the Indies, the streets of London, the beautiful ebony-skinned people of Africa, the bright birds and exotic plants of the Amazon...

When Uncle Jim's last letter had arrived, telling me that his ship would call at Jamnagar towards the end of the month, I felt a deep thrill of anticipation. Here was my chance at last! True, Uncle Jim had said nothing about my joining him, but he was not to know that I was seriously considering it.

It was not simply a question of walking out of school and taking a quick ride down to the docks. Jamnagar, on the west coast, was at least eight hundred miles from my school. I doubt if I would have made the attempt if Daljit had not agreed to come too. It isn't much fun running away on your own. It is even worse if you have a companion who is full of enthusiasm at the beginning and then backs out at the last moment. This leaves one feeling defeated and crushed. Daljit was not that kind of companion. He meant the things he said. About a month earlier, when I had told him of my uncle's ship and my wish to get to it, he had said, without a moment's hesitation: 'I'm coming too!' Daljit lived impulsively. Sometimes, he made mistakes. But he never went halfway and stopped. Someone had to stop him; otherwise he did whatever it was he set out to do.

Running away from school! It is not to be recommended to everyone. Parents and teachers would disapprove. Or would they, deep down in their hearts? Everyone has wanted to run away at some time in his life: if not from a bad school or an unhappy home then from something equally unpleasant. Running away seems to be in the best of traditions. Huck Finn did it. So did Master Copperfield and Oliver Twist. So did Kim. Various enterprising young men have run away to sea. Most great men have run away from school at some stage in their lives; and if they haven't, then perhaps it is something they should have done.

Anyway, Daljit and I ran away from school, and we did it quite successfully too, up to a point. But then, all this happened in India, which, though it forms only two per cent of the world's land mass, has 15 per cent of its population, and so it is an easy place to hide in, or be lost in, or disappear in, and never be seen or heard of again!

Not that we intended to disappear. We were headed for a particular place, and as soon as I took my first step into the unknown, that first step on the slippery pine needles below the school, I knew quite definitely that I wasn't running away from anything, but that I was running *towards* something. Call it a dream, if you like. I was running towards a dream.

A narrow path ran downhill from the school to the road to Dehra, and we followed it until it levelled out, running parallel with the small stream that rumbled down the mountainside. We followed the stream for a mile, walking swiftly and silently, until we met the bridle-path which was little more than a mule-track going steeply down the last hills to the valley.

The going was easy. We knew the road well. And by the time we reached the last foothills, it was beginning to rain, not heavily, but as a light, thin drizzle.

We took shelter in a small dhaba on the outskirts of a village. The dhabawallah was sleeping, and his dog, a mangy pariah with only one ear, sniffed at us in a friendly way instead of chasing us off the premises. We sat down on an old bench and watched the sun rising over the distant mountains.

This is something I have always remembered. Not because it was a more beautiful sunrise than on any other day, but because the special importance of that morning made me look at everything in a new way, hence the details still stand out in my memory.

As the sky grew lighter, the pines and deodars stood out clearly, and the birds came to life. A black-bird started it all with a low, mellow call, and then the thrushes began chattering in the bushes. A barbet shrieked monotonously at the top of a spruce tree, and, as the sky grew lighter still, a flock of bright green parrots flew low over the trees.

The drizzle continued and there was a bright crimson glow in the east. And then, quite suddenly, the sun shot through a gap in the clouds, and the lush green monsoon grass sprang into relief. Both Daljit and I were wonderstruck. Never before had we been up so early. Hundreds of spiderwebs—which were spun in trees and bushes and on the grass, where they would not normally have been noticed—were now clearly visible, spangled with gold and silver raindrops. The strong silk threads of the webs held the light rain and the sun, making each drop of water look like a tiny jewel.

A great wild dahlia, its scarlet flowers drenched and heavy, sprawled over the hillside and an emerald-green grasshopper reclined on a petal, stretching its legs in the sunshine.

The dhabawallah was now up. His dog, emboldened by his master's presence, began to bark at us. The man lit a charcoal fire in a choolah, and put on it a kettle of water to boil.

'Would you like to eat something?' he asked conversationally in Hindi.

'No, just tea for us,' I said.

He placed two brass tumblers on a table.

'The milk hasn't yet been delivered,' he said. 'You're very early.'

'We'll take the tea without milk,' said Daljit. 'But give us lots of sugar.'

'Sugar is costly these days. But because you are schoolboys and need more, you can help yourselves.'

'Oh, we are not schoolboys,' I said hurriedly.

'Not at all,' added Daljit.

'We are just tourists,' I lied unconvincingly.

'We have to catch the early train at Dehra,' offered Daljit.

'But there's no train before ten o'clock,' said the puzzled dhabawallah.

'It is the ten o'clock train we are catching!' said Daljit smartly. 'Do you think we will be down in time?'

'Oh yes, there's plenty of time…'

The dhabawallah poured out steaming hot tea into the tumblers and placed the sugar bowl in front of us. 'At first I thought you were schoolboys,' he said with a laugh. 'I thought you were running away.'

Daljit almost gave us away by laughing nervously.

'What made you think that?' he asked.

'Oh, I've been here many years,' the dhabawallah replied, gesturing towards the small clearing in which his little wooden stall stood, almost like a trading outpost in a wild country. 'Schoolboys always pass this way when they're running away!'

'Do many run away?' I asked. I felt a little downcast at the thought that Daljit and I were not the first to embark on such an adventure.

'Not many. Just two or three every year. They get as far as the railway station in Dehra and there they're caught!'

'It is silly of them to get caught,' said Daljit disgustedly.

'Are they always caught?' I asked.

'Always! I give them a glass of tea on their way down, and I give them a glass of tea on their way up, when they are returning with their teachers.'

'Well, you won't be seeing *us* again,' said Daljit, ignoring the warning look that I gave him.

'Ah, but you aren't schoolboys!' said the shopkeeper, beaming at us. 'And you aren't running away!'

We paid for our tea and hurried on down the path. The parrots flew over again, screeching loudly, and settled in a lichee tree. The sun was warmer now, and, as the altitude decreased, the temperature and humidity rose and we could almost smell the heat of the plains rising to meet us.

The hills levelled out into the rolling countryside, patterned with fields. Rice had been planted out, and the sugarcane was waist-high.

The path had become quite slushy. Removing our shoes and wrapping them in newspaper, we walked barefoot in the soft mud. All these little out-of-routine acts simply added to our excitement and thrill, making everything quite unforgettable for life.

'It's about three miles into Dehra,' I said. 'We must go round the town. By now, everyone in school will be up and they'll have found out we've gone!'

'We must avoid the Dehra station then,' said Daljit.

'We'll walk to the next station, Raiwala. Then we'll hop onto the first train that comes along.'

'How far must we walk?'

'About ten miles.'

'Ten miles!' Daljit looked dismayed. 'It'll take us all day!'

'Well, we can't stop here nor can we wander about in Dehra, neither can we enter the station. We have to keep on walking.'

'Alright, we'll keep on walking. I suppose the beginning of an adventure is always the most difficult part.'

Soon, the fields were giving way to jungle. But there were still some fields of sugarcane stretching away from the railway lines.

'How much further do we have to walk?' asked Daljit impatiently. 'Is Raiwala in the middle of the jungle?'

'Yes, I think it is. We've covered about four miles I suppose. Six to go! It's funny how some miles seem longer than others. It depends on what one is thinking about, I suppose. If our thoughts are pleasant, the miles are not so long.'

'Then let's keep thinking pleasant thoughts. Isn't there a short cut anywhere? You've been in these forests before.'

'We'll take the fire-path through the jungle. It'll save us three or four miles. But we'll have to swim or wade across a small river. The rains have only just started, so the water shouldn't be too swift or deep.'

Heavy forests have paths cut through them at various places to prevent forest fires from spreading easily. These paths are not used much by people, since they don't lead anywhere in particular, but they are frequently used by the larger animals.

We had gone about a mile along the path when we heard the sound of rushing water. The path emerged from the forest of sal trees and stopped on the banks of the small river I had mentioned earlier. The main bridge across the river stood on the main road, about three miles downstream.

'It isn't more than waist-deep anywhere,' I said. 'But the water is swift and the stones are slippery.'

We removed our clothes and tied everything into two bundles which we carried on our heads. Daljit was a well-built boy, strong in the arms and thighs. I was slimmer. But I had quick reflexes.

The stones were quite slippery underfoot, and we stumbled, hindering rather than helping each other. We stopped midstream, waist-deep, hesitating about going any further for fear of being swept off our feet.

'I can hardly stand,' said Daljit.

'It shouldn't get worse,' I said hopefully. But the current was strong, and I felt very wobbly at the knees.

Daljit tried to move forward, but slipped and went over backwards into the water, bringing me down too. He began kicking and thrashing about in fear, but eventually, using me as a support, he came up spouting water like a whale.

When we found we were not being swept away, we stopped struggling and cautiously made our way to the opposite bank, but we had been thrust about twenty yards downstream.

We rested on warm sand while a hot sun beat down on us. Daljit sucked at a cut in his hand. But we were soon up and walking again, hungry now, and munching biscuits.

'We haven't far to go,' I said.

'I don't want to think about it,' said Daljit.

We shuffled along the forest path, tired but not discouraged.

Soon we were on the main road again, and there were fields and villages on either side. A cool breeze came in across the open plain, blowing down from the hills. In the fields, there was a gentle swaying movement as the wind stirred the sugarcane. Then, the breeze came down the road, and dust began to swirl and eddy around us. Out of the dust, behind us, came the rumble of cart wheels.

'Ho! Heeyah! Heeyah!' shouted the driver of the cart. The bullocks snorted and came lumbering through the dust. We moved to the side of the road.

'Are you going to Raiwala?' called Daljit. 'Can you take us with you?'

'Climb up!' said the man, and we ran through the dust and clambered on to the back of the moving cart.

The cart lurched forward and rattled and bumped so much

that we had to cling to its sides to avoid falling off. It smelt of grass and mint and cow-dung cakes. The driver had a red cloth tied round his head, and wore a tight vest and a dhoti. He was smoking a beedi and yelling at his bullocks, and he seemed to have forgotten our presence. We were too busy clinging to the sides of the cart to bother about making conversation. Before long we were involved in the traffic of Raiwala—a small but busy market town. We jumped off the bullock cart and walked beside it.

'Should we offer him any money?' I asked.

'No. He will be offended. He is not a taxi driver.'

'Alright, we'll just say thank you.'

We called out our thanks to the cart driver, but he didn't look back. He appeared to be talking to his bullocks.

'I'm hungry,' declared Daljit. 'We haven't had a proper meal since last night.'

'Then let's eat,' I said. 'Come on, Daljit.'

We walked through the small Raiwala bazaar, looking in at the tea and sweet shops until we found the cheapest-looking dhaba. A servant-boy brought us rice and dal and Daljit ordered an ounce of ghee, which he poured over the curry. The meal cost us two rupees but we could have as much dal as we wanted, and between us we finished four bowls of it.

'We'll rest at the station,' I said as we emerged from the dhaba. 'We'll buy second-class tickets, and rest in the first-class waiting room. No one will check on us. We look first class, don't we?'

'Not after that walk through the jungle,' replied Daljit.

But we did occupy the best waiting room and Daljit made himself comfortable in an armchair. A train eventually came chugging in, and we were soon on our way to Delhi.

It didn't take us long to find a hotel once we got off at the Old Delhi Railway Station. It was called the Great Oriental Hotel, and was just behind the police station in Chandni Chowk. It didn't pretend to be even a third-class hotel, and for five rupees we were given a small back room that had a window overlooking the godown of an Afghan spice merchant. The powerful smell of asafoetida came up from the courtyard below.

We were tired and hot, so we tossed our belongings down on the floor and took turns at the bathroom tap. Then we stretched out on the only cot in the room and slept through the afternoon, oblivious to the noises from the street, the attentions of the insect population in the hotel mattress, and the creaking of the old fan overhead.

It was late evening when we woke up, and we were hungry again. Daljit opened the door and shouted. Presently, a servant-boy appeared.

'Bring us tea, toast, two big omelettes and a bottle of tomato sauce,' ordered Daljit with a confidence that I wished I had.

The omelettes, when they arrived twenty minutes later, were tiny. Both had obviously been made from one egg. The sauce had been diluted with water, and the toasts were burnt. The salt was damp, and we had to prise open the salt-cellar to get to it. The pepper, however, came out in a generous rush and made up the major portion of the meal. As our hunger had not been satisfied by this poor fare, we ordered eggs again, boiled eggs this time. No matter how tiny, they would have to be whole.

'Let's go out,' said Daljit after we had eaten the eggs. 'It's stuffy in here.'

'I'm still sleepy,' I said.

'Then I'll go out for a little while. I may go to the gurdwara.'

'Alright, but don't get lost.'

Drowsy, I closed my eyes, but the sounds of the city's unceasing traffic came through the window. Ships and distant ports seemed very far away but so did hills and mountain streams.

I fell asleep and woke up only when Daljit returned.

'I've solved our problem!' he said, beaming. 'We won't bother with the train. I met a truck driver, and he has offered to take us as far as Jaipur. That's more than a hundred miles. It will be quite safe to take a train from Jaipur.'

'When can your friend take us?'

'The truck leaves at four o'clock in the morning.'

'There's no rest for the wicked,' I said. 'Still, the less time we lose the better. It's Wednesday, and my uncle's ship might sail on Saturday. What will we have to pay?'

'Nothing. It's a free ride. The driver is a Sikh, and I persuaded him that we are related to each other through the marriage of my brother-in-law to his sister-in-law's niece!'

◆

At four the next morning, we made our way towards the Red Fort, its ramparts dark against the starry sky. The streets that had been teeming with so much life the previous evening were now deserted. The street lamps shed lonely pools of light on the pavements. The occasional car glided silently past, but it belonged to another kind of world altogether.

Near the Fort, we found a couple of dhabas that were still open. They did business with the truck drivers who slept by day and drove by night.

Our driver, a tall, bearded Sikh, loomed over us out of the darkness. He had a companion with him, also a Sikh, who was still in his underwear.

'You can get in at the back,' said the driver in his thick

Punjabi, which I could follow sufficiently well. 'We'll be off in a few minutes.'

The truck was parked beneath a peepul tree. We pulled ourselves up into the back of the open truck, only to find our way barred by what seemed at first to be a prehistoric monster.

The monster snorted once, stamped heavily on the boards, and sent us tumbling backwards.

'Bhaiyyaji!' cried Daljit to the driver. There's some kind of animal in here!'

'Don't worry, it's only Mumta,' said our friend.

'But what is it doing in here?'

'She is going with us. I am taking her to the market in Jaipur. So get in with her boys, and make yourselves comfortable.'

There was now enough light to enable us to take a closer look at our travelling companion. She was a full-grown buffalo from the Punjab.

'An excellent buffalo,' said Daljit, who appeared to be familiar with the finer points of these animals. 'Notice her blue eyes!'

'I didn't know buffaloes had blue eyes,' I said dryly.

'Only the best buffaloes have them,' said Daljit. 'Blue-eyed buffaloes give more milk than brown-eyed ones.'

Fortunately for us, the Sardarji started the truck and an early morning breeze, blowing across the river, swept away some of the stench so typical of buffaloes.

We were soon out of Delhi and bowling along at a fair speed on the road to Jaipur. The recent rain had waterlogged low-lying areas, and the herons, cranes and snipe were numerous. Fields and trees were alive with strange, beautiful birds: the long-tailed king crow, blue jays and weaver birds, and occasionally the great white-headed kite, which is said to be Garuda, Lord Vishnu's famous steed.

As we travelled further into Rajasthan, the peacocks became more numerous; so did the camels loping along the side of the road in straight, orderly lines. And, as the vegetation grew less and the desert took over, the people themselves grew more colourful, as though to make up for the absence of colour in the landscape. The women wore wide red skirts, and gold and silver ornaments. They were handsome, tall, fair and strong. The men were tall too and the older among them had flowing white beards.

As the day grew older, and the sun rose higher in the sky, the traffic on the road increased; but our truck driver, instead of slowing down, drove faster. Perhaps he was in a hurry to dispose of the buffalo. Soon he was trying to overtake another truck.

The truck in front was moving fast too, and its driver had no intention of giving up the middle of the road. It was piled high with stacks of sugarcane.

'It's going to be a race!' cried Daljit excitedly, standing up against the buffalo, in order to get a better view.

The road was not wide enough to take two large vehicles at once, and as the other truck wouldn't make way, ours had to fall in behind it, almost suffocating us with the exhaust fumes. We were thrown to the floorboards as the truck lurched over the ruts in the rough road, and Mumta, getting nervous, almost trampled us. Then there was a tremendous bump, a grinding of brakes, and we came to a stop.

As the dust cleared, we made out our driver's bearded face gazing anxiously down at us.

'Are you alright?' he asked gruffly.

'I think so,' I said.

'Did you overtake the other truck?' asked Daljit.

'No,' grunted our friend. 'He would not give way. You had better come in front.'

We agreed without any hesitation and his assistant rather grudgingly joined the buffalo.

After a few miles, the driver became friendly and told us that his name was Gurnam Singh.

It was getting dark by the time we reached Jaipur, so we were not able to see much of the city. We spent the night in the truck, sleeping in the back with Gurnam Singh. Mumta had been disposed of on the way. Jaipur nights can be chilly, even in summer, so Gurnam Singh considerately shared his bedding with us. Because he was accustomed to sleeping in the body of the truck, he was soon asleep, snoring loudly and rhythmically. Daljit and I tossed and turned restlessly. He kicked me several times in the night. The floor of the truck was hard, and retained various buffalo smells.

We had hardly fallen asleep (or so it seemed), when Gurnam Singh woke us up, saying that it was almost four o'clock and that he had to start on his return journey, this time with a load of red sandstone.

'What a life!' exclaimed Daljit, sleepily rubbing his eyes with one hand. 'I'd hate to be a truck driver.'

'One has to live somehow,' philosophized Gurnam Singh. 'I like driving. I knew how to drive when I was merely six or seven. The money is not so bad either. Now, when I get back to Delhi, I will have two days off, which I will spend with my wife and children. Goodbye friends, and if you pass through Delhi again, you will find me near the walls of the Red Fort.'

We waved to him as he shot off in his truck, throwing up huge clouds of dust, making a great noise and probably waking the local inhabitants. Dogs barked, and a cock began to crow.

We were on the outskirts of the city, facing a large lake. On the other side was open country, bare hills and desert.

We could also make out the ruins of a building—probably a palace or a hunting lodge—among some thorn bushes and babul trees.

'Let's go out there,' suggested Daljit. 'We can bathe in the lake and rest. Then later in the morning we can come into the city and find out about trains.'

We set out along the shores of the lake, and it was a good half-hour before we reached the opposite bank.

There was no one in the fields, but a camel was going round and round a well, drawing up water in small trays. Smoke rose from houses in a nearby village, and the notes of a flute floated over to us on the still morning air.

It took us about twenty minutes to reach the ruin, which seemed like an old hunting lodge put up by some Rajput prince when game must have been plentiful.

The gate of the lodge was blocked with rubble, but part of the wall had crumbled apart and we climbed through the gap and found ourselves in a stone-paved courtyard in the centre of which stood a dry, disused stone fountain. A small peepul tree was growing from the crack in the floor of the fountain. Finding nothing to do there, we made our way to the railway tracks again.

Daljit and I snuck on to a goods train. It was a hard night's journey. The train was agonizingly slow and stopped at many places. At one small station, a number of sacks filled with what must have been cattle-fodder were tossed into the wagon, almost burying us in our fitful sleep. But we found they were comfortable to rest on and lay stretched out on top of them until the first light of morning.

As the sky cleared, we knew we were not far from our journey's end. The landscape had undergone a complete change. We had left the desert for the coastal plain.

The tall waving palms parted, and then I spotted the sea.

It was the sea as I had always dreamt of it ever since my days in Kathiawar with my father. It was vast, lonely and blue, blue as the sky was blue, and the first ship I saw was a sailing-ship, an Arab dhow, listing slightly in the mild breeze that blew onto the shore.

The train stopped at a small bridge spanning a stream that wound its way across the plain down to the sea. We got down there and trudged the rest of the way to our destination.

Two hours later, we were at Jamnagar.

We stopped near a small tea shop and watched other people eating laddoos and bhelpuri. We couldn't even afford a coconut.

'Where is the harbour?' I asked the shopkeeper.

'Two miles from here,' he replied.

'Are there any ships in the port?' I asked, relieved yet anxious.

'What do you want with a ship?'

'What does anyone want with a ship?'

'Well there's only one and it sails today, so you had better hurry if you want to go away on it.'

'Let's go,' said Daljit.

'Wait!' said a young man who was lounging against the counter. 'It will take you almost an hour to get there if you walk. I will take you in my cart.' He pointed to a shabby pony cart close by. The pony did not look as though it wanted to go anywhere.

'My pony is fast!' said the young man, following our glances. 'Never go by appearances. She may look tired but she runs like a champion! Get in friends, I will charge you only one rupee.'

'We don't have any money,' I said. 'We'll walk.'

'Fifty paisa, then,' he said. 'Fifty paisa and a glass of tea. Jump in my friends!'

'All right,' agreed Daljit. 'There's no time to lose. Fifty paisa and buy your own tea.'

We climbed into the cart, and the youth jumped up in front and cracked his whip. The pony lurched forward, the wheels rattled and shook, and we set off down the bazaar road at a tremendous trot.

'I didn't know you had fifty paisa left,' I said.

'I don't,' Daljit replied. 'But we'll worry about that later. Your uncle can pay!'

As soon as we were out of the town and on the open road to the sea, the pony went faster. She couldn't help doing so, as the road was downhill. The wind blew my hair across my eyes, and the salty tang of the sea was in the air.

Daljit shook me in his excitement.

'We will soon be at the harbour,' he yelled joyfully. 'And then away at last!'

The driver called out endearments to his pony, and, exhilarated by the sea breeze and the comparative speed of his carriage, he burst into song. As we turned a bend in the road, the sea-front came into view. There were several small dhows close to the shore, and fishing-boats were beached on the sand. The fishermen were drying their nets while their children ran naked in the surf. A steamer stood out on the sea and though I could not make out its name from that distance, I was sure it was the *Iris.*

The cart stopped at the beginning of the pier, and we tumbled out and began running along the pier. But even as we ran, it became clear to me that the ship was moving away from us, moving out to the sea. Its propeller sent small waves rippling back to the pier.

'Captain!' I shouted. 'Uncle Jim! Wait for us!'

A lascar standing in the stern waved to us; but that was all.

I stood at the end of the pier, waving my hands and shouting into the wind.

'Captain! Uncle Jim! Wait for us!'

Nobody answered. The seagulls, wheeling in the wake of the steamer, seemed to take up the cry—'Captain, Captain…'

The ship drew further away, gaining speed. And still I called to it in a hoarse, pleading voice. Yokohama, San Diego, Valparaiso, London, all slipped away forever…

THE TROUBLE WITH JINNS

My friend Jimmy has only one arm. He lost the other when he was a young man of twenty-five. The story of how he lost his good right arm is a little difficult to believe, but I swear that it is absolutely true.

To begin with, Jimmy was (and presumably still is) a Jinn. Now a Jinn isn't really a human like us. A Jinn is a spirit creature from another world who has assumed, for a lifetime, the physical aspect of a human being. Jimmy was a true Jinn and he had the Jinn's gift of being able to elongate his arm at will. Most Jinns can stretch their arms to a distance of twenty or thirty feet. Jimmy could attain forty feet. His arm would move through space or up walls or along the ground like a beautiful gliding serpent. I have seen him stretched out beneath a mango tree, helping himself to ripe mangoes from the top of the tree. He loved mangoes. He was a natural glutton and it was probably his gluttony that first led him to misuse his peculiar gifts.

We were at school together at a hill station in northern India. Jimmy was particularly good at basketball. He was clever enough not to lengthen his arm too much because he did not want anyone to know that he was a Jinn. In the boxing ring he generally won his fights. His opponents never seemed to get past his amazing reach. He just kept tapping them on the nose until they retired from the ring bloody and bewildered.

It was during the half-term examinations that I stumbled on Jimmy's secret. We had been set a particularly difficult algebra paper but I had managed to cover a couple of sheets with correct answers and was about to forge ahead on another sheet when I noticed someone's hand on my desk. At first I thought it was the invigilator's. But when I looked up there was no one beside me.

Could it be the boy sitting directly behind? No, he was engrossed in his question paper and had his hands to himself. Meanwhile, the hand on my desk had grasped my answer sheets and was cautiously moving off. Following its descent, I found that it was attached to an arm of amazing length and pliability. This moved stealthily down the desk and slithered across the floor, shrinking all the while, until it was restored to its normal length. Its owner was of course one who had never been any good at algebra.

I had to write out my answers a second time but after the exam I went straight up to Jimmy, told him I didn't like his game and threatened to expose him. He begged me not to let anyone know, assured me that he couldn't really help himself, and offered to be of service to me whenever I wished. It was tempting to have Jimmy as my friend, for with his long reach he would obviously be useful. I agreed to overlook the matter of the pilfered papers and we became the best of pals.

It did not take me long to discover that Jimmy's gift was more of a nuisance than a constructive aid. That was because Jimmy had a second-rate mind and did not know how to make proper use of his powers. He seldom rose above the trivial. He used his long arm in the tuck shop, in the classroom, in the dormitory. And when we were allowed out to the cinema, he used it in the dark of the hall.

Now the trouble with all Jinns is that they have a weakness

for women with long black hair. The longer and blacker the hair, the better for Jinns. And should a Jinn manage to take possession of the woman he desires, she goes into a decline and her beauty decays. Everything about her is destroyed except for the beautiful long black hair.

Jimmy was still too young to be able to take possession in this way, but he couldn't resist touching and stroking long black hair. The cinema was the best place for the indulgence of his whims. His arm would start stretching, his fingers would feel their way along the rows of seats, and his lengthening limb would slowly work its way along the aisle until it reached the back of the seat in which sat the object of his admiration. His hand would stroke the long black hair with great tenderness and if the girl felt anything and looked round, Jimmy's hand would disappear behind the seat and lie there poised like the hood of a snake, ready to strike again.

At college two or three years later, Jimmy's first real victim succumbed to his attentions. She was a lecturer in economics, not very good looking, but her hair, black and lustrous, reached almost to her knees. She usually kept it in plaits but Jimmy saw her one morning just after she had taken a head bath, and her hair lay spread out on the cot on which she was reclining. Jimmy could no longer control himself. His spirit, the very essence of his personality, entered the woman's body and the next day she was distraught, feverish and excited. She would not eat, went into a coma, and in a few days dwindled to a mere skeleton. When she died, she was nothing but skin and bone but her hair had lost none of its loveliness.

I took pains to avoid Jimmy after this tragic event. I could not prove that he was the cause of the lady's sad demise but in my own heart I was quite certain of it. For since meeting

Jimmy, I had read a good deal about Jinns and knew their ways.

We did not see each other for a few years. And then, holidaying in the hills last year, I found we were staying at the same hotel. I could not very well ignore him and after we had drunk a few beers together I began to feel that I had perhaps misjudged Jimmy and that he was not the irresponsible Jinn I had taken him for. Perhaps the college lecturer had died of some mysterious malady that attacks only college lecturers and Jimmy had nothing at all to do with it.

We had decided to take our lunch and a few bottles of beer to a grassy knoll just below the main motor road. It was late afternoon and I had been sleeping off the effects of the beer when I woke to find Jimmy looking rather agitated.

'What's wrong?' I asked.

'Up there, under the pine trees,' he said. 'Just above the road. Don't you see them?'

'I see two girls,' I said. 'So what?'

'The one on the left. Haven't you noticed her hair?'

'Yes, it is very long and beautiful and—now look, Jimmy, you'd better get a grip on yourself!' But already his hand was out of sight, his arm snaking up the hillside and across the road.

Presently I saw the hand emerge from some bushes near the girls and then cautiously make its way to the girl with the black tresses. So absorbed was Jimmy in the pursuit of his favourite pastime that he failed to hear the blowing of a horn. Around the bend of the road came a speeding Mercedes Benz truck.

Jimmy saw the truck but there wasn't time for him to shrink his arm back to normal. It lay right across the entire width of the road and when the truck had passed over it, it writhed and twisted like a mortally wounded python.

By the time the truck driver and I could fetch a doctor, the arm (or what was left of it) had shrunk to its ordinary size. We took Jimmy to hospital where the doctors found it necessary to amputate. The truck driver, who kept insisting that the arm he ran over was at least thirty feet long, was arrested on a charge of drunken driving.

Some weeks later I asked Jimmy, 'Why are you so depressed? You still have one arm. Isn't it gifted in the same way?'

'I never tried to find out,' he said, 'and I'm not going to try now.'

He is, of course, still a Jinn at heart and whenever he sees a girl with long black hair he must be terribly tempted to try out his one good arm and stroke her beautiful tresses. But he has learnt his lesson. It is better to be a human without any gifts than a Jinn or a genius with one too many.